DO OR DIE!

Cantrell eased his guns into their holsters and, holding his shotgun in a pistol grip with his left hand, stepped into the saloon. The Hardesters sat at a table in the middle, facing the front door.

The barmaid gasped, her breath sounding loud in the still room. Voice quiet, heart pounding, Quint spoke. "You lookin' for me?"

The Hardesters turned as one, each throwing himself to the side, hands streaking for their guns. Cantrell's right hand dipped to his side and came up spewing flame and lead. . . .

*Also by Jack Ballas
from Jove*

TOMAHAWK CANYON

DURANGO GUNFIGHT

JACK BALLAS

JOVE BOOKS, NEW YORK

DURANGO GUNFIGHT

A Jove Book / published by arrangement with
the author

PRINTING HISTORY
Jove edition / November 1992

ISBN: 0-515-10979-7

Jove Books are published by The Berkley Publishing Group,
200 Madison Avenue, New York, New York 10016.
The name "JOVE" and the "J" logo
are trademarks belonging to Jove Publications, Inc.

PRINTED IN THE UNITED STATES OF AMERICA

10 9 8 7 6 5 4 3 2 1

To my wife, Harriette, my best critic and strongest supporter, and to John and Joan McCord and all the members of the DFW Writers Workshop.

CHAPTER
1

Quint Cantrell pulled the big line-back dun to a halt at the north end of town. He had traveled through high mountain country in the past weeks and welcomed the sight ahead of him. He rubbed the dun's neck.

So this was Durango. There had to be two thousand people in this town, nestled at the base of the San Juan Mountains. He studied the long street and saw a mixture of buildings, some log, some brick, and a few rough hand-hewn structures. The brick gave the town an air of permanence.

Cantrell liked what he saw. The streets were filled with people on horseback, others afoot, and some in wagons. The town was all he had heard. Raw. Wild. Beautiful. Cantrell decided then he was through running. Let the Hardesters bring their gunfight to him. He'd had enough.

The Hardesters had dogged his trail for eleven years, following him on trail drives, into small cow-towns, onto isolated ranches. At first he avoided meeting them because he wasn't their match with guns; later he stayed ahead of them so as not to involve people who befriended him; now he was through with the camps in isolated valleys or hidden ravines. He would not seek them out, but if they wanted a fight, he'd give them one.

They'll be surprised to find they've cut out a pretty hard job for themselves, he thought. It wasn't but about two hundred miles on down the road to home where he'd started running, but it had taken a few thousand miles to get here. This is where we're gonna find us a new home, he said to himself. Grave or ranch, I ain't runnin' no more.

The big horse, perhaps sensing a comfortable stall and feed

1

close by, started down the street. Cantrell let him go his own pace.

As he moved between the rows of buildings, his flicking glance searched out every shadowy alcove. Even in a town this big he would be noticed. There were not many men his size, nor were there many horses as good as the one he rode. People might not know he was Quinton Cantrell, but they would see him.

That Wanted poster, eleven years old now, showed a scrawny kid of seventeen and described him as six feet tall, a hundred and sixty pounds. It stated he was wanted for murdering Chat Hardester and offered a reward of two thousand dollars, *Dead or Alive*.

At first there had been many who tried to collect that money, but the word soon spread—dead men had no use for money.

Cantrell shifted his six feet, four inches in the saddle. He didn't think anyone would recognize him, but if they did, they wouldn't be dealing with a scared seventeen year old.

That had been eleven years ago. Now, he'd taken three herds to rails-end in Kansas, spent two years in Old Mexico, and ridden the Outlaw Trail. Today there were few, if any, who could match him with handgun, rifle, or Bowie knife, thanks to the teaching of Cole Mason, maybe the fastest gun alive.

There had been many times, Cantrell reflected, that he'd avoided his home territory, but he did it because he hated to kill; he'd done more of that than he liked to think about, and then only when pushed into it.

Now he thought this was the place he'd stay. He had a good stake, more than most cowhands could save in a lifetime. It was time to find a job and look the country over. If a small ranch came available, he thought to take a look at it. If he could get it cheap enough, he might have enough left over to put a few head of stock on it.

Cantrell passed no less than fifteen saloons and a number of prosperous-looking businesses before he saw a livery stable and reined the dun toward it. The usual array of buckboards, a couple of surreys, and three buggies stood in front of the stable without horses hitched to them.

People staying overnight, probably ranch families, Cantrell

thought. He dismounted and led his horse into the stable.

"Howdy, what ye be needin' today?" a wizened old man asked.

"After I take care of him, give him some grain, hay, and water," Cantrell said, and continued loosening the cinches.

"That'll cost ye fifty cents a day, but if ye take it by the week it'll be two dollars." The old man's voice was hopeful.

"Reckon the week sounds fine. Let's give him a good rest."

The old man grinned, showing toothless gums. "Big as that hoss is, I might've not charged you enough. Bet he can eat as much as any two hosses around here."

He squinted up at Cantrell as though trying to gauge whether his humor was being accepted as such, then cackled. "Aw, young feller, I was joshing ya. I'd almost take care of that big hoss for nothin'. Ain't he a beauty though."

Cantrell nodded. "Caught him runnin' wild up Wyoming way 'bout six years ago." He finished taking care of his horse, and said, "I'll stop in every day and check on him."

Although the sun was shining, the wind coming off the mountains was cool, almost chilly. Before leaving the stable, Cantrell took his sheepskin coat from his bedroll, and carried it and his Winchester in the crook of his left arm.

A general store across the street drew his attention. He decided to get new clothes. The ones he had on were clean but almost thin enough to read a newspaper through. He had one more outfit in about the same shape as the one he wanted to shed.

When he had water, he kept himself and his clothes clean, but as he looked down at his worn and faded Levis, he knew a man could wash dirt out, but he just couldn't wash more cloth in.

He made his purchase, went to the hotel, signed for a room, and took a bath. Finished, he decided to have a drink, a good meal, and a walk about town. This was his kind of town. He wanted to see it and listen to it howl.

He swung his gunbelt around lean hips, buckled it, and tied the holsters snugly to his thighs. He hoped he wouldn't need his guns, but reckoned he'd feel naked without them. If the Hardesters found him, he'd need them for sure.

Cantrell stood on the boardwalk and looked along the street. Looks like there ought not to be any thirsty men in this town, he thought. He had never seen so many saloons in one place before. He turned and started toward the north end when he saw the sign across the street for the Golden Eagle Saloon and Dance Hall.

Don't look like there's anybody much in there judging from the horses in front, he thought, and reckoned he'd try it.

After standing inside a moment to get used to the changed light, he saw he was the only customer. He walked to the corner of the bar and stood, his back to the wall.

A pretty, dark-haired woman, tall, slender, but with curves in all the right places, asked for his order.

"Whiskey."

While waiting for his drink, he studied the room. It was large, with several smaller rooms down one side; they looked like they were set up for private card games. The main room had a bandstand and a good-sized dance floor surrounded on three sides with tables and chairs. A wide staircase at the back of the bar led to the second floor, which overlooked the bottom one. The smaller rooms upstairs, Cantrell decided, were where the dance hall girls entertained their guests for the night.

"Nice place," he said when the pretty woman put his drink in front of him.

"It's mine. I built it when I saw the town fathers of Animas City, which is up the road a short piece, weren't going to let the railroad have free land for a depot. The town started moving down here where the depot was being built. I was one of the first."

Cantrell tossed his drink down and placed the glass on the bar.

She laughed, a nice laugh he thought, then reached under the counter and brought out another bottle.

"I'm Faye Barrett," she said, pouring him another drink. "Perhaps you won't cringe when you drink this one. It's some of the best we get in this part of the country." She placed his drink in front of him and held out her hand.

Cantrell folded her hand in one of his big ones. "Name's Quint Cantrell; thanks for the drink."

When he said his name, her hand trembled and tightened. *She'd heard the name before.* He wondered when and where. Too, neither her face nor her eyes changed expression. Ain't never gonna play poker with her, he thought.

"What're you doing in Durango? I could use a good man to help keep the peace in here."

Cantrell said. "I'm a cowhand, ma'am. I like towns once in a while, but a steady diet of them don't give me much room to breathe."

This time he did see her eyes change. She was disappointed, and he reckoned he knew why. He'd seen the same look in other women's eyes.

For reasons he couldn't figure out women liked him, but he'd stay clear of this one, since his name seemed to mean something to her. That could be trouble.

"If you're looking for a job riding," she said, "I might be able to help. I know most of the cattlemen around here. They come in pretty often."

"Thanks, but I might keep ridin'. If I decide to stick around, I'll let you know. Figure on staying here about a week. By then I'll make up my mind what I want to do." He didn't want to let on that he'd probably settle somewhere close by.

He tossed off his drink. "Thanks again for the drink, a lot better'n the first one."

"Things get livelier after dark. Why not stop by later?"

"I might do that." He tipped his hat and left.

He walked from one end of the main street to the other. There were more people in town than he would have thought would be at this time of day—mostly miners, but he did see a few in range garb like himself.

At the end of the business area, he angled off to see the river, which had a haunting, lonely name, one the Spanish had given it: *Rio de las Animas Perdidas*—River of Lost Souls.

He walked down, stood on a large boulder at water's edge, and nodded his approval. It was a stream as wild and untamed as the mountains that spawned it. He dipped his hand in the icy water; it tasted sweet and pure as mountain air.

It would take a lot of doing to get him away from this part of the country. He turned and headed for main street.

A shortcut between two buildings brought him back to the center of town. A large crowd drew his attention in front of the store in which he'd bought his clothes.

His height allowed him to see over the heads of the men gathered in front.

A man as tall as but heavier than Cantrell swung his fist in a roundhouse loop that connected with a beautiful, but terrified, bay horse. The bay screamed and reared, pulling on the reins wrapped around the man's left hand. The man swung again. The horse staggered under the blow.

Before another blow could land, Cantrell pushed people roughly aside to get to the bully. He grabbed the man's fist at the back of a swing and twisted. The ruffian spun, got his feet tangled, and fell. He reached for the .44 at his side, but was too late. Cantrell had his in hand.

He pushed the muzzle against the horse beater's temple, slipped the man's pistol from its holster, and threw it in the watering trough a few feet away.

"Ain't no business of yours what I do with my horse. Put that gun away an' I'll beat you to death."

The man started to roll to his feet. Cantrell caught his shoulder and slammed him to the ground again. "Stay down."

Through narrowed lids, Cantrell looked directly into the bully's eyes. "Now I'm gonna tell *you* how it is. If I ever hear of you mistreating a horse again I'm gonna find you, and *I'll* do the beating. When I get through, you'll never swing at anything else again." He jabbed his .44 hard against the horse beater's temple, then walked away.

CHAPTER
2

The crowd had been silent during the exchange between the two men. When Cantrell turned his back and walked away, voices, shrill and raucous, burst from the throng.

Cantrell twisted to look over his shoulder at the crowd and saw a slim man, a cowhand like himself, hurrying to catch up. He waited.

"Hot damn! I'll bet that's the first time Moose Lawson ever got throwed. Mister, you'd best be mighty careful. Don't let him get you in a fight without no guns."

He stuck out his hand. "They call me Stick McClure. Don't rightly know whether they call me Stick 'cause I'm the bronco-buster out at the McCord ranch and can stick to almost any bronc, or 'cause I'm so skinny."

"Quint Cantrell." Cantrell shook McClure's hand. "Thanks for the warning. Lawson and I should be about even though—I've never been whipped either." Then as an afterthought, he said, "That is, ain't been whipped since I was a full-size man."

"C'mon," McClure said, "I'll buy you a drink. I like to drink in the Golden Eagle. Miss Faye don't put up with no roughhousin' in her place."

McClure looked back down the street. "No need to worry about Lawson. He'll be chasin' that bay of his till daylight."

They had a couple of drinks before McClure disappeared upstairs with a pretty little brunette. She'd apparently been his girl frequently, because as soon as they'd entered the door she let out a squeal and threw herself into his arms.

Cantrell leaned against the wall at the end of the bar, sipping his drink.

7

Faye worked her way down the bar, serving drinks and carrying on a continuous banter with the customers. She called most of them by their first names. She stopped in front of Cantrell.

"If you're looking for a riding job, get Stick to introduce you to Ian McCord. If he'll take you on, you'll be working for the best man around."

"I might just do that. I had a little trouble a while ago so maybe I'll get out of town for a spell. No point in pushing my luck."

"I heard about it. Fact is, the whole town's heard about it. Let it cool awhile." Then she added, "I wouldn't like to see you get hurt, Quint."

"That makes two of us, Faye." He pushed away from the wall and reached in his pocket to pay his bill. "Tell McClure when he comes down that I'm bedded down at the hotel, and if I'm not there, tell him to look in the livery stable." Even though he'd paid for a hotel room, he knew he'd be harder to corner at the livery.

With no apparent shame, she looked Cantrell straight in the eye. "He likely won't be down till morning," she said.

"I'll be around." He left, still wondering where she'd heard of him.

The next morning Cantrell was sipping his second cup of coffee with old Rawhide Doby, the livery stable owner, when McClure looked in the door.

"You had breakfast yet?" Cantrell asked.

"Naw, figured to have it with you."

"Let's go get it then." Cantrell said to Doby, "You eat yet?"

"Yeah, I et 'fore sunup. Go ahead. Big as you are, if you ain't et since last night you must be nigh on to starvin' by now."

"Don't know as that has anything to do with it, but yeah, I'm nigh on to starvin'." Cantrell grinned at the old man and turned toward the door. "C'mon, McClure, let's see if that cafe's got any fresh eggs. Ain't had a egg in two months."

They had eggs. Cantrell ate a half dozen of them. He swallowed his last bite of biscuit, washed it down with coffee so thick you could set a fence post in it, and leaned back, satisfied. Watching McClure finish, Cantrell raised his eyes in wonderment: McClure ate more than he did.

After stoking his pipe, he asked, "Your boss hirin'?"

McClure gazed into his cup, studying the bottom, then looked up. "Don't rightly know. Bad time o' year being fall and all, but can't never tell. If Lion—that's what we call the boss—takes a likin' to you right off, then to hell with the season. He's likely to take you on."

"I ain't just lookin' for a place to winter. I'm lookin' for a longtime job unless I can find me a cheap place to buy." He shook his head. "'Course I'm talkin' about mighty cheap."

"Lion hires you, it'll be 'cause he figures on you stayin' awhile."

"Tell me how to find his place. I may hang around town a couple of days before I come out."

McClure stared at him a moment before answering. "You ain't figurin' on pushin' that ruckus with Lawson no further, are you?"

"No, I figure to stay out of his way if I can, but if I can't, I'll take it as it comes."

"I didn't tell you he's about as good with guns as he is with fists. He likes to fight with his hands though; I reckon 'cause he likes to hurt people."

"Thanks for thinkin' about me, McClure, but I'll just have to chance that. See you at the ranch."

McClure stood. "Reckon I'll head on out then. Ask anybody around town how to find the BIM—that's what we call it, though it's really the Box I-M. 'Bout twenty-five miles southeast of here, so leave early."

Cantrell watched McClure ride out, then went to the newspaper office to buy a paper. He liked to read. As a boy, his mother, sitting by the fire at night, had read to him and made him follow along—then she had had him read to her. She had taught him well.

Since then, he'd read anything he could get his hands on: newspapers, books, labels on cans—anything. Right now he thought the local paper would tell him more about the town than would a week of wandering about talking to people.

He noted the sign above the door of the building, *The Durango Herald, Established 1881*. That was only last year. While purchasing the paper, he saw a new book, *Tom Sawyer*, written by that fellow who worked for the newspaper out at Virginia City. He bought it.

It was the first new book he'd ever owned, and he couldn't wait to find some place where he could hide from the world and start reading.

The livery stable proved to be the best place, so he climbed up to the haymow and hunkered down by the door, where the light filtered in. It was a warm place, and the smell of hay mixed with the odor of horse droppings made him think of the old barn back home.

He read every word in the paper, but found nothing in it to give him hope that he'd find the land he wanted at a price he could afford. Cantrell then read *Tom Sawyer* until the sunlight dimmed.

He marked the page with a piece of straw and went to the hotel to take a bath.

While bathing, Cantrell decided to take in the town after dark and maybe head out to the ranch tomorrow. In his new Levis, he felt fit to be with people again.

He went to the Golden Eagle first. Faye poured him a glass of her private stock, then leaned across the bar.

"Lawson's going all over town looking for you, Quint. Says he's going to kill you. Why don't you leave town now and give it a chance to cool?"

He put his drink back on the bar, untouched. A hard, cold knot formed in his stomach. He didn't try to squelch the anger bubbling in him. If Lawson wanted a fight, he'd give him one he'd never forget. One that'd fix him so he'd never beat another horse or man.

"Might as well go find him. If I could let it rest awhile, maybe let it die and never happen, I'd do it, but Lawson ain't the kind to forget."

The look in her eyes showed that she really was concerned. Cantrell thought she was quite a woman, but if she knew anything about his past, she could bring him trouble.

"Go meet him then. Your drink will be here when you get through." She paused. "So will I."

That "So will I" bothered him; she was too ready to give too quick.

He looked in three saloons and was headed for the fourth when he heard heavy footsteps behind him.

He spun in time to dodge a fist that looked the size of a beef shoulder. It grazed his upper arm.

Lawson had been running toward him, and as he went past, Cantrell stuck out his foot and clubbed him behind his ear. Lawson went to the dirt.

Cantrell had been in this kind of no-holds-barred fight before. Lawson would use every dirty trick he knew; probably learned them in one mining camp or another.

The big man rolled to his knees, started to push himself up, then grasped two hands full of fine dust from the street.

Cantrell didn't wait. He kicked Lawson as hard as he could swing his right leg. His sharp boot toe caught the other man in the lower ribs. Lawson ate more dirt.

Cantrell thought if he hadn't broken some ribs, the kick had at least damaged Lawson enough to slow him down. This gave Cantrell an edge, and he figured he'd need it.

Lawson rolled, landed on his feet, rushed Cantrell, and with sheer weight penetrated his defense. He connected with a right to the side of Cantrell's head.

White lights exploded in his skull. He spun and almost went down. His head, numb outside, seemed one huge mass of pain inside. He staggered sideways and only by sheer luck avoided another slam to the head. Shaking his head, he tried to clear the red haze from his eyes and caught a blow to the ribs. Pain clutched his chest in a vise.

He backed off, sucking desperately for air. His head cleared a little, enough that he saw Lawson lift his fist for another round-house swing. Cantrell stepped in close and triggered a right then a left to Lawson's gut, then slipped back out of range.

Those blows hurt Lawson; Cantrell heard the breath whoosh from his lungs. He didn't give Lawson the chance to suck in more. He stepped back in and pounded Lawson's gut again, feeling his fists sink to his wrists.

Soft, Cantrell thought. Those gut shots were the ones that would finish him.

Lawson tried to back off. Cantrell followed; he swung, shuffled forward, swung, shuffled.

Lawson ducked his head, and, in desperation, tried to wade in.

Cantrell shifted his attack to the head. His left opened a cut over Lawson's right eye, and blood spilled down his cheek. He swung his right to Lawson's nose, and the cartilage flattened under his fist. Lawson would go down with almost any kind of blow now.

Cantrell threw one more to the gut. Lawson bent from the blow. Cantrell stepped in with clubbed fists, brought them down behind Lawson's neck, and at the same time brought his knee up to meet Lawson's face. He stepped aside, letting Lawson fall to bury his face in the dirt.

Lawson would be one hell of a long time getting well enough to fight again.

Cantrell grasped Lawson's right arm, put his boot on the back of Lawson's elbow and pulled. He heard the bone snap, then did the same to the other arm. "Now, you son of a bitch, try using your fists on a horse or man." The words came out slurred; blood had glued his lips together.

Cantrell staggered to the hitching rail and leaned against it, exhausted and gasping for air. *He* wouldn't fight anytime soon either.

He'd wanted this fight, wanted to get it behind him, and now that he had, he glanced at the mound of beaten flesh laying in a heap out there in the dirt. He felt no guilt.

He'd beaten a man to near death and deliberately crippled him. A bullet would have been more merciful. But he'd not wanted mercy for Lawson. Cantrell wanted the beating to stay with the bully, wanted him crippled, knowing that now Lawson would only be able to fight with guns—rifles probably, and not very well.

To hell with him, Cantrell thought. If he wanted guns, he'd get guns. His anger cooled slowly.

A crowd gathered around him, miners judging by their dress. Cantrell wasn't sure how they'd take to one of their own being whipped, almost killed.

He knew soon enough. They slapped him on the back, most wanting to buy him a drink. Lawson had beaten and bullied too many of them. They were glad to see him dethroned.

Cantrell tried to say he'd have a drink with them some other time but found he still could not make words come out. He didn't remember getting hit in the mouth.

Carefully, he ran his tongue around his teeth; each of them was there and in one piece. He tried to push away from the hitching rail but didn't quite make it. Then he felt a cold, wet cloth pressed to the back of his neck.

"Just take it easy a few minutes, big fellow. You took a few licks in that fight too." He recognized Faye's voice. The cloth felt good. He leaned his head back against its coolness—then he saw the buggy.

It stood at the outer ring of spectators. Standing in it, holding a tight rein on the horse, was a woman. No, she was more like a goddess: tall, willowy, blond, and green-eyed. Regal, he'd heard that word somewhere and thought it would fit.

Cantrell, accustomed to seeing a lot with a glance, didn't hurry this time. Their gazes met and locked. He saw a series of emotions cross her face: savage enjoyment of the fight she'd witnessed; interest in the winner; and then cold aloofness as she turned and flicked her whip lightly against the flank of her horse. She left so suddenly he wasn't sure but that he'd imagined her.

"You feel like going back to my place for that drink now?"

He turned his head to look at Faye. Even his neck hurt when he twisted it. "Might be just what I need." He pushed out from the rail and stepped up on the boardwalk. He offered his arm, but instead of taking it, Faye put her arm around his shoulders and steadied him.

When they walked into the cool darkness, Faye guided him around the bar and through a door. She said to the girl behind the bar, "Margie, I'll be in my room for a while. Bring me that bottle under the counter."

Cantrell wasn't surprised when he studied the room. Beautifully appointed in fine drapes and carpeting, it indicated the best of taste. And money couldn't buy better furniture than that he looked at. He felt a sense of relief to see it wasn't her bedroom.

Cantrell's sixth sense told him to be careful of this woman. She could be big trouble. She knew who he was; he had no doubt of that. Her hand tightening and trembling in his when she heard his name was the only indication he had had—but it was enough. He'd spent too many years reading sign of people and nature to ignore this one. Knowing he was Cantrell was enough for her to call down any number of gunfighters on him. And not least, he didn't like pushy women. Any pursuing to be done, he figured to do it.

The blonde he had seen in the buggy pushed into his mind, but Faye's cool, gentle fingers on the back of his neck pushed his thoughts aside. She guided him to a large upholstered chair and eased him into it.

"Sit there awhile. I'll get some warm water and wash your face. It's a mess."

He leaned his head back and closed his eyes. That fight had taken a lot out of him. It felt good to lay back and wait for the gentle touch of a woman, something he'd not had in years. Cantrell felt surprise that he missed something he'd had so little of.

The room had the delicate scent of lilacs, not at all like the typical musty, stale beer smell of most saloons.

He realized Faye had returned with warm water when he felt the washcloth gently sponging his face. She wiped the blood from his lips last.

He didn't open his eyes, but was aware her lips had brushed his, as light as a butterfly, sweet and soft. Then he slept.

Cantrell opened his eyes. He lay still, trying to get his bearings. A lighted lantern sat on a pedestal table across the room, casting a soft glow about him. He looked down and saw that Faye had spread a quilt across his knees.

He tried to sit up. A moan escaped despite his effort to suppress it. He felt as if he'd been thrown and stomped.

He lay back, sucked in a deep breath he had to force past the pain in his chest, then sat up, and stood, slowly.

The door from the saloon opened and Faye walked in. "Where do you think you're going? You're hurt much too bad to try to leave now."

He looked at her and saw the anguish in her expression. "No, Faye, you've already been too good to me. Know you don't take all strangers in like this and I'm right beholden to you for it, but don't reckon I better stay here."

"Would it make a difference if I told you you're the only man that ever crossed that threshold?"

"Aw, Faye, it ain't that. It's just—well, I gotta get things straight in my head." He said, "Hell, don't you think I want to stay? You're the prettiest woman I reckon I ever met, and you're nice, a lady. Don't want to start anything that would cheat you, maybe cheat us both." He crammed his hat down on his head and started out, then turned back.

"Gonna see if McCord'll give me a job. If he does, reckon I'll stop in when I'm in town."

She was standing, rigid, her face frozen, but her eyes said it all. She wanted him to stay, and despite his yearning for a woman, he walked quickly from the room.

CHAPTER
3

Cantrell saddled the dun and rode out. His thoughts returned to the scene in Faye's parlor. Knowing his words had given her hope that they could mean something to each other brought a brassy taste to his mouth. He hadn't meant them that way.

"Damn!" he exploded. The big horse threw his head around to protest the sudden noise. "It's all right, old hoss, it's just me figurin' out what kind of damn fool I am."

His gaze scanned the rolling hills flowing from the mountains, and moved on to the peaks that speared the flawless blue sky. He breathed the pine-scented air and felt it wash away the closed-in feeling towns gave him.

A man needs to go to town once in a while just so he knows he don't really belong there, he thought.

Out here was good grass, water, cows, all the game a man needed. Far as he knew there hadn't been Indian trouble since the Ute uprising at Milk River in 1879.

Out of habit, Cantrell continued searching the surrounding country. There might not be Indians, but some of the orneriest men anywhere had come west to prey on small ranchers, stagecoaches, and lone riders. He didn't intend to become a victim of their greed.

One of the many branches of the outlaw trail came down into this area out of the Uncompaghre Mountains. Cantrell knew the trail well, having ridden it quite a spell, and knew most who rode it. They left *him* alone. A man fast with his guns and quick to stand up to a hardcase didn't draw others close.

Cantrell had never gotten a dime he didn't work for, and thinking that, he unconsciously slipped his hand down inside his gunbelt to check that his bankroll was secure. It wasn't much, but it represented his life savings. It had to be his start for a place of his own.

When Cole Mason had taken Cantrell on as a partner, they had worked long and hard down in Texas rounding up mavericks gone wild during the War Between the States. They drove them to market across most of Texas and half of Kansas, and went back for more and did it again. Cantrell patted his money belt again. Yeah, he thought, they'll play hell gettin' this.

Mason had wanted to split fifty-fifty with him, but Cantrell wouldn't have it that way. Mason had furnished most of the know-how while Cantrell, just a spindly-legged kid learning the ropes, furnished the brawn.

He rode slowly, thinking another night would give his ribs time to work the soreness out.

Casting a glance at the sun, he estimated the time to be three o'clock. All he wanted was to be alone, a good place to camp, and to lay back against his saddle, look at the sky, and let the hurt leave his body.

He saw movement and thought it might be a deer or wolf, but then again it might be a man. He rode on.

The second time he caught movement, he saw a man—then he saw him again.

Cantrell, sure now that he had also been seen, knew an honest rider would ride over and join up. Just in case, he slipped the thong off the hammer of his .44 and pulled his Winchester from its scabbard.

He angled toward a stream, away from where he'd last seen the rider. Ahead, a thick stand of Aspen looked like a good campsite.

Riding toward it, he searched every shadow for a darker shade that might be a man. When certain he had the thicket to himself, he rode in, dismounted, and led the dun deeper into the tangled thickness.

After pulling several clumps of grass for his horse, Cantrell prepared his own meal. He continued searching the open range about him for sign of the rider.

"All right, hoss," he said. "I'm gonna enjoy my coffee. You keep watch." He sat so he could watch the downwind side, depending on the dun to warn him of anything upwind.

Dusk settled in. Cantrell stood, dumped the dregs from his cup, and walked toward the stream to wash it. Suddenly, the dun's head came up, ears rigid.

Cantrell slipped into the brush. He didn't have long to wait. First a shadow, then a man—pistol in hand—materialized in the glow of his fire. Cantrell recognized him.

The intruder was a tall, gangling man, with a scar that started at his hairline and cut across his left eye, stopping at his chin. He hesitated before stepping into the firelight. The scar gave him a sinister, evil look. Cantrell had put that scar on him. With recognition, he thumbed the hammer back.

"You lose something around my fire, Spider?" he asked.

Spider stiffened and peered into the shadows, trying to see him, trying to find something to shoot at.

"Drop your gun. Easy-like, and you might live to walk away." Cantrell watched the gun drop, and said, "Now turn around."

He waited for Spider's back to show in the dim light, then, with no more noise than a leaf makes as it flutters to the ground, Cantrell moved to within a foot of Spider's back.

He felt Spider for a hideout pistol or knife, found both, removed them, and threw them to the other side of the fire.

"You know my name. Who the hell are you?" Spider growled, no show of fear in his voice.

"Turn around."

Recognition *and* fear crossed Spider's face.

"Cantrell! You know I wasn't gonna do you no harm."

Cantrell just stared. Spider shrank under his steady gaze, and after a few seconds he had apparently stood the silence as long as he could.

"Aw c'mon, Cantrell, you know I'd face any man 'fore I would you. Gimme my gun and let me get out of here."

"Drop your gunbelt." Spider complied. "Now let's go get your rifle."

The last ray of hope faded from Spider's face.

When Cantrell had pulled the rifle from its scabbard, he motioned with his handgun. "This is your lucky day—I'm not gonna kill you. Get on that horse and put trail dust 'tween us. I promise—the next time I see you I'll kill you."

Spider climbed aboard and dug heels into his horse's sides. The night swallowed his shadow, and only then did Cantrell walk back to camp.

Spider wouldn't be back. He was unarmed; even better, he was scared to death. Cantrell collected Spider's guns and knife and pulled his own bedroll and saddle into the shadows. Wanting to be on the trail early, he lay down and went to sleep.

The next morning, he judged he'd put about three miles behind him when the sun, red through the haze, edged above the distant San Juan peaks.

He rode slowly, in no hurry. If McCord had a job for him, there would be nothing but sweat, dust, and bone-jarring tiredness in the long days ahead, or cold that ate into a man's gizzard.

Cantrell wondered why he missed the cow business. It was a dirty, man-killing life. But he wouldn't trade with anybody. He nudged the dun to a faster pace.

He rode into the ranch yard soon after the sun started its downward journey behind the western hills.

The tantalizing smells of fresh brewed coffee, baked bread, and fried steak reached him. He was hungry enough to eat a steer but wanted to get his business with McCord finished first. He swung off the dun and headed toward the main house. In midstride he heard a yell from near the bunkhouse.

"Hey, Cantrell, cook just rang the chow bell. C'mon an' eat 'fore you go up to see the boss."

He recognized the voice and turned toward it. "Thanks, McClure. Figured I might get here in time for grub. Need to wash up 'fore we go in though."

"Pump's over yonder. I'll wait."

McClure introduced the hands and told them Cantrell was looking for a job.

Shaking hands with them, Cantrell noted the firm handshake of each. They were a hard-bitten, efficient-looking bunch. The BIM was a large ranch, but even so he wondered why it carried such a large crew.

He also noticed that most of them wore their holsters tied down, and the fact that his were tied down didn't go unnoticed.

These men were not strangers to trouble, and Cantrell had a hunch it always rode pretty close to them.

He shrugged mentally, reckoning he'd bedded down with trouble a few times himself. Fitting in here should be easy, especially since most of them knew his reputation. They didn't say it, but it showed in their eyes. Yet they still made him welcome.

After eating and cleaning his gear, Cantrell thanked the cook for the good meal and spoke to McClure.

"Don't reckon I'm gonna find that job long as I hang around here. Might as well go see your boss."

"C'mon, I'll take you in to see him. I already told him about you puttin' Lawson on his back." He squinted at Cantrell. "You didn't happen to run into him again after I cut out, did you?"

Cantrell didn't want to talk about it. "Well, yeah," he said. "We had a little fight."

McClure danced from one leg to the other. "Hell, Cantrell, c'mon, tell me who won."

"The way I felt afterward I wouldn't say either of us did. Most would say I did though 'cause I was the one standin' when it was over."

"Hot damn! Knew you could do it." McClure sobered. "I better tell you a little about Lion. He's a hard man, but fair. He holds four things above anything else. First is his wife, the Señora Venicia. Her father, Don Esteban Alvarez, owned most of the land around here. When he died, Lion and the señora took over.

"The second is his daughter, Elena. She's stubborn as a old mossy-horn steer but pretty as a sunrise.

"Next, I'd have to say is this ranch, and then his crew. You ride for Lion, every man on the payroll'll side you no matter what kind of trouble you got."

"Sounds like my kind of outfit. Let's go see him."

In answer to McClure's knock, a tall blond lady answered the door. At first glance Cantrell thought it was the girl he'd seen standing in the buggy after his fight with Lawson. A closer look showed him she was several years older but just as beautiful.

Cantrell stared a moment. My God, he thought, this must be her mother, and Lion must be her father. McClure said something, and Cantrell realized he was introducing the lady.

"Cantrell, I'd like you to meet the Señora McCord. Ma'am, this here's Quinton Cantrell. I know the boss ain't hirin' right now but I'd sorta like him to meet Cantrell anyhow, just in case."

Her smile was radiant. She held out her hand for Cantrell's handshake. She was such a lady he almost kissed it, but shook it instead.

"Come in, Stick. Nice to know you, Mr. Cantrell." She nodded toward the back of the house. "Stick can show you to Ian's office. He's back there fussin' and cussin'. That's the way he works on his tally book." She smiled as she said it.

Sure not hard to see how a man could put this lady above everything else, Cantrell thought and, with a nod of thanks, followed McClure.

When Lion answered the door, it was obvious to Cantrell why the crew called him Lion. He was a handsome man, tall and ramrod straight, his hair a mane of white. He was almost as tall as Cantrell. After they had been introduced, Lion turned to McClure.

"You go ahead. I want to talk with your friend a little."

Lion closed the door and said, "Sit down. Take the load off your feet."

He went around his desk, sat down, opened the bottom drawer, took out two glasses, and poured a hefty drink of whiskey into each.

"Now tell me about yourself."

Cantrell nodded and looked at Lion straight on. "Just so I don't come in here with shadows on my backtrail, I want to say right off I got a Wanted poster out on me. It's eleven years old, but it's there.

"It's also a fact I never put a dime in my Levis but what I earned it in fair, honest work. Now if you still want to listen, I'll tell you my side of it."

A flicker of a smile crossed Lion's face. He leaned back in his chair. "Let's hear it."

Cantrell frowned—remembering. He took a swallow of his drink, leaned forward and began.

"I was seventeen at the time. Pa's outfit was a small one but we made out, didn't bother nobody. Then the Hardesters, they owned the biggest ranch around, started pushing on the small outfits. They wanted the water we had on our place.

"They tried to get Pa to sell, but he wouldn't.

"At first, they run our cows off, burned our haystacks, did anything to try to get us to sell, or just plain leave. Then they started beatin' up on Pa—every time they seen him.

"That wasn't enough to make us run so they took to insultin' my ma. I tried to take the shotgun an' go to huntin' 'em but Pa took it away from me. Then come the day.

"I was standin' out by the well when they rode in, all five of them. Chat Hardester slapped Ma. Pa grabbed for a rifle and they killed him.

"I run to get the shotgun, but they grabbed me an' whipped me with a bullwhip after tyin' me up. I still carry the scars.

"When they left, Ma cut me loose.

"I told her I was gonna kill Chat Hardester. She tried to talk me outta it but I wouldn't listen. I packed her things in the wagon and headed her toward her sister's place over in the next county. Told her I might never see her again.

"When she was headed out good, I went in the house and got Pa's old double-barreled twelve-gauge, loaded it with buckshot, and headed for town.

"Knowed I couldn't match Chat Hardester's six-gun speed. I was pretty good with a rifle but figured that old shotgun would even us up real good.

"Soon's I rode into town I seen Chat's horse tied to the rail in front of the saloon." Cantrell picked up his glass and took a swallow of his drink.

He continued, "When I got down from my horse I walked over to the undertaker's, told him Pa was lying out yonder an' needed to be buried. Give 'im a dollar to do it."

Cantrell put his glass on the desk.

"From there I went back to the front of the saloon and checked the reins to be sure I hadn't tied 'em so's I could leave in a hurry. Knew I'd be runnin' when I come outta there after killin' Chat.

"Them Hardesters didn't only own the biggest ranch. They owned the fastest guns *and* the law. I knowed I'd be on the wrong side of *that* pretty quick, but it was something I had to do.

"When I pushed through the batwing doors I sort of slipped off to the side in order for my eyes to get used to the darkness.

"Chat nor the barkeep noticed me. Chat was tellin' how he'd whipped me and the tall bit of squirmin' I done while he was doin' it.

"Soon's my eyes got so I could see I stepped to the middle of the floor.

" 'Hardester, you got no whip in your hand now, so fill it with that .44 you're packin'.'

"He turned around, slow-like. Then he says, 'Well now, kid, reckon I didn't give you enough. You ain't damn fool enough to believe you can beat me to the draw, are you?'

"I knew he didn't see the shotgun hangin' down straight at my side. All he could see was that old, beat-up single-action Colt I had in a holster on my right side. So I told 'im, 'Draw, Hardester. You've whipped up on your last kid.'

"Well, he sort of grinned at me. I knowed right then he figured I was gonna try to beat him to the draw. Right in the middle of that grin he went for his gun. He was fast, Mr. McCord, real fast, but soon's I seen his eyes narrow I knowed he was gonna draw, so I rotated that old shotgun and fired.

"Seemed like everything was happenin' real slow-like. I felt the gun buck against my side; then it looked like a great big red flower bloomed out of Chat's chest. The shot knocked him backward against the bar. When he slid down it I knowed he was dead.

"I swung the barrel a hair to the right, and centered it on the barkeep.

"I said to him, 'Move an' I'll kill you too.'

"He shook his head, his face about the color of that dough Ma used to make bread outta. He put his hands way up in the air.

" 'I ain't takin' no hand in this here fight.' He sort of squealed them words. Then he said, 'Get the hell outta here while you can, kid. This place'll be full of people 'fore you know it.'

"I turned and walked slow-like outta the door, like maybe I'd just been to see a friend. On the boardwalk outside I met a man comin' at a dead run.

" 'What happened?' he asked.

"I told him I was just showin' the barkeep that old shotgun of Pa's and it accidentally went off. Even though I was actin' sort of relaxed, I was scared to death.

"I eased over and got on my horse, walked him fast-like to the edge of town, then give him his head. And b'lieve me, Mr. McCord, that horse ran like the devil was after him."

Cantrell picked up his drink, took a swallow, and leaned back in his chair. "That was eleven years ago, Mr. McCord. I ain't ashamed of none of it. Reckon I'd've killed all five of them if there'd been any way to do it. Know I'm gonna have to do it someday.

"If you take me on I don't want to bring trouble down on you. If they find out where I am, it's my fight. I'll quit and go meet them. I'm through trying to dodge killing them."

When Cantrell had finished his story, Lion picked up his drink and sipped from it.

"I heard your story several years back, from a Texas man who drove a herd up here. His pa sold me the cows down in the Big Bend." He sipped his drink again. "Seems like he said you helped him drive a couple of herds to rails-end in Kansas. He thought you were one hell of a good cowhand.

"He's my friend, young man, and I might add Cole Mason's your friend too."

Cantrell felt his throat tighten. He took a swallow of his drink to hide his emotion, then smiled crookedly at Lion.

"Don't reckon he told you he taught me everything I know about cows. Why, I was just a raw kid trying to find some place to earn my keep. He talked his pa into letting me go on trail drive with him."

"No, he didn't tell me that, but he did tell me one thing. Said he taught you how to handle that .44 you're packin', and said you may be the fastest to ever buckle on a gunbelt. He didn't say it, but I got the feelin' that you're faster'n him."

"Aw, don't you believe that. We used to play games, and I figure he let me beat him."

Cantrell saw Lion's eyes smile back at him. "Glad you said that, son. Tells me you ain't a swaggerin', gun-totin' bully. One thing puzzles me though. If you're that good, why haven't you faced the Hardesters?"

"That's a fair enough question," Cantrell answered. "I've had to kill at one time and another, but I just plain don't cotton to it. Now, I reckon if I have to, it's got to happen.

"Soon after I left home, reckon I'd've killed all of them if I could. Had a little time to cool down 'fore I got so I could handle a gun pretty good. By then killin' got to be so I didn't like it. Never did like it for that matter."

Lion stood. "Tell Wyatt Mann, my foreman, you're the new hand around here and I said to work the hell out of you." He stuck out his hand. "Welcome to the BIM, and that last I said— Well, Mann'll do that anyway."

"Thanks, Mr. McCord. I'll make you a hand." Cantrell walked toward the door. Lion stopped him.

"The boys call me Lion. You can call me Ian, Lion, or McCord, but forget the mister."

"Thank you, sir." Cantrell left.

He had not pulled his rig from the dun when he rode in. Now that he had a job, he took care of his horse and put him in an empty stall.

CHAPTER
4

When he came out, he saw McClure and several other hands down at the corral and headed in that direction.

"Reckon Lion must've hired you," McClure yelled. "Figured that out for myself when I seen you stable your horse."

McClure tied the bay he'd been leading to a rail. "Reckon you'll be wantin' to find Wyatt Mann now. He's over yonder at the stock pens."

Cantrell nodded and changed his course. When he saw Mann, he knew this outfit had a working foreman.

Mann had a young calf up in his arms. He carried it to the gate and struggled to shift it enough to get the latch off. Cantrell lengthened his stride to a jog and opened it for him.

"Thanks." He slanted a look at Cantrell. "Reckon the boss hired you. Figured he would. You look like the kind of man we want around here."

Cantrell closed and latched the gate behind him. "Where you going with him?"

"Over yonder. The little critter got separated from its ma. She's in that other pen."

Cantrell ran ahead and opened the gate enough for Mann to shove the calf through. It didn't need coaxing. As soon as its hooves touched the ground, it headed for its ma and had an udder in its mouth quicker than scat.

Both men chuckled, while Mann brushed dust from his sleeves. "Reckon you'll be needin' a string of ponies. Get McClure to cut you out two or three. We cover a lot of ground out here. Stash your gear in the bunkhouse. If the bunk ain't got nothin' on it, it don't belong to nobody, so pick any one of them."

"Thanks." Cantrell turned to leave and almost ran head-on into the girl he'd seen in town.

"Oh! Pardon, ma'am." He tipped his hat. "Didn't see you."

Mann walked over. "This is Miss Elena, Lion's daughter. She's a fair hand around cows, but she's stubborn as a loggin' mule and got a temper like a rattlesnake. Aside from that I reckon she's all right."

It was obvious to Cantrell that Mann was used to teasing Elena, but he wasn't prepared for her reaction, and apparently, neither was Mann.

"Mr. Cantrell and I almost met the other day in Durango." Her eyes were like green ice. "But he was busy beating some poor miner to near death, and then his saloon girl gave him such tender treatment I'm sure he could see nothing else."

In her icy anger, she was regal and beautiful, Cantrell thought. Then she continued, "If Mr. Cantrell is as good with cows as he is pursuing saloon girls I'm certain he'll make Papa a good hand." She turned on her heel and left.

Mann pushed his hat back. "Wh-What the hell was that all about?" he sputtered.

"Damned if I know," Cantrell replied, "but she shore don't cotton to me."

He squinted into the afternoon sun, watching until Elena disappeared into the stable.

"Reckon I'll stay clear of her. That shouldn't be a problem though. Lion said for you to work the hell out of me."

"Kinda figured on doin' that." Mann's dry grin, along with his words, dripped sarcasm.

"Well, tell me what you want done and I'll get after it."

"C'mon in the bunkhouse. I'll sketch a map and some landmarks on the BIM, along with the location of the line shacks. It's comin' on time to start hazing the cows back down to winter range."

Mann glanced toward the bunkhouse. "I reckon you noticed—the crew wears their handguns tied down. You do the same, but I don't reckon I have to tell *you* that.

"We sit right straddle the trail to Santa Fe. Some pretty salty characters use it. They slaughter our cows and use what little they need for a couple of meals, then let the rest rot. And if you cross their path they're likely to kill you for your horse, or anything else you might have."

Mann shook his head. "Cantrell, we've even had 'em bust in the door of our line shacks. They come in a-shootin' without any thought of givin' them inside a chance. They know a cowpoke ridin' the line won't have any money, so all they kill 'em for is guns and saddles. Reckon there's some place where they get a pretty good price for guns and loads for them. You be careful."

Cantrell returned Mann's look straight on. "I usually cover my backside. I might even run into some of my old friends in those hills."

When he rode out the next morning, Cantrell didn't expect to come back until all the cattle had been hazed to lower ground.

He had been working the far northeast section of the ranch for about a month, and it looked as if there was yet another month's work before they completed the gather.

His partner, a tall, taciturn man, looked to be part Apache. His bowed legs, lean, high-cheekboned face, and straight black hair gave Cantrell that idea. He used the name Art King. He'd been with the BIM about fourteen years, and Cantrell had never seen a better man with cows. He seldom said much more than "Mornin', might rain," if that was the case, and then he would stick his thumb toward the sky. Cantrell liked him.

They had put in a hard day chasing cows out of Aspen brakes, ravines, and brush. It was King's turn to cook. He was silently mixing biscuits on the table by the stove when Cantrell heard what he thought to be a twig snapping.

"Keep doin' what you're doin'," he said. "We got company."

King never changed expression or missed a beat in rolling the biscuits. Cantrell moved back into the corner shadows of the line shack. Night had settled in, and the lantern cast a soft glow over the cooking area. The old cast-iron wood-burning stove made little light.

Cantrell had hardly gotten set, his .44 drawn, when the

door crashed inward, followed by two gunmen. They came in firing.

Cantrell fired at the first one through the opening. King dived for the floor. With him out of the way, room opened up for Cantrell.

Lead, smoke, and wood sliver filled the room. Cantrell thumbed back the hammer for another shot. The second gunman turned toward him and fanned his gun. Cantrell slipped thumb from hammer and watched the gunny's skull explode behind his still-snarling face.

"Damned hardcase ought to know better'n to fan a gun," he muttered, then walked over and toed the two onto their backs. They were dead. He turned his attention to King. He had been hit.

Cantrell squatted for a closer look.

King, his hand pressed to his shoulder, blood seeping between his fingers, cursed a steady stream, stopped to get his breath, and started again.

"Boy! I didn't even know you could talk, and here you've said more words in one string than I've heard you say in the last month."

King grimaced at him, obviously in pain. "Aw, go to hell. I just never had nothin' to say before."

"Sit still and let me look at that."

He worked his fingers along the bone. It seemed to be all right, and the bleeding came in a steady ooze. Cantrell guessed the arteries had escaped injury.

"Gotta clean this out. It's gonna hurt like hell. Where you keep that bottle of rotgut you nip on so sneaky-like?"

"Over there under my bedroll. Clean it, but don't waste none of my whiskey," King growled. "If you're as good fixin' bullet holes as you are puttin' 'em in folks, I ought to be good as new by sunup."

Cantrell dug through King's gear and brought the bottle back.

"Here, take a swig of this. It'll help kill the pain."

King took several healthy swallows while Cantrell held the bottle to his lips. When Cantrell pulled it away, King gasped, trying to get his breath.

"Damn! That's good. Now you take a drink."

Cantrell felt himself go warm inside. King had never offered him a drink before. It was probably rotten whiskey, but he'd have taken a drink if it had been rat poison. It looked like he had a friend.

He took a healthy swig and felt it curl his toes before he went to work on King's shoulder.

Neither said anything until Cantrell tied the bandage in place, patted it, and stood.

"That's it," he grunted.

King let his breath out, sweat streaming down his face. "Hope I can do the same for you sometime."

Cantrell chuckled, and cleaned up the mess. Finished, he stripped the two gunmen of their guns and went through their pockets. He checked them for money belts; each of them had one, and they were both heavy.

He took a blanket, made a pack of it, piled the gunmen's belongings into it, and tied the ends together.

"Now to find their horses." He slanted a look at King. "We'll turn this stuff over to Lion when I get you back to the ranch tomorrow. Full day's ride. You feel up to it?"

"Ain't nothin' wrong with me. You ain't takin' me back to the ranch like some milksop city feller. I'll handle my end of it right here."

"Like hell. You want me to hogtie you and take you back? You could get infection in that shoulder right easy with nothin' to put on it but that rotgut."

King didn't say another word. He just looked at Cantrell, and by that look, it didn't appear their friendship had lasted very long.

Cantrell found the gunmen's horses, rubbed them down, and fed them. He took their saddles, bridles, and rifles into the cabin.

"We'll leave in the morning." Cantrell's tone brooked no argument. "I'll bury those two before we leave."

He got up a couple of hours before daylight. It would take all day to dig a hole deep enough to bury the two men. Maybe he could find an easier way.

A cutbank downstream of the line shack looked like an ideal

place. He dragged the bodies under it and caved it in. Some future gullywasher might wash them out, but he'd worry about that if it happened.

Now, he had to get King to the ranch. Cantrell didn't look forward to the long ride with all the extra gear he'd be taking back.

He stopped several times to let King rest despite his grumbling denial that he needed it. He had the extra horses on a lead rope and traveled slowly to allow King, trailing behind, a chance to ease the bounce of his saddle.

He searched every nook and cranny for sign they were not alone. The extra gear, horses, and the wounded man made keeping a constant vigil more difficult, but when they finally sighted the ranch buildings, they had encountered no trouble.

Mann opened the gate to the corral. "What happened?" He looked at the two extra horses and raised his eyebrows. "That's damned good horseflesh. Where'd you get them?"

"Have somebody take care of our horses and unpack these. I'll tell you about it after we get King in a bunk."

He dismounted and reached to catch his partner. He was just in time. King slumped into his arms.

While Cantrell told Mann the story, they undressed King and got him into a clean bunk.

Mann looked at Cantrell across King's chest. "Now you know why I told you to wear your gun tied down. This kind of thing happens all too often; only it's not always them as gets hurt."

Cantrell nodded and pulled the blanket up under King's chin. "I reckon you all have eaten so I'll see the cook. Gonna turn in early. Wantta head back 'fore dawn."

Mann shook his head. "No. You've been up there over a month. Take a couple of days off, go to town and raise a little hell. It'll do you good."

"But . . ."

"No but about it. Take some time off."

"Well, all right, but I need to see Lion 'fore I go. Want him to keep something for me, and I want to give him these money belts I took off them outlaws. Reckon it'll be all right to try to corner him tonight?"

"Yeah, he ain't much for puttin' off seein' his men if they want to talk." Mann gave Cantrell a look born in hell. "Stay away from Miss Elena. Way she acted last time, she might shoot you."

"Ain't never figured that out yet." Cantrell shook his head. Before heading for the main house, he told Mann to lay the guns out so the men could pick what they wanted of them. They were very good weapons.

He swept his hat from his head when the door opened. "Evenin', Miss Elena. I need to talk with Lion a few minutes if it's all right."

"He's in his office. Go on back. He sees *anybody*."

Cantrell felt his face harden but nodded his thanks. He was getting a little tired of this high and mighty, spoiled female. He stared into her eyes a moment, said nothing, and headed back to Lion's office. Someday, he figured to find out just what he'd ever done to her. He reached the office and knocked.

"Cantrell! Come in, boy. What're you doing back here? Thought you and King were out at the northeast line shack."

He didn't want to tell the story again—but what the hell.

"We were, but we had some trouble with a couple of gunnies an' King took a bullet through his shoulder. I brought him back. Figured y'all would make him stay still long enough to get well. Knew I'd play hell keepin' him down."

"Tell me about it."

He told Lion about the cabin gunfight, and that he'd brought the gunmen's belongings back for any in the crew that might need them. He tossed the two money belts onto Lion's desk. "Figured those belonged to the ranch. They're pretty heavy."

Lion stared at him a moment. "This money is rightfully yours. You want me to keep it for you?"

Cantrell shook his head. "Ain't mine. What's in those belts belongs to the ranch. Help pay for what cows them hombres has stole off you. It's yours, Lion."

"I hope the word gets around and they'll stay clear for a while. Those bastards don't give a man a chance, an' seems like they're gittin' braver all the time. Wish I had the guns to ride into their hideout and get rid of them all."

"Don't ever try it, Lion. There's a whole bunch of them.

It'd take a army to ride in there an' do any good. But what I really came to see you for—I want you to keep something for me. Someday I'll ask for it back."

"Sure, son, what is it?"

Cantrell stripped the money belt from under his shirt and handed it to him.

Lion hefted it a couple of times. "Pretty heavy, son. How much is it?"

" 'Bout twenty-seven hundred dollars, give or take a couple hundred I spent."

"That's a lot of money. You sure you want me to keep it for you?"

Cantrell stared at him a moment. "Don't you want to know where I got it?"

Lion pursed his lips, then looked at Cantrell. "Hell, yeah, but it ain't any of my business. If you want to tell me, go ahead."

Cantrell returned his look. "If you'd asked me, I probably wouldn't have told you. I worked for it, Lion. Me an' Cole Mason, we rounded up mavericks down in the Big Bend, pushed 'em into Kansas and sold 'em. We made more than one drive, and after payin' off the trail hands we split up what was left." He nodded toward the belt. "That's my share. Mason wanted me to take half of it but I wouldn't stand still for it. It was his cow savvy that let us make it, so what's in that belt is what I took, and even at that I think he gave me too much."

"Whew! You got enough to start yourself a nice little spread." His nod was emphatic. "Yep, I'll keep it for you. You want a receipt?"

"Nope. You know you got it. An' I'll guaran-damn-tee you I ain't gonna let nothin' happen to you while I'm around."

Lion opened a drawer and took out a piece of paper. "I ain't plannin' on it but something might happen."

He scribbled awhile, signed it, and handed it to Cantrell. "Just in case. Now you take care of that as good as you would if it was gold."

"You can bet on it." Cantrell said and held out his hand. "Thanks a lot. That thing out at the line shack made me kinda leery of hauling that much around with me." He stuck the scrap of paper in his pocket without reading it.

He said over his shoulder, "Mann said I should take a couple of days off and go to town. Reckon I could have a couple of those double eagles back?"

Lion laughed and reached in his pocket. "Here, I'll mark it off your pay. You have more than that coming anyway."

"Thanks," Cantrell said, thinking he'd wait until the next morning to head for Durango. It wasn't until he sat on his bunk that he read the receipt Lion had written. It read, "Received three money belts from Quinton Cantrell, all unopened. One has at least twenty-five hundred dollars in it. They *all* belong to him, and will be given to him if anything happens to me." He had signed and dated it.

"Well," Quint mumbled, "I'll argue with him about this later."

CHAPTER
5

Venicia watched Cantrell close the door behind him before she walked into Lion's office. "What did Quint want this late, Ian?"

He scooted his chair back and patted his knee. "Come sit down, *querida mia*."

Venicia walked around his desk, sat on his lap, and put her arms around his neck. "All right, Ian McCord, now I'm at your mercy. Tell me what Quint wanted."

He laughed. "Mercy? Venicia, you've never been at anybody's mercy in your life." He gave her a peck on the cheek and leaned back to see her better. "Cantrell and King had some trouble up at the line shack. Cantrell killed two men up there and brought me the money belts they were wearing. I tried to get him to keep them, but he wouldn't hear of it. Said that money belonged to the ranch. Said it would help pay for the cattle they been stealin' from us."

"Did either of them get hurt?"

"King took a slug through his shoulder so Cantrell brought him back. Said he knew he couldn't keep him down long enough for him to get well and that we could. From what he said, King ain't hurt bad."

"Thank goodness for that." She peered intently into Lion's eyes. "You told me a while back we had an outlaw riding for us. Quint's that outlaw, isn't he, Ian?"

He nodded. "Yeah, but I know how he got to be one, and that don't make no difference to me. I trust him."

"He brought that money to you; somehow that doesn't fit my picture of an outlaw." Venicia leaned close to Lion and kissed his cheek. "Now, tell me about him."

He pushed her away. "No you don't. You start cuddling up to me like that and you know I'll do anything you want. I'll tell you his story some day—but not now. Matter of fact, I reckon when the time comes I'll have *him* tell you." He looked thoughtfully at her. "You have a reason for wanting to know. What is it?"

"No, I really don't—but, well, yes I do. I-I'm afraid Elena is—No, I can't say that. Oh, I don't know what I mean." Venicia sighed. She knew what she wanted to say, but even thinking it seemed preposterous.

"Yes you do. Now, say what you mean."

Venicia stared at him, wide-eyed, and took a deep breath. "Now, don't you laugh, Ian, or so help me you'll sleep in a cold bed for a week."

"Laugh at you, my love? You know I'd never laugh at you."

She studied his face a moment and decided to say it. "Ian, Quint is the kind of man a woman could very easily fall in love with. Oh, she might know she shouldn't, but the mind never makes that decision for a woman. Women respond to emotions, not reason, and Elena is a woman in every respect. Right now she's fighting what she feels—but she's falling in love with Quint."

"Falling for Cantrell? You—you're dreamin', *querida*. Have you seen how she treats him? I ain't never seen a woman treat a man like that. Why, she treats him like dirt. I been meanin' to speak to her about that. He's one of the best men I ever knew."

Venicia had a mysterious little smile at the corners of her mouth. "*Not* the best *I've* ever known, but I've thought while watching him that he'd come close. You mark my words, Ian McCord, Elena's mighty close to admitting to herself she's found her man—and right now she's fighting it. I'm afraid of what will happen when she accepts the idea. Elena's as bullheaded as you, and if she gets the bit in her teeth—well, it scares me."

Lion folded his arms around her and stood, lifting her as though she were a child. "We'll worry about that when I see her change. Might not be anything to your worries. Come on, let's find something to warm us."

Venicia looked at his craggy face and fell in love with him all over again. She leaned her face into the bend of his shoulder, reached up, and nipped his earlobe. "Something warm, Ian? Were you thinking of a cup of coffee?" She giggled and snuggled closer.

The next morning, when Cantrell walked to the corral to saddle up for town, three men were there with Mann. Two of the men busily hitched a spirited bay to the buggy. Mann came over before Cantrell could open the corral gate.

"Miss Elena decided she's gonna go to town. I always send two or three riders along when she goes. Want you to ride with them. From what King says you could give Jim Courtright and John Wesley Hardin the draw and still beat them."

"Aw, don't believe that. He was layin' on the floor and couldn't see anything."

"Anyway—you ride with them."

"Mann, I'll ride *with* 'em, but I shore as hell ain't gonna *drive* that buggy."

"She drives her own. Don't worry. Just stay close enough to see no harm comes."

Cantrell nodded, opened the gate, and looked for his horse.

While saddling, he told the men how he wanted them to arrange themselves around the buggy. When they rode away from the ranch, they hit a hard steady pace and held it for several hours.

From memory Cantrell studied the surrounding hills and estimated they were still about an hour out of Durango. He avoided contact with Elena, riding ahead of her buggy, carefully scanning the terrain. Mann had put him in charge of the escort, and he'd die before letting anything happen to her. Peering into the distance, Cantrell saw dust, then riders. Estimating they were about two miles away, he dropped back to the side of the buggy.

He looked at Elena. It was the first time since leaving the ranch that their gazes had met. "Stay behind us. Keep out of handgun range. Riders comin'."

Her chin started to come up in that proud, disdainful way. "Stay here." His voice brooked no argument.

Her eyes widened. She apparently had never been spoken to in that tone. Her face flushed. Her eyes sparked fire, but Cantrell thought she would do as told. He rode to the others. He nodded to one of them. "Stay here with the buggy. We're gonna ride ahead. Empty the saddle of any that gets close."

To the rest of the men he said, "Get your handguns out but keep them out of sight. Don't fire unless I do. Let's go."

When they got closer, Cantrell counted eight men riding in a tight bunch. Closer still, he recognized three of them. One was Spider.

When within twenty or thirty feet, Cantrell held up his hand. "This is as far as you go. You're on BIM range. We don't cotton to the likes of you."

The one leading the pack leered. Cantrell had heard him called Curly Farlow somewhere on his backtrail.

"Who the hell are you to tell us where we can go?"

"*I'm* not tellin' you. These .44s trained on your gut are doing the talkin', but if you want to push your luck I'll get about three of you." Cantrell nodded toward his men. "They'll get the rest."

Farlow slanted a glance at Cantrell's men. The leer disappeared. "This is the road to Santa Fe. You can't block a road."

"The hell I can't." Cantrell squinted into the middle of the pack. "You, Spider, ride out to the side. I told you not to ever let me see you again."

Spider didn't move.

"C'mon out, Spider, or I'll kill you in the pack. Your friends won't take kindly to you squeezin' off a shot that might hit them."

"Hell, Cantrell, I don't want no trouble with you."

"You got trouble. Ride out of there." Cantrell figured he'd have to kill Spider now or risk getting shot in the back from ambush later on.

Spider had no choice. He kneed his horse clear of the crowd.

"Now, pull that handgun anytime."

Spider's hand flashed to his side—but much too late. Cantrell put two slugs in him before his gun cleared leather.

Cantrell didn't watch him fall. He swung his gun to cover Farlow. "Feel lucky?" The leftover rage from the shooting at the line shack and Spider's attempt to hold him up combined to make Cantrell cold, killing mad. He hoped Farlow would be a damned fool and try for his gun.

Farlow held his hands clear of his holsters. "Not today, Cantrell, but the time'll come."

"I hope so—soon. Now drop your guns." He waited until they dropped. "Now your rifles, and don't get any ideas about trying your luck. You'd be dead before the idea took hold." He motioned to the rider closest to him. "Gather those guns and put them behind the seat in the buggy."

His attention turned to Farlow. "Tie Spider across his saddle, then ride ahead of us—we're all going to Durango. Soon as I get Miss McCord safely to town, you and your scum can go on your way."

Farlow cast him a sneer and jerked the reins to turn his horse. They took care of Spider and he motioned his men to head out as Cantrell had told them.

On the outskirts of town, Cantrell rode close to the back of the seven and said, "I'll tell you when to break this little party up. You'll peel off one at a time, and when I get back to the BIM, I don't want ever to see any of you on it."

He rode back to the buggy. "Miss Elena, when do you want us ready to leave here?"

She looked at him steadily for several seconds before she replied. "You know they're going to kill you, don't you?" The cold aloofness was gone.

"Well, ma'am, maybe so, but there's been them who tried it 'fore now. They ain't never had much luck."

"Anyway, I'll stop at the hotel if you'll have one of the boys take the buggy on to the livery. I'd like to be ready to leave for home day after tomorrow, early."

"Yes, ma'am. Anything you want us to do for you while we're here?"

"No, nothing except—well, please try to stay out of trouble."

"Yes'm, I always do. It just don't always happen that way." He turned and rode back to Farlow's bunch.

As they traversed Main Street, Cantrell poked one, then another of Farlow's bunch in the back and waved them to the side. By the time they reached the hotel, none of the outlaws rode with them.

He helped Elena down and signaled one of the men to take her bag in. Assured she would be all right, he tied the dun behind the buggy and headed for the livery.

Rawhide Doby met him outside the stable door. "Looks like you hooked up with the BIM. Seen you ride by with Miss Elena. Good outfit."

Cantrell stripped the gear from his horse, then looked at Doby. "Reckon Lion's the best man I ever rode for 'cept one. I don't s'pose I'll ever figure anyone to be the equal of that one."

"Must've been one hell of a man. Don't reckon I ever seen one I'd put in the same stable with Lion McCord."

"Cole Mason's that kind of man, and Lion would agree with me. I'm going to get me a room in the hotel. Don't feel like sleepin' in your haymow tonight. Need a bath anyway."

"Well goshding it, looks like you mighta just took one the last few days. Whatcha need one now for?"

Cantrell smiled to himself. "Old-timer, I don't rightly know when I might get a chance for another, so I figure to take one now 'fore winter sets in. Might catch cold then."

Doby apparently took him seriously. "You can bet on it. I took one once right after Christmas an' dang near caught the pewmonia."

Cantrell headed for the hotel, chuckling to himself. Through habit his glance flicked from doorways to windows, to alleys. He was not aware of doing it. Vigilance was as natural to him as breathing.

He reached the hotel, went in, signed for a room, and told the boy at the desk to have warm bath water carried to his room in a couple of hours. He left and went to the general store down the street.

After selecting three pairs of Levis and four shirts, he was about to leave, when he saw the suits. He hadn't owned a suit since his last one burned in a grass fire over in Kansas—outside of Dodge City.

According to the hands, the Señora Venicia always had a big fandango New Year's Eve. Cantrell pondered getting a suit, dress shirt, and string tie, and decided it was a good idea. After adding some long-handles and socks to his growing pile, he told the storekeeper to tally his bill. It came to twenty-one dollars and eleven cents.

"Whew! Things sure are costly anymore."

"Yeah, but remember your suit came to almost eleven dollars."

Cantrell shrugged, paid his bill, and went back to the hotel.

Dark had settled in when Cantrell walked back out on the street. Clean from the skin out he felt better. Hoping Faye would let it slip why his name had upset her, he headed for the Golden Eagle.

The saloon was just ahead when he crossed the opening between two buildings. Out of the corner of his eye he saw shadowy movement. He threw himself forward at the instant orange flame blossomed from the darkness.

He hit the ground, drew, fired, rolled, and fired again. He thumbed the hammer back for another shot, but held it. His attacker was lying, unmoving, the upper part of his body on the boardwalk, his legs dangling between the buildings. Cantrell stood. A crowd had gathered.

He walked to the ambusher and kicked his gun beyond reach, a needless task—the man was dead.

A miner, the closest person to Cantrell, stood with his mouth open, staring.

"Get the law," Cantrell told him, and looked down at the man he'd killed. Cold, controlled anger flooded him. This man had brought it to him. He felt no sorrow for killing him.

A brawny stranger sidled up. Cantrell figured him for a miner. "Seen the whole thing. Started to yell for you to watch it but didn't have time. He fired an' you'd done killed him 'fore I could get a word out."

"Thanks, stranger. I'd take it kindly if you'd tell the law that when he gets here. After he gets through talking to me I'll meet you in the Golden Eagle—buy you a drink."

Still cautious, Cantrell pushed his toe under the gunman's shoulder and rolled him over. As he suspected, the man was one of Farlow's bunch. This would not be the last of them he'd have to face. His rawhiding them back to town would stick in their craw.

A grizzled, crusty old man wearing a marshal's badge walked up, peered at the corpse, grunted, then looked around the circle of men. "Who done it?"

Cantrell stepped clear of the crowd. "Reckon I got to stake claim to it, Marshal," he said.

"You'd better—"

"I seen it all, Marshal Nolen," the stranger cut in. "That there man alayin' there had already fired 'fore this here one even drew his gun. I can swear to that."

The lawman looked at the crowd. "Anyone else see it?"

Two others, miners by their dress, stepped forward. "It's like Bronson there said," the taller of the two grunted.

The shorter one looked at Cantrell, then shook his head. "I didn't figure you had a chance. Never seen a body git a gun in action so fast. Who are you?"

Cantrell looked directly at the marshal. "Quint Cantrell's the name." Now the sheriff would be wanting to talk with him.

"I knew who you was when I walked up, Cantrell." The marshal's gaze was cold. "The three of you, and you too, Cantrell, come on over to the office." The marshal walked behind them and said, "I want the three of you to sign a statement, and I want to talk to you a mite, Cantrell."

Cantrell followed in the wake of the other three. He held his shoulders straight, head high, while inside he felt sick and limp.

Knowing the marshal would have to do something about the Wanted notice on him, he figured the Hardesters were finally going to corner him. Something turned hard and mean deep in his gut. He'd surrender to this old-timer, but damned if he would stick around and be turned over to any of the Hardester brothers.

Reaching the marshal's office, the old lawman opened the door, stepped, aside, and waved them in.

After they were seated, the marshal questioned them as a group, wrote his report, and had them sign it. Cantrell was in accord with the way the others told it so he signed it as well. The paperwork finished, the marshal dismissed them—all but Cantrell.

CHAPTER
6

Cantrell didn't wait for the marshal to open the conversation. "Reckon you're gonna hold me on that old Wanted notice." He shrugged. "You got your job to do."

The old man's eyes crinkled at the corners. "Cantrell, that notice is over eleven years old. How old were you then?"

"Seventeen."

"I know the story behind it. Can't say I blame you for killing Chat Hardester." He pulled an old, charred, corncob pipe from his desk, packed it, and put a light to it. He puffed until a cloud of smoke engulfed half the room.

The silence built until Cantrell wanted to reach out and tear into it.

Finally, the marshal, his voice deep in his throat, broke the silence. "Son, I've been upholding the law for thirty years now. A wanted man? Well it's my sworn duty to arrest him. I—"

"I understand, Marshal." Cantrell stood. "Where's my cell?"

The old man's eyes again crinkled at the corners. "Ain't got one that'll fit you, son. I said any man wanted by the *law* I'd arrest, or die trying, but you ain't wanted. That poster wasn't put out by no law officer. It was put out by the Hardester brothers. I don't do their bidding. They ain't throwed their rope around me." He stood. "Want a cup of coffee?"

Cantrell felt as though a great weight had lifted from his shoulders. He wanted to hug the old man—or run out in the street shouting that he was free. Instead he shot the marshal a straight look and said, "No, sir, but it'd make me right proud if you'd let me buy you a drink."

"No thanks, son. If you're still there when I shut down for the night, I'll stop and have one with you." He looked across at Cantrell. "You were heading for the Golden Eagle, wasn't you?"

Cantrell nodded. "Yep, and I'll be there when you close down."

It was still early when Cantrell pushed through the batwing doors. He glanced around the room and saw none of Farlow's bunch. An empty table in the back corner attracted him. He sat with his back to the wall.

A pretty girl wearing too much face paint came to take his order.

"Whiskey, good whiskey," he answered in response to her smile. He watched as she walked back to the bar, liking the way her hips rolled under her skimpy dress—looked sort of like a couple of cub bears playing in a gunnysack.

She leaned across the bar and said something to Faye, who looked across the room at him, reached under the shelf, and poured from the bottle Cantrell knew she kept there. Faye said something to the girl and brought him his drink herself.

"Why didn't you let me know you were in town, Quint?"

He felt his face harden and flush, not liking the possessive way she had put the question to him. He wanted to answer that he didn't know he had to keep her apprised of his where-abouts.

"Marshal had me," he answered.

"And he didn't arrest you on that old . . ." Faye stopped and bit her lower lip.

"What were you going to say, Faye?"

She stammered. "Oh—oh yes, on that old fight you had with Moose Lawson."

It wasn't like her to lose composure. He knew she'd intend-ed to say, "that old Wanted notice." How could she know about that?

He looked directly at her, then motioned her to have a seat. "No," he answered as she seated herself. He didn't bother to stand and instantly regretted that he hadn't. He believed in always showing good manners.

"A man took a shot at me soon after I got to town. The marshal wanted to talk to me about it." He tossed down his drink, put money on the table, and stood.

"Where are you going? Aren't you going to stay awhile?"

He shook his head. "Haven't had anything to eat since morning. Gonna find me a steak to surround."

"I haven't eaten yet. Mind if I come along?"

Anger welled in his throat. He swallowed. "Sure, glad to have company," he lied, hoping she'd let it slip how *much* she knew of him, and *how* she knew.

They walked to the hotel in uncomfortable silence.

On entering the dining room, Cantrell saw Elena. She sat alone, and it looked as though she had finished her meal. He removed his hat and nodded, wishing Faye was anywhere but at his side. Their gazes clashed. Not acknowledging his nod, Elena looked away.

Well, it looks like I'm back where I started with that lady, he thought. Don't seem like she's ever gonna treat me like she does the other hands. Maybe she heard about the gunfight and just plain don't cotton to men who get in trouble all the time.

He seated Faye before sitting down himself. When he again looked toward Elena's table she was gone.

"If you've got eyes for that lady you might as well forget it, cowboy. The likes of you don't stand a chance with her."

He didn't bother to hide his anger this time. "Just what the hell do you mean by 'the likes of me'? You don't even know me. I ain't never said ten words to her—besides it ain't none of your business."

Faye stood, knocking her chair over as she did. "Maybe it isn't my business but there are things that are. I think I'll go take care of them right now." She threw her napkin on the table, cast him a furious look, and stomped toward the door, her heels sounding as though they would punch holes in the floor.

Her words were a threat, and Cantrell had the uneasy feeling she would make one hell of an enemy. But, he thought, he'd had a few enemies in his time, so what difference would a few more make? Unless they were like the Hardesters.

The last place the Hardesters tracked him to was Leadville, and he'd left there only after planting several false clues that would lead them to San Antonio. With luck, that's where they'd gone. The thought made him feel better. He hadn't wanted to do it this way, but he hoped he was rid of Faye.

He ate slowly, thinking, trying to sort out what Faye might know. She couldn't know anything that would hurt him, unless the Hardesters were friends of hers. The marshal knew about the Wanted poster and didn't intend to do anything about it. Cantrell didn't know of anything else on his backtrail that might get him in trouble with the law.

"Oh, well, what the hell," he growled, paid his bill and left. Faye had succeeded in spoiling his dinner, and if he had known what she was about, he would have continued to worry.

Sitting at the desk in her office, she scribbled hurriedly on a sheet of stationery. Anger bubbled just below the surface. She had been nice to—to that outlaw and he'd shunned every advance she'd made. Never in her life had she deliberately shown a man how she felt about him. Now, when she'd let down all her defenses, acted like one of her whores, thrown herself at him, he'd insulted her.

She finished writing, folded the paper, stuffed it in an envelope, and addressed it to the Five-H Ranch, New Mexico Territory. After melting sealing wax on the flap, she walked from the room.

Fearful she would change her mind, she walked to the post office and dropped the envelope in the slot along with some change for postage. *That* should take care of Mr. Quinton Cantrell, she thought. Wait until the Hardesters get *that* letter.

Cantrell saw her come out of the post office when he stepped into the marshal's office. He wondered what could prompt a woman to walk on the streets this late at night.

He told Nolen he'd not be in the Golden Eagle, and asked him to suggest a saloon where they could have a drink.

" 'Bout ready to close the office for the night. C'mon, I'll show you."

The marshal led the way to a small saloon around the corner from his office. They had the place to themselves. The tables were rough-hewn, the chairs handmade, but comfortable, and the bar was a large pine trunk, cut in half lengthwise and planed smooth. Cantrell liked the coziness of the place.

When they had their drinks, the marshal cast a troubled look at Cantrell. "You figure to stay in this part of the country?"

Cantrell nodded. "Reckon so, Nolen. Got a good job with Lion McCord, and I'm sorta lookin' to start my own spread if I find the right place at a price I can afford."

"Glad to hear it, son, but you know the Hardesters are gonna find you sooner or later. Then it's gonna be hell to pay."

"Yeah, I know, but I'm through dodging them. Ain't lookin' for a shootout, but reckon it's gotta happen sometime."

The old marshal looked worried. "I wish it didn't have to happen in my town," he said. His voice was so soft Cantrell had to strain to hear him.

Cantrell took a swallow of his drink and placed it back on the table in front of him. "I wish there was something I could do to change it, Marshal. The only thing I could do would be to drift again and that I ain't gonna do." He tossed the rest of the drink down and held up two fingers to the bartender.

"One more, then I gotta get to bed," Nolen said. He laid his hand on Cantrell's arm. "Son, I ain't askin' you to leave town. I don't blame you for what you have to do." He shook his head. "I just wish it didn't have to be here."

"Yeah, I wish it didn't have to be anywhere, and along with that I've made myself some more trouble. The whole Farlow bunch would like to see me laid out with a few well-placed slugs in me."

They finished their drinks in silence and stood to leave. Before parting, Nolen said, "Son, I can't do anything to help you, but I want you to know I'll not do anything to hurt you neither."

"Thanks, Marshal, I appreciate that."

Cantrell went to his room wishing for something to read. He went to bed determined to buy a paper and another book when he awoke. He had read *Tom Sawyer* twice since he bought it and wanted something new.

On reaching the middle of the street the next morning Cantrell had a clear view of the mountains to the north. They were shrouded in black, forbidding clouds. A lot of snow's falling up there, he thought. Gonna be a cold ride home. He hunkered deeper into his sheep-skin.

The warmth of the newspaper office folded around him. The tingle in his nose and ears slowly warmed, and with it came a feeling of well-being. He walked to the counter.

"Well, young feller, you read that last book you bought already?"

Cantrell was surprised that the tall, gray-haired man behind the desk remembered him. Despite the threatening weather outside, the day suddenly seemed filled with sunshine. He was making acquaintances in this town.

"Read it a couple of times and started on the third. Reckoned while in town, I might find something new. Can't just keep on readin' the same old thing all winter. This might be my last trip in until spring."

The proprietor turned to a shelf. Cantrell didn't know what title the owner of a newspaper went by.

"I don't have any books right now, but I do have something I believe you'd like. It's just a collection of loose pages some-body pulled together. I put a cowhide cover around them." He handed the folder across the counter. "It has a bunch of writings by Tom Paine, the feller who pulled the colonists together to whip the British. All of his 'Common Sense' papers are in there, and a few of his 'Crisis' papers."

He looked up from the packet he had pulled from the shelf. "You know, if Paine wasn't the first to think of getting out from under the British, he may very well have been the first to write about it. This is something I think you'll read many times."

Quint paid thirty-five cents for the folder and the latest newspaper on hand, then headed down the street.

Heavy clouds moved in to shut out the sun and the blue of the sky. Cantrell felt his gut tighten. They could be in for the first bad snowstorm of the season. To reach the ranch, a long ride even in good weather, would be a cold and dangerous journey in a snowstorm.

He changed his course. He'd thought to walk down Main Street, but now he walked quickly toward the hotel. He'd better see Miss Elena.

Before reaching the steps in front of the hotel, Cantrell saw Elena coming toward him, her arms full of packages. He turned to intercept her.

"May I carry those packages for you?"

Her icy stare was answer enough, but she said, "No, thank you. I can manage very well."

Well damn her anyway, he thought, but he had to talk to her, so he followed along. "Miss Elena, I need to talk to you." She didn't slow down, so he talked as they walked briskly to the hotel door.

"Ma'am, this weather's gonna turn awful nasty pretty soon. I think I better find the rest of the men and make sure they have money to last till the weather clears. Be safer to sit out the storm here in town."

They reached the hotel door and he opened it for her. Inside, she faced him. "I'm certain you'd like to have another night or two to carouse with your saloon women." She shifted the packages for a firmer grip on them. "*You* may think we'd better stay in town, but *I* think you'd better find the men and prepare to leave right away."

"Ma'am, as late as it is, you know we won't make it home by dark. We'll have to camp somewhere along the way. I think we shouldn't leave."

She knew better than this. She'd been raised in this part of the country. Cantrell didn't know why she was being so obstinate, but he thought he must be the cause of it.

"Nevertheless, Mr. Cantrell, we'll leave as soon as you get the men together."

"Yes, ma'am, I'll carry out your *orders* right away." His answer was short, crisp—and angry.

He spun on his heel and walked out the door. Spoiled brat'll get the bunch of us killed, including herself, he fumed to himself.

He had no doubt but what *he* could make it, regardless what the weather did, but now he was saddled with a hardheaded woman.

Yeah, she ain't no kid, she's a woman full-grown, so she ought to have better sense than to take out her grudge against me on the men.

He found Bob Bentree in the second saloon he peered into. "You take the other side of the street. I'll take this one. Find the other men and meet me in the hotel lobby. Miss Elena wants to leave as soon as possible."

"Cantrell, when I come in here it looked like one helluva storm was blowin' in. Reckon we oughtta be leavin' 'fore it gits here?"

"I told her. She don't give a damn."

He reached in his pocket and pulled out the few dollars he had left.

"When you find the others, put your money with this and get extra blankets, a slab of bacon, beans, coffee, and some dry lucifers wrapped in oilskin. See you as soon as we can get ready." He went out to begin his search.

It took about an hour to locate the men and hitch up the buggy. They gathered in front of the hotel. Cantrell's glance flicked across horses, men, and buggy. He mentally checked off saddles, rifles, handguns, buggy spokes and rims, and last—the provisions.

He asked Bentree, "Did you have enough money to get provisions?" At his nod, Cantrell continued, "Tell Miss Elena we're ready."

Bentree disappeared through the hotel doorway. I'm gonna try one more time to change her mind, Cantrell thought. It was getting nasty and promised to get worse.

When Elena came through the doorway, Cantrell walked to the front of the buggy to help her up.

"Miss Elena," he said before offering his hand, "I wish you'd think on it again."

She looked at him, her face and voice expressionless. "Please help me up, Mr. Cantrell."

He helped her into the buggy seat, then walked to his horse.

CHAPTER
7

Cantrell swung into the saddle, saying, "We'll get as far as we can by dark, 'less we're forced to hole up 'fore then."

They put about three miles behind them before it began to snow—only a few feathery flakes at first.

Well, here she comes, Cantrell thought. The dun swung his head and shook it, as though wondering why his big master had brought him out in this.

Now the snow began in earnest, and the animals braced against the gusting wind. Cantrell rode close to the men. "If this gets any worse, we won't be able to see ten feet. Ride next to the buggy. Stay close enough so you can touch it. Don't want you getting lost." He cupped his hands around his mouth to help them hear words the wind tried to blow away.

"Long as you can see what's ahead, look for a cutbank, blowdown, anything that'll shelter us." He gave them all the same message, then returned to the head of the horse pulling Elena's buggy. He'd lead as long as he could see.

The years spent on the open range and in the mountains had honed his sense of direction. He would not get lost, but they'd soon have to find shelter. He judged the temperature about zero.

He dropped back abreast of Elena. "You doin' all right?" he shouted.

She peered out of her parka, her nose and chin red. She nodded. Her eyes showed a hint of concern. Well, he thought, she brought it on herself. He felt no satisfaction that she worried or suffered from the cold. Lion and Mann gave him the job to get her safely home, and he would do it.

He thought sundown still a couple of hours away, but with

the overcast so heavy, darkness shrouded them. His guess as to the time could have been off significantly, and he felt a twinge of anxiety.

Cantrell had led them off the trail a long way back. He tried to remember each foot of the trail from town to the ranch and could think of no line shack, or any form of shelter, so he led them closer to the hills. The drifts were worse here, but chances for shelter better.

By his reckoning they were about seven or eight miles out of town, still close to twenty miles from ranch headquarters. The weather wasn't the only threat. The closer they rode to the hills, the more they were in jeopardy of running into some of the lawless bunch.

In this weather, if they found shelter, others might be there ahead of them. He shrugged. He'd face that when it happened.

Bob Bentree rode alongside. "Tom-Buck figures he smelled smoke back yonder, just a whiff, but he says he'd bet on it."

Cantrell signaled a halt. He motioned them to gather where Elena could hear.

He looked at each of them. "Tom-Buck figures he smelled smoke. May mean a cabin close by, or just somebody else caught out in this storm—whichever, remember, they may not be friendly."

His eyes, narrowed against the wind, looked at the men, then directly at Elena. "Whoever it is, we got to have shelter. We locate the smoke, I'll ride in and scout it. Keep your guns ready."

They covered close to another two hundred yards before Cantrell smelled a stronger hint of smoke. He guessed the direction from which it came and signaled the others to stay where they were. He dismounted and ground-reined the dun.

He disappeared into the white shroud that engulfed them. Running half-stooped-over so as to be less visible, he moved in on the source of the pungent odor.

Soon after leaving the dun, he entered a thicket of young pines and slowed, feeling his way, so as not to step on a twig and warn those ahead. Here among the trees it seemed quieter; a sound would carry. As it turned out, the thicket was only a windbreak, barely twenty yards wide.

About to step from the shelter of the trees, he saw a dilapi-dated old cabin in the small clearing and stopped.

Slowly, he sank to the ground. Smoke billowed from the crude stone chimney. The gusty wind tore it to stringy wisps and blew it away.

Whoever occupied the cabin might be friendly, but Cantrell would have bet his poke they were not.

The wooden shutters on the windows lessened his chance of being seen, but that didn't mean there might not be an eye pressed to a crack.

Three horses stood in the lean-to at the back of the cabin. This indication of three men inside didn't give Cantrell reason to rejoice.

The men who roamed this part of the country were salty. They lived by the gun. Cantrell would give them no chance to do harm to Miss Elena.

Fading back into the trees until sure his movements were covered, Cantrell worked his way around to the blind side of the cabin.

He dropped to his stomach and slowly snaked his way across an open area, sweating despite the cold. With his gloved hand he brushed the frozen sweat-cicles from his eyebrows and nose. He inhaled, trying to relax muscles pulled taut as a bowstring, bracing for the possibility of a bullet. The deep breath didn't help.

He slithered to the back wall, expecting the horses to announce his presence. Instead, they looked at him curious-ly, listlessly, and again munched on the little bit of hay in the rack.

Some of the tension flowed from him. He stood and care-fully searched for a crack through which he might see into the room.

He passed up a knothole. To cover it with his eye would shut off light. Even in this semi-dark that might be noticed. Then he found what he was looking for—a crack about as thick as a silver dollar.

The fireplace and the area in front of it were visible through the crack. Two men huddled close to the roaring flames.

Cantrell studied every inch of the room in his view and found the third man. Had it not been for the wall Cantrell could have touched him. He was lying on a bunk built against the wall. His chest rose and fell evenly.

Cantrell eased himself to the ground. He'd seen two of these men before. He couldn't remember where, but if he'd seen them, he would bet on the kind of men they were. He pondered going to the door, knocking it in, and with luck and surprise, blowing them to hell.

That idea ain't worth a damn, he thought. Elena and the boys wouldn't know what was happening, whether to come on in or not, and if he got unlucky, they'd be in a real fix. Too, breaking in and shooting, without giving the men inside a chance, wasn't his way.

He wriggled his way back to the pine thicket. His tracks had not drifted over, so he followed them to the buggy.

"There's a cabin over yonder in a clearing. Three hardcases have staked claim to it."

His glance searched each of them. They were cold, shivering, freezing—and blue. To hell with the hardcases, he thought, Miss Elena needs a fire and shelter.

"Ma'am, we gotta get in out of this. You won't be able to stand much more." Where before, her face had been red, it was now pinched and drawn. "What I'm gonna do might get some of us killed, but we're sure as hell gonna die if we stay out in this, so listen and do like I tell you—all of you."

Cantrell stated his plan. Bob Bentree gave him the only argument, trying to persuade him to stay behind and let him do the job.

"No. Do it my way. If I have it under control, I'll fire one shot. If y'all hear more than one shot, get the hell out of here, but if just one, then ride in." He grinned crookedly at them, and somehow found himself looking straight into Elena's eyes. He nodded. "I'll have coffee boilin' when you get there."

He made his way back to the cabin, then sat with his back to the wall and removed his gloves. He blew on his hands, trying to warm them.

Finally, feeling them tingle as with the prick of a thousand needles, he pushed them down inside his Levis and held them against his belly. When he felt he could hold a gun, he grasped the handle of the one he had shoved inside his belt. He wouldn't chance gripping his holster gun, because his hand might freeze to the metal.

He stood, bent so as to move under the windows unseen, and made his way to the door.

Well, Quinton Cantrell, let's see if we can pull this one off, he thought. Straightening, he pounded on the door and stepped quickly to the side, expecting lead to blow the door to slivers.

"Quint Cantrell here," he yelled. "Wantta share your fire."

The latch bar scraped the door as it was removed. The door swung open on stiff, weathered leather hinges. Cantrell held his hands clear of his guns.

"All right, c'mon in. We'll let you warm up a mite, but we ain't sharing our grub with you." The man who'd answered the door looked over his shoulder. "It's Cantrell all right. I seen him before. Seen him in Denver, and up in the park."

Cantrell slipped in and moved to the side to keep the wall at his back, thinking that if they hadn't palmed their weapons as soon as they saw him, maybe his scheme would work after all.

He waited, hoping they'd gather into a tighter group. The odds were already in their favor without having one of them to his side when he made his play.

"Got my own grub. Don't need none of yours. I'll fetch it after I warm up." He walked to the fire and squatted, holding one hand over it at a time, the other close to his side, where he could get at his .44.

He figured that the one who answered the door was the one he'd seen lying in the bunk. He hoped he wouldn't crawl back into it. That would make it impossible to draw and cover them all without having a blind side.

He lucked out. He didn't know the names any of them were using, but one of those he'd seen by the fire went to the wall and picked up a pair of saddlebags.

"Who's gonna cook? I went out and brung this stuff in. I done my part so one of you is gonna cook."

The other two sidled up and peered into the bag. All three stood bunched together.

Cantrell's right hand flashed to his gun. "Hold it right there," he said. His six-gun didn't waver. "Don't look up, don't move even your eyelids, or I'll separate you from them."

"What the—"

"Don't do it," Cantrell cut in. "Now, slow-like, drop your gunbelts. No fast moves. My thumb might slip off this hammer.

"Now drop those saddlebags in case you got a handgun in them." Guns, gunbelts, and saddlebags fell to the floor. "Move to this side of the room, and put your face against the wall. If you look around, I'll kill you."

Sullenly, they walked to the wall and did as directed.

Cantrell slipped his right handgun from its holster, pointed it at the ceiling, and thumbed off a single shot.

"Damn you—"

Cantrell moved his pistol a fraction and fired into the wall next to the face of the man who had cursed and looked over his shoulder.

"Said to keep your face to the wall," he ground out. "The next one moves gets a slug in the back of his head." He knew as he said it that he'd never shoot one of them from behind— but they didn't know that.

"Stand there awhile. Got friends comin'. One of them's a lady, and I don't want her gettin' upset when she sees y'all." He cocked his head slightly, then moved so he could cover the door as well as the three men. Damn, he thought, remembering the directions he'd given those back at the buggy. One shot, he'd said, and he'd fired two.

"Cantrell! You all right?" The shouted query was some distance from the cabin.

"Yeah! C'mon in," he yelled, glad for once that they had disobeyed him. While he waited, his glance swept every corner of the cabin. They needed more firewood. Still looking, he saw four bunks in tiers of two against the wall where the man had slept when he peeked through the crack.

One of those bunks would have to be fixed for privacy so nobody could look at Elena while she slept.

Outside, the snow squeaked and crunched under feet, then Cantrell heard Bentree tell one of the others to take care of the horses.

The door swung open, and seeing them, Cantrell knew he'd found shelter not a moment too soon. They'd had about all a body could stand. He stepped to the side to clear a path to the fire, and to insure an unobstructed line of fire at the outlaws. "Get to the fire and warm up. Bentree, soon's you thaw out, check those three there for guns or knives. I didn't want to chance it alone."

Elena, shaking like an Aspen leaf in a spring breeze, looked at him and said, her teeth chattering so she could hardly talk, "Wwwell, wh-wh-where's that coffee you promised us?"

Cantrell felt himself go mushy inside. If she could joke at a time like this, nearly frozen, she would do to ride the trail with. Spoiled and hardheaded she was, but she had more guts than a platoon of soldiers.

He glanced at the fire, thinking that the three he'd barged in on must have a pot brewing.

"Why it's right over yonder sittin' on the coals, Miss Elena. Tom-Buck," he said, not taking his gaze off the men still standing against the wall, "pour Miss Elena a cup of coffee while I figure out what to do with these three."

"Cantrell, what you got against us?" one of the three said, not turning his head. "You come in here an' throwed yore gun on us without nary a one of us doin' nothin' to you. Besides if'n you're worried 'bout yore lady, ain't a one of us ever done wrong to no woman. We done a lot o' things but harming womenfolk ain't one of them."

Cantrell stared at the backs of their heads, thinking that it was a fact that, hardcases or not, there were few men in the West who would harm a woman. He mulled over all he knew of the men he'd met on the shady side of the law. He decided to chance it.

"All right, turn around and look at me 'cause I'm gonna read to you from the book." They turned as one.

"I ain't gonna give you back your guns but we'll share this cabin till the weather lets up. If a one of you makes a move that don't look right, I'll tie you, and you can spend the rest of your time lyin' yonder in the corner."

Bentree collected pocketknives from each of them. With them totally disarmed, Cantrell rested easier.

"I don't know you men, but you seem to know me, so you know I ain't gonna take even a little chance with you. We'll split this cabin down the middle. That side's yours, this'n's ours. We get the bunks 'cause of Miss Elena. One of us'll cook and we'll all eat what's fixed.

"Tom-Buck, sit there and keep a gun on them. I'm going out and get more firewood. When I get back, you go get some, and when you get back, Bentree'll go."

An hour or so later, Cantrell sat on the floor against the wall. Firewood, plenty to last the night, formed a stack almost to the ceiling alongside the fireplace. Too early to cook supper, they all sat soaking in the warmth of the cabin.

Cantrell felt the gaze of one of the outlaws on him and shifted his eyes to look at the man.

"Tell me something, Cantrell. I heard about you for some years now, and I ain't never been told you'd shoot a man in the back. You wouldn't've shot us with our back to you—would you?"

"Nope, but you didn't feel like takin' a chance, did you?"

The outlaw grinned and shook his head. "Not me."

Cantrell stood. "Reckon I'll fix some grub." He looked at Tom-Buck. "Where'd you put it?"

Tom-Buck nodded toward one of the lower bunks. "Right there, Cantrell. I'll cook though. From what Art King told us, you can't cook near as good as you handle a gun."

Elena rose abruptly. "*I'll* cook."

Cantrell looked at her, his eyebrows raised. "Aw, now you don't need to believe Tom-Buck, Miss Elena. I can put a passable meal together."

"Afraid of my cooking, Mr. Cantrell?"

He was, but didn't dare tell her he'd bet a month's pay she couldn't boil water. "No, ma'am. I figure if you made up your mind to it you could do most anything." Seeing a spark of anger show in her eyes, he turned away before she could scald him with her tongue.

Surprised, he watched her go about preparing their meal as

though very much at home in the kitchen. She had Bentree
open several tins of beans while she used Cantrell's sheath
knife to slice strips of bacon, putting some in the beans and
frying the rest.

She mixed biscuits, patted them out, and placed them close
to the fire to rise and bake, but not burn. Watching her, Cantrell
thought it would be hard to mess up canned beans. Maybe the
biscuits would be like rocks.

If he had really hoped she would flop, he was disappointed.
The biscuits were fluffy. The fresh coffee she'd brewed lay on
his tongue soft as a maiden's dream—some of the best he'd
ever had—and of course the beans and bacon were what he'd
expected.

After eating, he sat leaning against the wall, thinking that
now he knew how that old sow felt all sprawled out in the
sun with her belly full, the one he used to watch when he was
a kid. He slanted a look from under his hat brim at Elena. She
returned his look.

"You seem surprised, Mr. Cantrell, that I didn't burn everything to smithereens. If you'd bothered to ask, the boys could
have told you that Papa often lets me go on roundup—as the
cook."

"You? On roundup?" It slipped out before he could stop
it. "Uh, I'm sorry, Miss Elena. Reckon I just always pictured—"

"Pictured me as the sheltered, pampered daughter of the rich
cattleman?"

He squirmed. "Well yes'm. Reckon that's about it. Sorry."

"Don't be. We both know you were *partly* right." Her voice
had softened and she turned away.

Damn, Cantrell thought, that woman is the most befuddling
female creature I ever did know. He stood, took his mess gear
to the fireplace, and scooped up ashes with which to scour it.

They settled into a routine for cooking, eating, sleeping, and
standing watch. It snowed for two days and stayed bitter cold
for this early in the fall, even for the high country.

Cantrell was convinced by the end of the first day that the
three outlaws were like so many who rode the wrong side of
the law. As young cowhands, they either shot someone in a

Saturday night brawl, or swung a wide loop and got caught at it. As a result they had run, and been running ever since. They were, most of them, pretty decent men. These three, he judged, were in that category, just wild.

The morning of the third day dawned bright and sunny, but frigid. Cantrell checked the horses and broke the ice in the trough so they could drink. He looked at the sky.

"Well, you sad-looking bunch of horseflesh, I don't reckon we can spend the winter here, so get ready to earn your keep, poor as it's been lately."

Walking back to the cabin, he thought it would be hard going at times for the horses. He pushed through the door into the warmth. "Get the gear together," he said. "We're headin' out."

"But hell, Cantrell, it's still cold enough to freeze the horn off an anvil out there," Bentree said.

"Yeah, I know. But don't look like it's gonna get any better. So long's it's clear, we better make the most of it."

He looked at Elena. "You feel up to givin' it a try?"

Her chin rose defiantly. "If you think you can make it, I'll be there as long as you are."

He allowed himself a slight, ironic smile. "Yes'm."

He said to Tom-Buck, "Leave their guns, but make sure none is loaded."

His glance shifted to the outlaws. "You stay here. Don't try to follow. When the weather thaws a little, you can make it to Durango in less'n a day. We'll leave you as much food as you had when we found you."

One stood and looked him in the eyes. "You and me, Cantrell, we got something to settle. I ain't gonna mess with it here 'cause of the lady, but we're gonna meet someday."

Cantrell stared at him a moment. "I hope not, cowboy. I don't want to kill you, and I will if you push it, so think about it awhile. Leave it alone."

Bentree went out to hitch the horse to Elena's buggy. The others gave him enough time to get the job done, then followed.

The snow, dry and powdery, didn't give the horses as rough a time as Cantrell had anticipated.

"Reckon we'll make it to the ranch by mid-afternoon," he said to no one in particular. "Bet Lion gives me hell for bringing Elena out in this." Well, he thought, he'd been cussed out by the best of them. One more time wouldn't matter—and he was sure it wouldn't be the last time.

Even though he didn't figure they'd be followed, he cast occasional glances to their rear. He saw no sign, there or along the ridges.

About mid-afternoon the outline of the ranch buildings loomed in the distance, looking black in contrast with the stark white blanket of the landscape.

"Guess my reckon was pretty good, old hoss." The big dun just twitched its ears.

Another half hour and they rode into the ranch yard.

"C'mon in," Lion roared from the *galéria*. He turned his head toward the bunkhouse. "Mann, get somebody out here to care for these horses."

Cantrell would have bet that Lion's yell shook snow off trees in the next county.

As soon as they entered the big front room, he roared at Cantrell, "What the hell you mean bringing my daughter out in this weather? I send you along to make sure she's safe, and here you pull a damn fool stunt like this."

Cantrell spread his hands helplessly. "Lion, I made a dumb decision. Sorry, reckon you trusted the wrong man. Got no excuses."

He stood there while Lion gave him about as good a tongue-lashing as he'd ever had, aware all the while that Elena looked at him with a puzzled frown. In the middle of Lion's harangue she walked to the center of the room.

"Enough of this." Obviously she had never spoken to her father in this manner. His jaw dropped and he stood in stunned silence. Elena looked at Cantrell. "Why don't you tell him why you brought us out of town in a threatening storm?"

He returned her look, careful to keep his face blank. He didn't answer.

She turned back to her father. "He doesn't deserve this, nor do the other boys. Cantrell brought us out because I told him to.

"He asked what I'd do if he just told the boys to go back to whatever they were doing and stay put till the storm blew itself out." She looked her father right in the eyes. "I told him I'd leave anyway."

Her gaze dropped before Lion's angry stare. "I reckon, Papa, my temper almost got us all killed. Cantrell's as good a hand as you thought him, or we might not have made it."

"Why didn't you tell me this?" Lion growled at Cantrell. "Or you men? You should have told me."

"Oh, Papa, be reasonable. You don't have a man working for you who would lay blame for *anything* on someone else. It was my fault. They bear none of the blame."

"Lion," Cantrell interrupted, "Miss Elena's being nice about it. I must've made her mad about something, I don't know what, but she was mad at me an' just didn't stop to think. Lay the blame on me and if I'm fired I'm sorry, 'cause I like it here. I'll get my gear and ride out."

Lion cleared his throat. "You will like hell. You think I don't know my own daughter. Spoiled and hardheaded she is, and I'm damned if she's gonna cause me to lose one of the best hands to come down the trail in a long time. Go get your supper."

Cantrell, glad to get out of there, led the way, and when safely outside, grinned at the others. "Whew! I thought I'd had the bark scrubbed off by the best of them, but I'm here to tell you Lion's so damn far ahead of the rest that he makes 'em seem like kittens. Probably tell my gran' kids about this one."

He stopped suddenly. "Say, just thought of something. When I fired the second shot back there at the cabin, why didn't y'all get the hell out of there like I told you?"

Tom-Buck grinned. "We was gonna, but Miss Elena raised so much hell 'bout us leavin' when you might need us, that I reckon we decided whatever you done run into wasn't gonna be near as bad as listenin' to her. So we went to see what you got yourself into."

Cantrell's throat tightened and he wondered why he felt so good. He couldn't figure Elena out. One minute she did something to make him want to turn her over his knee, and then she followed it up with something to make him all mushy inside. He knew he didn't know much about women, but this one made the rest seem like an open book.

Damn it anyway, he thought, she's a woman but she's Lion McCord's daughter. That told him he had no right to think of her as a woman—but he did it anyway.

Reckon I better get my gear together and head back to the line shack, Cantrell thought. Ain't gettin' nothin' done here.

Stick McClure cut out the two extra horses Cantrell told him he wanted. One was a hammer-headed, deep-chested gray. It looked meaner'n hell, but, Cantrell thought, it looked like it would stay with him all day if he needed it. The other, a rangy bay, probably could outrun a jackrabbit.

Boy! That Stick can really work horses, he thought, as he watched. Mann walked up beside him and leaned on the top rail of the corral.

"Who you want to take with you this time, Cantrell? King ain't up to it yet. 'Course he's been raisin' hell, says there ain't nothin' wrong with him."

"Well, I'll take McClure there if it's all right with you," he said, tongue in cheek.

"You know damned well I ain't gonna let you take *him*. He's the best wrangler in the country."

"Aw, Mann, reckon I know that. Just figured to pull your rope a little." Cantrell, looking at the side of Mann's face, said, "How 'bout Bob Bentree? He talks a lot, so when King's shoulder gets all right, send him out and I'll send Bentree back."

Mann nodded. "Good, but have Bentree go over to the south line shack when you're through with him. Tell him to haze anything he sees back toward the center of the spread."

Walking away, Mann said, "The boys told me about that run-in you had with Farlow. He won't come here close to headquarters but you can bet he ain't gonna forget you crossed him. Ain't nobody out there to help ya."

Cantrell sighed. "Mann, the way I been goin', anybody what wants my hide's gonna have to stand in line to get at me." He unconsciously eased his .44 in the holster. "Anyway—yeah, I'll watch my backside."

CHAPTER
8

After checking on King and getting a dozen reasons why he was able to go back to work, Cantrell and Bentree rode out.

The ride seemed twice as far as Cantrell remembered it. The cold crawled down his collar, up his Levis, around the buttons of his sheepskin, and his saddle felt like ice. The sun shone, but gave no warmth. When it finally slipped below the mountains to the west, they rode still another hour before reaching the line shack.

Cantrell cut wood while Bentree got the fire started. A pot of coffee and a couple of tins of beans made up their meal. Soon after eating, they turned in.

The morning dawned still and cold. Times like this Cantrell wondered why he liked ranching so much. He put his knee into the side of the bay and pulled the cinches tight, then said over his shoulder to Bentree, "You take the ravines and trees east of here; I'll work those hills to the north. Figure there ought to be a few head ain't got sense enough to make for lower ground on their own."

Cantrell searched brush, clumps of mountain cedar, aspen thickets, and the depths of each ravine. He looked for stray cows, but also for man-sign. He'd made some pretty mean enemies since coming to this country, and as a result there were eleven men out there somewhere, counting the Hardesters, all of whom wanted him dead.

To hell with them, he thought. Didn't ask for trouble; they brought it to me.

He found single cows, a few in pairs, and started them

toward the line shack, thinking that about noon he'd head back and keep them moving.

A nice sized bunch, fourteen head, huddled together in a ravine. He kneed his horse down the slope and started them moving. " 'Bout all I can handle, old hoss. I'll start 'em back and gather the rest, at least as many as I can find, and get on back to the shack."

He worked the small herd onto open range. As usual, there was one old mossyhorn that took the lead.

Out on open range again, Cantrell felt a cold, hard knot between his shoulder blades. The feeling was not new to him. Someone watched, or followed him.

His look searched the skyline, rocks, even clumps of brush that might hide a rifleman. He saw no one—but wasn't fooled. Something, someone, had him under their gaze.

Whoever waited had not found the right place to shoot from. That, or they were looking for a cinch kill.

He slipped his saddle gun, a Winchester .44–90, from under his leg. It was as accurate as any rifle he'd ever fired. If they knocked him out of the saddle, he wanted his long gun with him.

Cantrell kept to flat ground as much as possible. Finally the cabin came in sight. The knot still twisted his stomach and bunched the muscles between his shoulder blades. He tried to blame it on the cold, but he knew better.

Reaching the cabin, he found Bentree there ahead of him. Cantrell took care of his horse before going to the shack, hoping whoever had stalked him would not try for him there. These were *his* enemies. He wanted Bentree out of it. Cantrell thought they'd wait and try to get him alone.

The next day the feeling of being watched persisted, and he used extra caution. Even when he knew there were cattle in an area, he left them alone if cover existed for those on his trail to shoot from.

"Damn, old hoss, whoever they are, they're good. I ain't even seen a shadow." Cantrell rode the dun today and felt more comfortable talking to him. He seemed to understand more than that gray, or bay, McClure had singled out.

Cantrell had not told Bentree about his feeling of being shadowed, but he knew he suspected something because Cantrell had taken extra precautions to make the cabin secure the night before.

Smoke swirled from the chimney at the end of the day. Cantrell circled the cabin wide to come up behind the horse shed. Bentree's horse was there, so he figured all was well. Nevertheless, he slipped to the cabin from the blind side and squirmed to a crack in the chinking to peep inside. Seeing Bentree, he stood and walked to the door.

Hunkered down in front of the fireplace, spreading coals evenly under a haunch of venison, Bentree looked over his shoulder at Cantrell. "Took you a while to come in. What's the matter?"

Cantrell told him about his feeling and said, "Probably nothin'. Probably spooked from so much trouble lately."

He'd been in similar situations too many times. He just didn't want to get Bentree involved. He'd ride his own trouble, in his own way—but he did wedge a piece of wood against the door before turning in for the night.

The next morning Bentree suggested they ride together. Cantrell refused, but knew his excuse for feeling spooked had not fooled Bentree. Saddling the hammer-headed gray, Cantrell rode out—alone.

Despite constant vigilance he saw nothing he could identify as a man, not even a track. Riding, he tried not to follow a pattern. He took unpredictable turns, doubled back, and rode the roughest trails.

There *were* tracks of wolf, deer, bear, even a mountain lion in among some rocks, but none of man.

For three days he'd been riding with his saddle gun resting on the pommel. Riding the gray today, he needed patience, *knew* he'd need it.

"You hammer-headed son, the right thing to do would be to turn hunter 'stead of bein' hunted," Cantrell said to himself. The gray tossed his head and snorted as though he disagreed.

"Yeah, reckon you're right. They know where I am. 'Bout the only thing I can do is hope they'll show themselves. We start huntin' them and we're likely to stumble right into their middle."

Cantrell had hardly gotten the words out when he felt the blow. He fell, hearing the sharp report of a rifle. Quick, sick, pounding numbness paralyzed him. The gray bolted.

The shot had come from high up. He'd been riding beside a stream with a cliff to his left. He'd chosen this trail because of the smooth rock underfooting, knowing his horse would leave little or no sign. It hadn't been good enough.

Still clutching his rifle, he dragged himself up hard against the cliff's base, where a slight overhang furnished shelter from the guns above.

A couple of extra shots, one right after the other, hit the trail where he had been only moments before. They couldn't see him or the slugs would have been closer. In time, they would circle for a better shot.

The pain hadn't started yet, only a deadly numbness flowing down his left side. He felt to see where he'd been hit. The bullet had entered high on the left side of his chest and come out under his arm.

Sweat streamed down his face. The temperature was close to zero, but he sweated. He knew he would die if he stayed here. He had to gamble. The two shots they'd fired were meant to keep him still until they could reach a better vantage point. If he let them get position on him, he'd take their lead without having a chance to fight back. He was damned if he'd go without taking them with him.

The creek crashed and gurgled about fifteen feet from where he lay. He rolled to his right side, hoping to reach the bank before blood started to spill from him to the trail.

Pain—sharp, penetrating—stabbed at him. He had to reach the creek bank before passing out. Dragging along, using his right arm and pushing with his leg, he reached the bank. His breath came in great, racking sobs.

He rolled down the incline and into the water, breaking a thin crust of ice at the stream's edge. They would find where he had entered the water. He dragged himself farther, heading upstream.

Finally, he saw a place to hide if he could reach it.

Cold and pain made holding the Winchester unbearable, but he gripped it with the fear of death. Without it he'd stand no chance at all if it came to a shoot-out from distance.

Agonizingly, pushing the pain to the back of his mind, he crawled to a hollow under the bank. Brush washed to it had snagged on an old tree skeleton's roots growing in a tangle down the bank. He pulled himself under the cutbank.

Cantrell could see little between roots and snagged brush, but he thought his pursuers could see even less into the darkness that surrounded him.

He lay back, fighting off the nauseous blackness of unconsciousness. He must stop the bleeding. Maybe if he stayed busy, he wouldn't pass out. He turned his head slowly from side to side, searching for something to staunch the flow of blood. Only thick, claylike mud lay within reach. Maybe that would do it.

With his right hand, Cantrell dug fingers into the bank, then held his clenched fist in front of his eyes. Everything blurred, but he knew he held a handful of sticky gray clay.

Reaching inside his shirt, he packed it into the hole in his upper chest, then dug another handful and pushed the mud into the hole under his arm. Finished, he stretched out, stifling a groan.

He didn't know how long he'd been there, but he knew he hadn't passed out, because every second had been pure hell. Then he heard them and slipped his .44 from its holster.

Cantrell stared at his handgun, thinking they would have to get damned close to see him, and that close he could do more damage with his pistol than he could with his rifle. Besides, he didn't think he could lever a cartridge into the rifle's chamber.

"C'mon, you gutless, ambush-shootin' bastards," he grunted. Two of them were walking upstream toward his hiding place.

Cantrell's sight cleared. Some inner will pushed all aside except the threat, and the pain receded to the back of his awareness.

They came closer, sloshing through the cold water, searching the creek bank on each side for sign, close enough now to be recognized. There were two of them—Farlow's men.

"I don't know how the hell he got away," the one closest to Cantrell said. "I know where I hit him, and besides, when we found his horse his saddle had blood on it." He stopped and peered closer at the bank.

Cantrell's stomach tightened. He wanted them closer, needed them closer for his handgun to be effective.

"Thought maybe I seen some sign," the one who had been talking said.

"Nah, that bastard's layin' somewhere, dead. He couldn'ta lived. I seen where you hit him," the other said, taking another couple of steps. "We know he come in this here stream from that broken ice back aways. It's gettin' too dark to see now so let's come back in the mornin' an' find what's left of him."

He'd hardly finished his sentence when the first one pointed at the bank directly below Cantrell. "He come outta the water here." The gunman looked at the brush piled against the roots and grabbed for his handgun. Cantrell fired.

A round, black hole appeared in the man's forehead. Simultaneously, a slug plowed into the mud at Cantrell's side.

He shifted his .44 a hair and fired again. He missed. A second shot burned his leg and he fired again. This time the third button on the other man's shirt disappeared into his chest.

Knocked back, the gunman caught himself and staggered forward, convulsively pulling the trigger of his handgun, his bullets blowing holes in the water at his feet—then he fell face down in the roiling stream.

Cantrell lay back, opened the chamber of his .44 with his right hand, pushed his pistol into his left hand, and in sheer agony, punched out the spent shells. He reloaded—and let his eyelids shut out all in front of him. There were no more of Farlow's bunch to worry about, judging by the way those two talked.

The world went away; only a deep velvety darkness remained. There was no cold, no pain—nothing. He slipped into unconsciousness.

He must have gone from unconsciousness into natural sleep. He awoke and from long habit, before moving, he opened his eyes a slit, his senses alive and seeking. He didn't wake confused as to where he was or how he got there, as many do in a strange place. He knew instantly where he was and what had happened.

He heard the cry of an eagle and an almost inaudible sigh of wind through the trees. He smelled the fresh scent of pine. Through his slitted lids he saw that a powdering of snow had dusted the land during the night, and the temperature seemed warmer. It *was* warmer, much warmer. A chinook wind blew down the slopes and warmed as it came. He began to *feel*. The cold ground rendered him so stiff he couldn't move, and pain pushed in on him.

Cantrell tried to ignore the pain—but couldn't. Gut-wrenching agony tore at him. He almost blacked out again. "Don't do it, Quinton Cantrell. You ain't gonna see another sunset if you give in to this."

He tried to move but was so stiff he could move only his head. He looked toward the stream. The bodies of the two gunmen lay where his bullets had dropped them. The shallow water had kept them from washing downstream. They were stiff, their eyes staring sightlessly at a sky they'd never see again.

Cantrell swallowed the flow of hot bile that welled behind his tongue.

He couldn't bury them. Every man deserved to be covered so animals couldn't get at their bones, but these wouldn't be. He would be lucky to keep his own bones from being gnawed on.

Fighting pain, he rolled over, wanting to find where the gunmen had picketed the horses. "Old gray horse, wherever you are, I hope they left you saddled," he ground out from between clenched teeth. "That's the only way I'm gonna stay on you—if I can *get* on you."

He tried to stand, but got only to his knees.

"Gotta crawl then." Talking aloud seemed to cover his pain a little. He tried lifting his head but couldn't manage it, so in order to see, he turned his head from side to side.

Cantrell crawled downstream—moved an arm and a leg, fought off pain, and did it again. "Better get up over the bank while I can still move." His words slurred.

He tried to angle up the bank and slipped, then decided it might be easier to go straight up. He had only a couple of feet more to go. His knees again skidded from under him, and he worked them beneath his body.

Back on all fours, he saw a small splash of red and knew he was bleeding again. He'd have to stop the blood upon reaching the top. His thinking came as though the body he worried about belonged to another.

Cantrell reached the lip, and slowly, very slowly, pulled himself over. He lay there, exhausted, pulling in great gulps of air.

For the first time he thought of his lungs and reached to wipe his lips with the back of his hand. He held it out and looked at it. No blood. "That slug missed my lungs, gonna be all right. Gotta stop bleedin' though," he said—and passed out.

Light filtered through his eyelids. He didn't know how long he'd lain there, but thought it must have been several hours because the sun hung low in the west. "I'll lay here just a few minutes and rest," he said, and then thought, Hell, I been layin' here a long time, don't need no rest.

He tried to push his arms under him, tried, then tried again. Where had his strength gone? Couldn't get his arms and legs to do what he wanted. Darkness closed in.

When next he opened his eyes, the sun had set. A tinge of red still showed in the west, so the hour was early.

Still gotta find the horses, he thought. He tried again to get his arms and legs under him. He made it.

"Can't see very good—wonder if the bleedin' stopped." Then he saw them, not *them*, but their eyes glowing in the half light. Wolves. If they were hungry, he was in a lot of trouble—more trouble than he already had.

He made it to the cliff base and rolled over, his back against a smooth slab of rock. "Now if I don't pass out again, you got more trouble than me," he said, wishing the big gray beasts could understand him.

He counted four sets of eyes and assumed there would be more. He fingered the shells in his belt and found plenty. "Hope the barrel don't split on me." After dragging it in the mud, he wasn't sure whether his gun was plugged or not. He held the rifle as steady as his one arm permitted and fired. It was a good, clean shot—but he missed. The wolves melted into the darkness.

"You'll be back, but if I can stay awake, you ain't gonna feed on *my* bones."

Like most men who spent their lives outdoors, he would not kill unless he had to. Those animals were like him, they were trying to survive—but it might boil down to them or him.

The hours passed, and with the night, the temperature dropped. The cold penetrated to Cantrell's bone marrow, seemed to freeze his guts. He'd lost blood, a lot of it, and if the temperature continued to plummet, he'd pass out. If he did, the cold would end it for him, or the wolves would.

He shook, then got so cold he couldn't shake. He tried flexing his muscles to generate warmth. It seemed to help.

The wolves were back.

He nodded, fought off sleep, and again saw them, their bellies close to the ground, creeping closer. He fired again and creased one, judging from the yelp. They moved back a little, so he fired again. They didn't retreat at all with that shot.

CHAPTER
9

Elena looked out the kitchen window and saw Bob Bentree running his horse hard enough to kill it. He reined to a sliding stop by the bunkhouse.

Elena's breath caught in her throat. A vise clamped her breasts. Where was Quint? Why had he not come back too? Elena didn't know when she'd started thinking of Cantrell as Quint.

She threw the dishrag into the soapy pan of water and ran for the door.

Arriving at the bunkhouse, she heard Bentree tell Mann that Cantrell was missing, that he hadn't returned to the shack the night before.

Elena took charge. "Wyatt, get three or four men. Bob, help them saddle up, then get some sleep. First tell Wyatt the area Quint was working. Saddle me a horse too. I'm going with them."

"We can handle it, Elena. You tell the señora we're leavin'."

"I'll tell Mama, Wyatt, but *I'm* going. Where's Papa?"

"He rode out this morning—went down to the south pasture."

"We can't wait for him," Elena said, and at the same time saw that Mann wasn't going to argue with her.

She headed for the house and heard Bentree tell Mann he was damned if he would stay here; he could rest later.

Elena rushed into the house, calling for her mother.

Venicia met her in the hall. "What's happened, Elena? You look scared to death." Venicia was, as always, cool and calm.

"Mama, something's happened to Quint. He didn't come back to the line shack last night. We're going to look for him."

"*You're* going?" Venicia asked, her face showing no surprise.

Elena's chin came up, stubbornly. "Yes, Mama, *I'm* going. Papa thinks highly of that man and I'm going to see that nothing's happened to him."

"*Papa* thinks highly of him? What about you, Elena?"

"I . . . I . . . Oh, I don't know. I haven't time to talk about it now anyway. I've got to change clothes."

She spun, and rushing toward her room, she heard her mother say, "We'll talk about it when you return—as soon as you return."

While changing, Elena wondered at herself. Why did she worry about Quint? He was just one of the hands, even if Papa did seem to hold him in high esteem. Oh, oh, dammit, I just don't want any of the men hurt, she thought—and knew she lied to herself.

Frantically trying to hurry, she had trouble with the buttons on her blouse, and after taking far too long, she thought, she finished with her clothes, buckled a gunbelt around her waist, and took a rifle from the gun case as she passed through the living room.

The men were mounted when she reached the corral. Each of them had an extra horse in tow, and Mann handed her the lead rope for hers.

"Don't want to kill these horses," she said. "We gotta put some miles behind us. Let's go."

Without waiting for Mann to take the lead, Elena led out.

They had been in the saddle about an hour when Mann came alongside. "Slow down, Elena. We got extra mounts, but at this pace none of them'll last till we get to the line shack. *That* won't do Cantrell any good."

She cast him a worried look. "Wyatt, suppose he's broken a leg, or maybe some of that Farlow bunch drygulched him. Bentree said Quint's been worried the last couple of days, had a feeling of being stalked."

Mann nodded. "Yep, told me that too, but we still got to slow down or we won't get there at all."

Elena knew the wisdom of Mann's words and slowed her horse, although it took a lot of willpower to do it. Her stomach churned and her breathing came hard. Her imagination worked overtime. She thought of ambushes, mountain cats, horse trouble, and each of them made her more miserable.

Bentree had ridden all night and gotten to the ranch house about ten o'clock in the morning. They rode up to the line shack about eleven that night.

"We're not gonna be much good if we don't eat," Mann said. "Let's fix some grub."

"I think we should go ahead, Wyatt," Elena said, hoping he wouldn't argue.

"We're stopping to eat, Elena. It won't take long and we'll be able to do Cantrell more good if we're in good shape."

Mann's words were an order, and Elena knew it. He had helped raise her, and she knew just how far she could push him.

In less than an hour they were back on the hunt. Bentree showed them the way Cantrell had gone the morning before. Even though dark surrounded them, their horses would sense anyone, or other horses, in the area.

They stopped about midnight, boiled coffee, chewed jerky and dried biscuits, then climbed back on their horses and rode deeper into the hills.

Elena, for the dozenth time, caught herself chewing her lower lip and stopped. They had found no sign and they were riding blind. She forced herself to admit that every passing minute made it less likely they'd find Quint.

We've got to find him, we just have to, she thought urgently. She didn't question why it was so important to her. Even when she wiped tears from her cheeks, she blamed it on her concern for one of their riders—one that Papa thought a lot of.

The sun rose, shouldering its way above the mountains, giving welcome light, light that might show them a track or other sign that Cantrell had passed their way. The air, crisp, pure, and cold, along with sunlight brought them new hope, new energy, new determination to keep looking. Any suggestion that they quit and Elena had already decided to continue alone.

"Papa says I'm stubborn, and they're all going to find out just how stubborn I am if they try to call off this hunt," she mumbled.

"What's that, little one?" Mann asked from a pace behind her shoulder.

"Nothing, Wyatt. I was just talking to myself."

They rode all that day and into the night. Men and horses were tired, woefully tired. "We're gonna have to stop and give these animals some rest pretty soon. We need it as bad as they do," Mann said.

Elena knew he was right. She hated to stop now. Quint might be just over the next hill, in the next ravine, or alongside the trail.

"Wyatt," she said, "let's fire a rifle periodically. If Quint is where he can hear it, maybe he'll answer."

"Just thinkin' that, little one. I'll fire off a shot every ten minutes or so."

The wolves inched closer. Cantrell fired again, and the sound of his shot had hardly died when, he wasn't sure, but he thought he heard an answering one. Probably just the echo of his own, but he fired again. Then he was certain. Someone answered.

Every few minutes he fired a round into the night sky. Suppose it's more of them Farlow men, he questioned. Hell, if it is, I'm a goner either way. Might as well lead them to me.

Two more shots, and he still hadn't killed a wolf, but they hadn't gotten close enough to attack. Then he heard a shout. He had no strength left to answer, but he kept firing until he saw the wolves melt into the darkness and heard the ring of shod hooves on the granite trail.

Jacking shells into the chamber of his Winchester had taken all of his strength. He was sweating as though from a hard day's work.

As soon as he saw the dark shapes of horsemen take form, he placed the rifle on the ground beside him and pulled his .44. He held it ready until he recognized Elena in the lead. His hand holding the .44 dropped weakly to the ground at his side.

She apparently saw the shadowy movement as his hand dropped, and she said over her shoulder, "We've found him."

"What took you so long?" He grinned weakly up at her, his voice no more than a whisper. Then darkness again closed around him.

When he opened his eyes, he felt warm. Someone had built a fire and wrapped him in blankets. He lay in the same spot as he had when he passed out. It was still dark, so he had not been out long.

He tried a deep breath and felt something tight around his chest. He'd been bandaged. Turning his head, he saw Mann on the other side of the fire talking with Elena.

"We gotta rig a travois to carry him outta here. Wagon can't make it over some of the country 'tween here an' the ranch; besides, it'd take too long to get one," Mann said.

"We're not moving him until we can see the trail clearly," Elena responded. "I don't want him hurting anymore than he is."

She pulled the coffeepot off the fire and poured herself a cup. "You and the boys get some sleep. I'll watch over Quint. Like Papa said, 'He's too good a hand to lose.' "

Cantrell felt good. Something had happened to change her opinion of him. He couldn't imagine what, but he was glad that now she seemed to think highly of him.

"Ma'am, less you figure to drink all that coffee yourself, I shore could use a swallow or two of it. That is if y'all got a spare cup."

With a surprised look she glanced across the fire at him. "Awake, huh?" Then he saw her face turn red as she apparently realized he had heard her. "I s'pose if you aren't afraid to drink after me, we could share this cup."

"Yes'm, reckon I'd like that pretty good."

She put her hand under his head, lifted it, and placed her cup to his lips. He took a quick sip of the steaming liquid.

He pursed his lips and blew his breath out slowly. "Whew! Mann must've made that. Almost need a knife to cut it. I like it like that."

"I'll have to remember that," Elena said, and looked him squarely in the eyes when she said it.

Now what the hell did she mean by that? he wondered. Unless things change a lot, she sure won't be making coffee for *me*. He turned his head toward Mann. "Mornin' comes, there's a couple of gunnies down in that streambed needs buryin'."

"And my gray and their horses are around here somewhere. Might have somebody find them tonight and take care of them. They're probably tied, or picketed. Chances are, mine's still saddled. Been that way for a couple of days now."

Elena held his head and gave him another sip. He had hardly swallowed it before he slipped off into sleep.

He awoke to bumping, bouncing movement. He was on his back, and tied down. On turning his head to the side, he saw that a long, straight sapling bore his weight and knew he was on a travois.

"We'll take him to the line shack. I'll stay with him along with a couple of the boys," Elena was saying. Cantrell couldn't see her. She must have been riding alongside the horse pulling the travois.

"Wyatt, you go back to the ranch and tell Papa what's happened. Then if Art is able to ride, send him to me. He learned a lot about healing and the right herbs and roots to use from his Apache mother." Cantrell heard her hesitate. "Too, he seems to think a lot of that cowboy lying yonder, and I'm beginning to realize why."

"Yes'm, I'll git him out soon's I git back. Fact is, I've damn near had to fight him to keep him from comin' back anyway." Cantrell heard Mann ride off.

It was mid-afternoon when they reached the line shack. Elena had not permitted them to increase the gait of the horses, saying she didn't want to start Quint bleeding again.

They untied the ends of the saplings, moved the horse from between them, and laid Cantrell gently on the ground.

"Easy now. I want four of you to handle that. Let's get him inside to one of the bunks."

Cantrell looked up. Elena was standing to the side, a worried frown creasing her forehead. "Gently, boys," she said. Then she shifted her gaze down and, seeing his eyes open, asked, "How're you feeling?"

"Why heck, ma'am, I'll be ridin' in a couple of days." His voice didn't come out as strong, or convincing, as he had intended.

"You just try it, cowboy, and we'll tie you down." She wasn't joshing.

He woke in the middle of the night shivering. The cabin was warm, so he knew he had a fever. He'd always heard a fever meant your hurt was festering. Damn, he thought, that could only mean he'd be down longer than he'd figured.

A cool hand touched his brow, and Cantrell knew Elena touched him. He opened his eyes and looked at her. The creases between her eyes were deeper.

"Ma'am, don't frown so. I don't want to be the cause of worry wrinkles on your pretty face, so smile at me."

"Quint, you're feverish. It's nothing to josh about." Abruptly, she walked to the wooden pail sitting on the table, untied her scarf, dipped it in the water, wrung it out, and came back to his side.

"I'll sponge you off and maybe it'll help drive your fever down." She lifted his head and rubbed the cold cloth along the back of his neck, then lowered his head gently to the bunk and sponged his face. She again went to the pail and back again. She opened his winter underwear down the front and sponged his chest.

"Aw now, ma'am, it ain't rightly decent of me to be layin' here, an' you washin' my, uh, my chest." Suddenly he felt his face heat up and he knew he'd turned red. "Now don't you go no farther."

She laughed, the sound almost like music. Cantrell thought he'd never heard a sound as pretty. He'd never heard her laugh before, and certainly not with him.

"Quint Cantrell, I'm not the sheltered, fragile little thing you seem to think me. I've doctored broken legs, bullet wounds, and cuts and bruises on almost every hand we've had, and I've looked on most—well almost," he saw that now *she* was blushing, "all of their body."

"I promise you one thing, ma'am, you ain't gonna look on even *near* almost all of mine."

She sighed. "All right, but I'm going to sponge you until Art gets here. He'll know what to do—and you better let him do it." She looked puzzled. "How in the world did all that mud get into your wounds."

"Reckon I put it there, ma'am—it was either that or bleed to death."

King rode in soon after sunup, ground-reined his horse, and hurried into the cabin. "Left m'horse out there," he said. "Somebody take care of him."

King felt Cantrell's forehead. "See you been bathin' his face," he muttered in Elena's direction. He looked down at Cantrell. "Now it's my turn, muchacho. Hope I hurt you like you did me."

"First off I ain't no little boy, an' next, Miss Elena's already fixed me up, so you don't need to mess with me."

"The hell I don't, amigo. Something's wrong or you wouldn't be burnin up." He opened Cantrell's underwear. "Here, Miss Elena, hold him up while I peel this off'n him."

"You damned well ain't gonna peel me right here. Wh-where's my damned gun?"

"If you don't lay still, I'll lay the bar'l of *my* gun across your stubborn head." King winked at Elena. "An' then I'll take all your clothes off."

Cantrell groaned and squeezed his eyes as tightly closed as he could get them, trying to shut out his embarrassment.

King unwrapped his bandages and looked at the holes the bullet had made. The one where it had come out was larger and festering badly.

"Ain't got no proper roots or nothin', but fat pork ought to draw that poison out. We got any bacon? Salty if we got it."

Elena went to the cupboard and found the bacon slab Cantrell had brought with him from the ranch. She walked to where his clothes hung from a nail, got his sheath knife, sliced off two pieces of the fat pork, and took them to King.

He bent over Cantrell and turned his head to look at her. "Miss Elena, I'm gonna change these bandages every mornin' an' night. I'll stay with him, so why don't you go on back to the ranch an' get rested up? Tell Lion I'm gonna keep a couple of the boys to do the work around here."

"I'm staying. I'll send all but two of the riders back."

King shrugged. To Cantrell, watching from under half-closed lids, it seemed King knew that to argue with her was futile.

Under the care of King and Elena, Cantrell began to mend. First his temperature returned to normal, and after that the bullet holes healed—slowly. One day drifted into the next.

It seemed to him that Elena and King were with him every minute, fussing over him like mother hens.

After he sat up on the fifth day and announced that he was getting out of bed, they raised hell, but he did it anyway—and they continued to fuss over him.

At the end of the second week he said he was going to start riding again. When he told them *that*, he found out they really knew what they were doing in the hell-raising department, but he could raise hell too.

"You want to tear it open, and start it bleeding again?" Elena asked, standing in front of him, her fists clenched.

"No, ma'am, Miss Elena, I reckon—"

"Don't call me ma'am, or—or Miss Elena," she interrupted. "Can't you just call me Elena?"

"Don't reckon so, Miss Elena. Don't recollect any of the other hands that don't put a handle to your name." He muttered under his breath, "Damn! Wonder what's got her so fired up. I shore ain't done nothin' wrong to her."

"What did you say?"

"Uh, nothing, ma'am."

"Quinton Cantrell, when are you going to get it through that hard head of yours that you ain't 'just one a the hands'," she mimicked him. "You ain't to Papa, and you ain't to me. So . . . so," she stammered, getting madder all the time, "damn it, treat me like a woman."

He looked around the cabin, knowing no one, King or any of the hands, were there, but wanting to make sure.

"Miss Elena, I don't reckon there's anything in the world I'd rather do than treat you like the beautiful woman you are, but I *am* just a hand. *You* are Lion's daughter. *You* are a lady, and *Lion* is not just my boss but my friend as well." He shook his head hopelessly, then repeated, "I'm just a cowhand, ma'am."

He noticed that Elena avoided being alone with him after that, and two days later she left to go home.

Before she left, he heard her tell King to try and make him take it easy until he healed. He grinned to himself. King was going to have one hell of a job trying to carry out those orders.

CHAPTER
10

Elena rode into the yard, tossed her horse's reins to McClure, and strode purposefully toward the house.

Venicia met her at the door. "How's Cantrell?"

"He's going to live—if he'll let himself." Elena stamped her foot. "Uhhh! That's the hardest headed man in the whole state of Colorado. He won't do *anything* I tell him to do."

Venicia smiled, mockingly. "Met your match, huh?"

"Oh, mama, he's even worse than that. He's gone back to work and . . . and he calls me ma'am, and . . . and Miss Elena." Tears streamed down her cheeks. She told herself she cried because she was so mad. "I tried to tell him not to, but he refused. Said none of the other men called me Elena. He's . . . he's just a hard-headed male animal and I hate him."

Venicia folded Elena into her arms. "Oh, *niña mia*, I'm so sorry. I knew this would happen. No, you don't hate him, *niña;* you're in love with him. I told your father you would fall in love with Cantrell soon after he came to work for us. Your daddy thought I had lost my mind, but I knew, dear."

"Mama, how can you say such a thing?" Elena sniffed, pulled a handkerchief from her pocket, wiped her eyes, and blew her nose. "Mama, he doesn't even look at me like I'm a woman. Maybe I caused him to feel this way, the way I treated him. He . . . he just tells me he's a cowboy, one of Papa's ranch hands."

Venicia pushed Elena back and looked into her eyes. "Elena, there is something you must know. This is for the best. Cantrell is an outlaw. He has a price on his head. You could never be happy with him."

84

Elena squared her shoulders and returned her mother's look. She had quit lying to herself. Yes, she loved Quint. Yes. Yes. Yes. And she didn't care if he was an outlaw. She didn't care what he was, but she knew something her mother didn't.

"Mama, Quint isn't an outlaw."

"Wishing it weren't so will not help, *niña*. Your father told me, and he had no reason to say it if it were not so."

Elena was shaking her head before Venicia finished her sentence. "Mama, when he was so feverish, delirious, he talked a lot. He rode the outlaw trail for years but never did a dishonest thing in his life."

"Elena, stop that. You're only wishing now. No. I don't think he ever stole anything. He's wanted for killing a man down in New Mexico Territory."

Again Elena shook her head. "Mama, the sheriff in Durango told Quint that that reward on him, dead or alive, was put out by brothers of the man he killed. The sheriff said Quint's not wanted by the law, never has been."

Venicia stared hard into Elena's eyes. "Are you sure of this? If it is really true, it makes a lot of difference."

"Yes, Mama, it's true. I asked Quint about it when he became lucid. He told me the whole story." She smiled, tears welling into her eyes again. "And, Mama, I'm not going to find excuses any longer. Yes, I love him. I suppose I have from the first time I saw him or I wouldn't have gotten so angry when I thought he looked at other women, but . . . but it's too late. I never gave him a chance to even *like* me, let alone love me. I am just a hot-tempered, selfish brat." She threw herself into her mother's arms again and sobbed, thinking her heart would tear itself from her breast.

Venicia hugged her and smoothed her hair, crooning softly, as she had done when Elena was a little girl.

When Elena had cried herself dry of tears, Venicia pulled her handkerchief out and gently wiped her face. "Now, little one, stop crying and let's talk. If what you say is true, and I believe that it is, you and I have work to do. We'll not tell anyone, but we have fences to mend. I've always been your best friend, have I not?"

Elena tried and succeeded in giving her mother a brave smile, even though she didn't see what might be done. If she hadn't been such a shrew, they might have had a chance, but it was too late.

"Mama, I just don't see what we can do this time."

"Come, let's have a cup of coffee and talk about it. I've never seen anything two strong women couldn't do if they made up their minds to it."

Despite his resolve not to, Cantrell caught himself thinking of Elena as a woman, just as she'd told him to do, but he was determined to put those thoughts to rest. She had just let the woman come out in her and tried to mother him.

Despite his argument with himself he continued in the passing weeks to hold thoughts of her close and private, while at the same time telling himself he was a damned fool.

At the end of the third week he was putting in a full day's work, and then some. If they got another snow soon, he wanted to have the breaks, creek beds, and ravines clear of cattle so he and King could herd their gather and start them toward winter pasture.

"Reckon I got my area cleared," he said over the rim of his old granite cup. He and King had finished supper and were drinking the last of the coffee.

"Give me a hand tomorrow an' we can finish the whole thing by sundown if we get at it 'fore daylight," King said.

"All right, let's turn in." Cantrell stood and cleared his side of the table.

They scoured the kitchen gear and blew out the lantern. As was his habit, Cantrell picked up his rifle, went to the door, and stepped outside.

He always liked to check the area. The room was dark behind him, and the door opened onto darkness. He was sure he'd not be seen if the cabin was watched.

Standing there, listening, not moving, he sensed all that surrounded the line shack. There was no sound; that was what worried him. Even the usual night sounds were missing.

Cantrell knew every clump of brush, trees, and rocks around the shack. His gaze slowly searched them, looking for shadows that might be thicker or darker than normal, or a shape different than he remembered.

About to move on and end his search, he saw what looked like a clump of brush move, as if the wind had swayed it—but there was no wind.

If there's one out there, I'd bet on there bein' more, he thought.

Studying the area again, he saw what appeared to be two others. Ought to wait and let 'em make a move, he thought. But even as he did, the Winchester came to his shoulder.

He fired at the darkest shadow to his far right, levered a shell into the chamber, and fired at the next spot he'd picked as concealing one of them.

Not wanting to fire at the same spot twice, he moved his sights a little farther left and fired again. With every shot he moved his position.

Three bullets hit the wall a couple of yards from him. They were firing, hoping for blind luck. Cantrell triggered off five quick shots and saw two dark forms stand and run for the timber behind them. He levered and fired fast enough that the echo of the shots merged as one report.

A man fell. The other stumbled to the side, but kept running. Cantrell fired again—but missed. The last of the three went into the trees.

Two down, but maybe not dead. A little daylight would have helped, Cantrell thought.

The door at his back snicked shut. King had joined the party.

"What you run into?" he whispered.

"Three of them out yonder. Two down. Hit the other but he got into the woods 'fore I could drop him."

"Who you figure they were?"

"Don't know. Probably some of Curly Farlow's bunch. Reckon anybody else would've hailed the cabin an' rode on in."

Cantrell faded toward the back of the cabin. "You stay here. Cover me. I'm gonna circle around and see if they're dead." He stopped and cocked his head to the side, listening.

A horse was leaving in one hell of a hurry—but that could be a trick. Cantrell mentally marked the spot where he thought the hoofbeats came from. He'd check there first.

As he reached the back of the cabin, at least fifty yards of open, snow-covered ground spread before him. He had to cross that to reach cover.

Cantrell started to drop to the ground, but stopped. His Levis were dark blue, and his sheepskin black. He'd make a prime target against the snow dressed as he was. Thinking a moment, he shook his head in resignation.

Damn! he thought. Nothin's easy. He peeled off his clothes. His long winter underwear, white, or gray from so many washings, would not furnish near as good a target against the snow. Stripped to his underwear, he kept his boots and gunbelt on.

Dropping to the ground, he snaked his way to the windbreak, a strip of Ponderosa pines about twenty yards wide. There, against the dark needles, he could be seen easily; the light color of his long johns was no help now.

Sure hate to get shot with nothin' on, he thought.

Cantrell moved slowly. Snow, scooped up by the front of his long johns, slipped in next to his skin, down his body. He gritted his teeth, but he'd felt worse than this. Those Comanches down Texas way had used fire. Snow wasn't near that bad.

After what seemed forever, he reached the trees, got to his knees, frowned, and slipped back to the ground. Another hundred yards of crawling, and he was close to where the horse had been whipped into a run. Cantrell stopped, hardly breathing, his gaze searching for a shadow that might be a man.

Back in the trees, finding nothing, he changed his course toward the fringe that looked out on the line shack. He'd found the two downed rider's horses on the other side of the windbreak and left them there.

The man he looked for had not stayed close to the horses. He would be where he could watch the cabin—if he was still anywhere around.

Cantrell moved slow enough that he, looking right at his arms and legs, could not see movement. That's what would give him away every time—and it was what showed him the remaining rider.

The man stood against the bole of one of the larger trees and, apparently tired of standing, slipped down the trunk to sit. He blended in with the tree, so Cantrell might have slithered right up to him had he not moved. Cantrell didn't want to kill the man unless he had to, but, what the hell, this man wanted him dead—had already tried and missed.

"Don't move." His voice was soft. He didn't want to startle the gunman into sudden movement.

The shadow at the base of the tree twisted, and flame lanced toward the spot from which Cantrell had spoken. He had vacated the spot even as he spoke.

He levered and fired once in the middle, then bracketed the shot with two more, the sound of the three blending. The man rose about halfway and then sprawled facedown in the snow.

On the chance that his shots had missed doing the job, Cantrell stayed down and wormed his way closer. Reaching the man, he put the muzzle of his rifle against the outlaw's head, felt for a pulse, and found none.

Cantrell stood and reloaded his rifle. He hated wasting shells like that, but in these shadows he hadn't been sure he'd put his lead in the right place. He pushed the gunny to his side and rolled him over. He recognized another of Farlow's bunch.

Sure figured that bunch right. Every one of them seems determined to make buzzard bait of me, he thought. There're only two left—then the Hardesters. The thought didn't give him much comfort.

A glance toward the cabin told him King was staying put until he heard a yell to come out.

He was pretty sure the other two outlaws had cashed in their chips, judging from the way they dropped when he put lead into them. He looked at the dead gunman next to him and decided to leave his guns and belongings with him until he was sure about the other two.

They were dark blotches against the white blanket on the ground. If either moved, Cantrell would fire before he got his gun in action. He checked one, then the other. They were both dead.

"C'mon out, King," he called and walked quickly toward the cabin. "Gather their guns and belongin's. Their horses are the other side of them trees yonder. Gonna get some clothes on."

He dressed and huddled near the fire waiting for King to come in. It wasn't long until the door opened.

"Was hopin' you didn't try crossin' that open area with your clothes on. Mite chilly out yonder without them though. Shore wish Miss Elena could've seen you. Bet she'd start babyin' you right off. Maybe even unbutton yore long johns and put a plaster on your chest."

King ducked Cantrell's cup as it sailed past his head, then laughed as though it were the only funny thing he'd experienced in a month.

Cantrell marveled at how King's usually stoic features lighted up when he smiled.

CHAPTER
11

The next day they finished working the rough country and hazed their gather toward winter pasture.

Cantrell figured they had about a hundred and eighty head. He thought it was a pretty good gather. A yearling broke free of the herd, and Cantrell kneed the gray over to bring it back.

Funny thing about cows, they seemed to all have minds of their own, what little minds they have, he thought.

King rode over. "Gonna take most of tomorrow 'fore we git this bunch to winter grass." He flipped a thumb toward the mountains. "Gonna get wet doin' it."

"Yeah." Cantrell looked toward the higher peaks. "That lightning up yonder looks like a good one comin'. One thing about it though—with the wind comin' down off the mountains, it'll cause a warm up."

"Hell, Cantrell, I'd just as soon be cold as wet."

Cantrell nodded. "Yeah, but I sure don't cotton to being cold *and* wet."

"Reckon you're right."

They pushed the herd slowly, not wanting to work the summer fat off.

The rain started as a cold, penetrating drizzle, then by mid-afternoon set in to rain steady.

Cantrell reined toward King. "Ain't no lightnin' down here to spook 'em, so let 'em go. We'll find a cutbank or trees to make camp under."

King nodded.

They spent a cold, wet night under a big ponderosa pine that channeled rain down their necks and kept the fire wet down to a smouldering, sputtering excuse. Cantrell was glad to roll out of sodden blankets and saddle up. King slanted a look at him.

"Quick outta your blankets this mornin'." His mouth split into what would pass for a grin.

"Didn't notice you as bein' slow to roll out either." That was the only conversation until about four o'clock, by Cantrell's reckoning.

"This's far enough. Reckon they ain't gonna go nowhere," King said, and rode past Cantrell. "Let's head for home."

They opened the corral gate and drove their extra horses in, including the five they'd rounded up after Cantrell killed the three Farlow gunmen. It took the better part of half an hour to strip off the packs and unsaddle. Finished, they headed for the bunkhouse.

Cantrell opened the door and pushed King ahead of him into the welcome warmth. He dropped the packs of the three gunmen inside the door.

"There's more gear you can turn over to Lion," he said to Mann, who was playing penny-ante poker by the stove. "Three more of Farlow's bunch ain't around no more."

"Damn, Cantrell." Mann looked down at the dripping pile of gear. "You're thinning out people faster'n we can populate it up. What happened?"

"Mann." Cantrell looked at him, straight on. "Reckon I'm gonna git on some dry clothes, an' then me an' them dry clothes're gonna surround about a half a cow, some taters, an' biscuits. If the cook ain't got it fixed, I'll fix it myself. *Then* I'll tell you what happened."

"Cantrell's done said it for me too," King said.

The weather stayed gray and rainy. Mann held the outside jobs to a minimum, but most jobs simply could not be done anywhere else. Now it was after dark of the third day Cantrell had been working out of ranch headquarters.

He rode in tired and wet, stabled his horse, and was forking fresh hay down to him when Mann came into the barn slapping his hat against his thigh to rid it of rain.

"Lion wants to see you. Get cleaned up an' eat first. He ain't in that big a hurry."

"What's he want?"

"Didn't say."

When Cantrell knocked on the door, Lion answered it and ushered him into the sitting room. Elena and Señora Venicia were sitting in chairs pulled close to the big stone fireplace.

"Señora. Miss Elena." Cantrell nodded, then said to Lion, "I ate and cleaned up 'fore I came. 'Cording to Mann, you wasn't in any hurry."

"Sit by the fire, Cantrell." Lion went to a cabinet in the corner. "You look like a drink would knock the chill out of your bones."

Cantrell allowed his eyes to crinkle at the corners. "Yes, sir, reckon I ain't gonna turn one down on a night like this." He sat in a chair on the far side of the fireplace. Lion brought him a drink and then sat next to the señora.

Cantrell took a swallow of his drink, waiting—Lion would tell him what he wanted in his own good time.

Lion packed his pipe, took a sliver of kindling from the tinderbox, held it in the flame, then held the lighted sliver to his pipe bowl. He squinted through the smoke at Cantrell.

After a moment, he broke the silence. "Cantrell, my señora and Elena want to sashay down to Santa Fe 'fore Christmas. I can't go." He sipped his drink, took another puff on his pipe, and exhaled a huge cloud of smoke.

"I'm taking the train to Denver. Gotta speak before the state legislature about some laws they're talking about that would raise hell with ranching." He leaned forward. "I want you to take my womenfolk down yonder an' bring 'em back to me—safe."

Cantrell leaned back, not taking his gaze off Lion's. He emptied his glass. This had caught him in a bear trap.

It wouldn't do for him to be around Elena for that long at one sitting. He was already thinking too much about her and didn't have any business doing that, what with his reputation and several men out yonder doing all they could to kill him. He cleared his throat again.

"Lion, I don't want to do it. You're the boss an' I'll do anything you tell me, but that's tough country." He stood and walked to the other side of the room, turned, and came back.

"I don't think Geronimo and Victorio, along with their band of renegade Apaches, are operatin' far enough north to be a threat, but we'll be crossin' Jicarillo Apache land, not to mention that some of the worst outlaws in the country hang out down that way.

"I've been prisoner of the Apache and seen firsthand what they do to women—especially beautiful white women, and your ladies are the most beautiful I ever seen."

He stopped and spread his hands lamely. "Besides that, Miss Elena reckons I'm a troublesome man. She wouldn't want me along."

It had seemed to Cantrell that Elena wasn't listening to the conversation, but she must have been, for she stood suddenly, and there was no question but what she was angry—boiling.

"You don't have to take me if I'm so much trouble." Elena's eyes were spitting green fire. "I asked Papa if he'd let you take us because," she stammered, "because you seem to know what to do when trouble jumps squarely on your back." She looked at her father. "Give me somebody else. *I'm* goin' to Santa Fe."

"Whoa now, little wildcat." Lion held up his hand as though to stop her words. "What got you turpentined? Cantrell's just thinking of your safety."

"Oh—oh, nothing." Now, Cantrell saw, she was looking him squarely in the eyes. "Except this . . . cowhand is the most exasperating man I've ever seen."

Cantrell thought she'd really tied a can to his tail.

He stood. "Lion, let me back down this trail a little." He rubbed his jaw, then ran his fingers through his hair. "If the ladies are set on going, I'd rather it was me that took them."

Lion took Cantrell's glass, filled it, and handed it back. "How many men do you want with you?"

"Ten—of my choosing. There's talk that the Denver and Rio Grande Western is gonna hook up with some other railroad down Chama way, but that ain't happened yet, so reckon we'll have to horseback it. You gonna send the coach along for the ladies?"

"Yeah. Thought about getting a railcar to take y'all as far as Chama."

"Sounds good. It'll cut down on travel time. If we leave here with ridin' stock and the coach, it's gonna take over two weeks goin' an' comin'. Using the train far as we can'll cut three, maybe four days off travelin', even with loading and unloading the horses and coach."

"Pick your men." Lion held out his glass in a toast. "Safe traveling."

Cantrell tossed down the remainder of his drink and nodded to the señora and Elena. "Good night, ladies, Lion." Leaving, he said, "I'll need a couple of days to get the coach and gear ready—and find somebody to do the cooking."

"You afraid of my cookin', Quint?"

He couldn't suppress a grin as he faced Elena. "No, ma'am, reckon I've eaten worse." Then he frowned thoughtfully. "Or have I?" He whirled toward the door and left before Elena could get her hackles up again.

It took a full two days to get everything ready, but when the coach and horses were loaded aboard the railcar, everything needed was there and in good shape.

Four of Cantrell's riders had never been on a train. They marveled at the speed and comfort of it, while the rest of them cursed the coal dust and smoke.

Elena told Cantrell her mother wanted to stay in Chama overnight and leave early the next morning. He was pleased with that decision because, he thought, it would take the better part of the night to scrub the grime and cinders out of his hair and skin.

The little narrow gauge engine shuttled their car onto a sidetrack. Cantrell told King to have the boys off-load the horses and coach while he found a hotel room for the señora and Elena.

He got them situated, signed for rooms for himself and the men, and directed that a tub of hot water be brought to his room in an hour or so. He then went back to the sidetrack. They had everything off-loaded and stowed in, or on the coach, when he got there.

"King, see that the horses are taken to the livery," he said. "The coach too. I want all of them grain-fed tonight. Set up a watch on the gear unless the hostler will watch it properly. If

we stand watch, include me. We ride at six in the morning."
Cantrell went to his horse, saddled him, gathered the lead lines
of several of the horses, and led them to the livery stable. After
that, he returned to the hotel.

The next morning, when he came down the stairs into the
hotel lobby, the regulator clock on the wall read quarter past
five. The coach was standing by the hitching rail.

Bedroll over his shoulder, Cantrell went to the livery for his
horse and rode him back to the hotel. He had ordered breakfast
and was drinking his first cup of coffee when the señora and
Elena came in and walked to his table.

He stood, almost knocking over his chair.

The señora asked, "May we join you, Mr. Cantrell?"

"Yes'm, be pleased if you would," he answered and walked
around to hold her chair, then barely got to Elena's in time to
help her.

Cowboy, he thought, this ain't the usual thing. Wonder why
they're gonna sit with a hired hand? Sure am glad some of
the boys are in here and seen that they sat with me, not me
with them.

For the first time in years he was glad his mother had taught
him proper table manners, and was surprised at how nice it felt
to eat with ladies. He squirmed though, thinking that a cowboy,
especially him, just wasn't cut out for this sort of thing.

Cantrell didn't reckon they'd be wanting to do it again,
because he was pretty rough around the edges. He looked
across the table at Elena and found her looking at him.

"Ma'am, I figure we're gonna get to Tierra Amarilla about
noon; might be good if you want to stop an' eat there, an'
maybe stretch your legs." He felt his face turn red. "Er—I
mean rest a little."

Elena laughed that tinkling bell-like laugh that he liked so
much. "That's all right, Quint. We do have legs, although
many women refuse to admit it." She laughed again and said
to her mother, "Mama, didn't I tell you Quint was refreshing
to have around? So stern and dangerous in a man's world, and
so naive with women." She cocked a mocking glance at him.
"With some women that is."

Damn that woman! She's always saying things that mean something else. He wondered what it was she thought she knew about him. Then, he thought of Faye and wondered if Elena really thought there was anything between them.

"Yes, Quint," Elena continued, "Mama and I think it would be nice if you'd let us rest awhile then."

"Then that's what we'll do." He drank the last swallow of his coffee. "If you ladies will excuse me, I better make sure everything's ready outside. Be a few minutes, so take your time."

Outside, he looked over the saddle cinches and walked around the coach for a last-minute check. He did it automatically, and while doing it, he wished Lion hadn't said it so strong to them, right in front of him, that he, Cantrell, was in full charge an' they were to do exactly as he said.

He had thought Elena would bust a gut from trying to keep that volcano inside her from exploding.

He was glad Tierra Amarilla was close. It gave them the morning to settle into the routine he wanted to maintain. He had the riders stay close to the coach, while he and King took turns scouting ahead of the main party.

There was a slight chance that the Jicarillo would cause trouble, but a much greater chance existed that his party would encounter outlaws.

The small cavalcade drew considerable attention as it moved down Main Street, between stores lining each side of Tierra Amarilla's business district. The coach, glossy black with gold-embossed trim, was especially large and luxurious for this section of the country.

Cantrell would have rested easier had they not looked so affluent. Outlaws would be drawn to a party like this.

He signaled the driver to stop in front of the café, the only one in town. He dismounted and helped the ladies down, then turned his attention to the riders.

"You men go on an' eat. King, have them fix me whatever they're special on today an' bring it out. I'll stay around the coach. Do that first so's I can be through eating when you are."

King brought him a plate of frijoles, tortillas, and a slice of roasted venison about an inch thick. Cantrell nodded his thanks,

then said, "Tell 'em I'll come in an' pay before we leave."
Lion had given him money for such things, with instructions
that neither he nor the men were to stint on what they ate—
or anything they might need.

Lion had said that he didn't want the señora or Elena to
worry about paying for anything other than their shopping
purchases. Cantrell leaned against the side of the coach to eat
his meal.

A grizzled old-timer ambled up and peered at him through
shaggy brows. "Whew! You shore are a big'un, ain't you?"
He chuckled, obviously wanting to talk.

"Heck, old-timer, I'm the runt of the litter." He chuckled at
the look of dismay that crossed the old man's face. "Naw, not
really. Ain't got no brothers or sisters."

"Boy, I was thinkin' I shore wouldn't want to meet up
with y'all. Why just one of you could about pop'late a whole
town." He danced from one foot to the other. He didn't wait
for Cantrell to answer. "Damn you got cold as ice blue eyes,
ain't ya?"

The old man moved around in the shade so, Cantrell thought,
he could see him better.

He turned his head away from Cantrell and spat a stream
of tobacco juice halfway across the boardwalk, looked steadily
at his artwork a moment, and then said, waving at the coach,
"Ridin' round the country in a fancy rig like you got here,
outlaws're likely to try to rob you."

"Yeah? You know of any that might try such t'ween here
an' Santa Fe?"

"Just gonna tell ye that." He squatted down in front of
Cantrell and sketched some lines in the dirt. "Down here,'bout
a day's ride, you gonna come on a town by the name of
Abiquiu."

He sketched another line off to the side. "Over here, west of
Abiquiu, is a town called Coyote. Now that there's where the
pizen'est mean critters this side of Texas get together. Most of
'em are from Mora, Taos, and Rio Arriba counties. They go
to Coyote 'cause the law knows 'em and don't bother 'em."

He stood and looked at Cantrell. "Them's the ones you gotta
watch out for. For a peso they'd shoot you down like a dog."

He started to walk off, then turned back. "That there town of Coyote is only 'bout nine or ten miles west of the road you'll be travelin'."

Cantrell took the man's bony shoulder in his hamlike fist. "You eat dinner yet, old-timer?"

The old man stared at Cantrell, his back stiff, his head erect. "Sir, I didn't tell you that for no handout."

Cantrell had offended the old man, and he felt sick because of it. "Aw c'mon, if I hadn't eat yet, I would sure like to sit and talk with you, but you can see I just now finished, an' I gotta stay with this coach or the señora'll skin me alive. You go in and talk with the boys. Tell 'em you're my friend an' that I said for you to eat with 'em. They'll like talkin' to you much as I did."

A snaggle-toothed grin crossed the old-timer's face. "You reckon they would—you really reckon they would?"

"Why, heck, I sure enough reckon they would."

The grizzled old form hobbled toward the door of the café. That's a hungry man and too damned proud to take a handout, Cantrell thought, and decided that he liked him.

"Say, old-timer, when we come back through here, if you want a job, I'll take you back with us."

"Reckon I'll be right here lookin' for ya." The old man's words floated toward Cantrell.

Well, Cantrell thought, he could give the old man half his pay. If it didn't cost Lion anything, he ought not to mind.

Cantrell glanced back the way they'd come. Dark clouds with lightning in them lay close to the ground. A lot of rain was falling in the hills, he figured. If they got any, it would settle the dust and he'd not be spitting mud while riding drag.

Then he thought that both he and King had better ride ahead and look for a camp spot. He took his slicker from the bedroll.

A couple of hours out of Tierra Amarilla, it started raining. The trail would be a hogwallow by nightfall.

Cantrell spurred his horse. The sooner he found a campsite, the better. King had been scouting ahead and was now coming back.

"See anything?"

"Yeah. Seen a couple a moccasin tracks. Don't think we need to worry though. The Jicarillos ain't give us no trouble lately."

Cantrell dipped his head to let the rain run off the brim of his hat. "Ain't worryin' 'bout Indians much as I am a place to camp right now."

"Seen a sort of hollowed-out place in the side of a hill up yonder a ways. Plenty of firewood." King tilted his head to the side, apparently trying to keep the rain off of his face. "It wouldn't pass for a cave, but close to it."

"All right, pull off and make camp when you get to it. I'm gonna ride ahead for a spell."

He had not gone a hundred yards when a Jicaríllo brave slipped out of the brush at the side of the trail.

The brave wasn't wearing paint, and he had his arm out-stretched in front of him, his palm facing Cantrell.

Cantrell returned the universal peace sign and rode toward him, aware King was not far behind.

Most Indians were honorable people. If they said they came in peace, then that's how it was. Cantrell greeted the brave in the Apache language.

"You got women in big house wagon." It was a statement, not a question, so Cantrell admitted it was so.

"You got smokin' tobacco? I smoke sumac long time, want tobacco."

Cantrell was about to reply that he smoked a pipe when King said, "I got a couple of bags." He dismounted and dug in his bedroll.

After a while he handed the bag of fine-grained Durham to the brave, who took it and tucked it somewhere inside his doeskin trousers.

"Keep dry." His face showed no expression. "I got gift for you."

Cantrell didn't see that the Indian had anything with him. "Aw, we don't need—"

"You need," the brave interrupted. "I give warning." Before Cantrell or King could question him, he continued, "White man war party hide on trail. Wait for you. Kill. Plenty badmans.

You," he motioned in a sweeping gesture, "keep guns ready." He turned and slipped into the brush as quietly as he had come.

"Well. How the hell you figure that?" Cantrell said.

"He knows the Jicarillo'll git blamed if those bastards pull it off. Most of them Indians are trying to live in peace." King gazed at the place where the brave had disappeared. "A whole lot of the young warriors have been killed. They know they can't win." He slanted a puzzled glance at Cantrell. "Where the hell you learn to talk Apache?"

"Had a couple Apache friends on my backtrail, ex–army scouts. They taught me a lot about the Apache."

King grunted something. Cantrell figured it was just as well he didn't understand.

They rode in silence for a while. King broke it.

"How come you don't smoke, Cantrell?"

"Don't rightly know. Oh, I smoke a pipe once in a while, but don't cotton to it much. I never could see what everybody saw in it. Too, I've seen a few like that brave we left back yonder, who if they couldn't git tobacco would smoke anything. Didn't figure to let anything get ahold of me like that."

CHAPTER
12

The camp was drier than Cantrell had thought it would be. The hollow on the lee side of the hill caused most of the rain to blow over them.

They built a large fire. The Indians were not hostile, and Cantrell was certain the outlaws knew where they were anyway. After he'd posted a watch and gotten out provisions, he said to King, "We need to talk." Elena and the señora were about to start supper. "Ma'am, reckon I need to talk to y'all too."

He called to one of the riders. "We gonna have to trust you to do the cookin' tonight, Barnes."

He spread his slicker on the ground and motioned the ladies to be seated, then squatted in front of them.

"King and me seen a Jicarillo brave a while ago." At the look of alarm that crossed the señora's face, he shook his head. "No, ma'am. We got nothin' to worry about from the Apaches, but he told us about some gunmen who know about our party. They're waitin' down the trail for us."

Elena looked at him with that direct gaze of hers. "What do you think we should do about it?" She showed no sign of fear. A surge of pride swelled his chest.

"Well, ma'am," he squinted into the darkness that surrounded them. "I figure, if it's all right with y'all, I'll leave King in charge here and I'll go pull a Indian raid on them."

"You! Just one man? I know you think you can handle about any situation, but—"

"Elena," the señora interrupted, "let him talk." Her voice was like steel.

Hmmm, this lady has a lot more than beauty, Cantrell thought, then continued. "One man will be able to do what I plan better than a whole army could." Then he sketched his plan. When he finished, King pulled his knees against his chest, folded his arms around them, and cocked his head toward Cantrell. "I'm the Injun in this bunch. I'll be the one to do it."

"No." Cantrell shook his head. "The Apaches taught me a lot more than how to talk their language. I've heard them argue that I had to've been born to an Apache woman."

He sobered. "No, King. I'm the one to do it. You take care of the ladies, and be damned sure they get to Santa Fe and home safe in case I ain't back here by daylight."

"Quint's the one to do it," Señora Venicia agreed. Then she looked directly at Elena. "And he *will* be back by daylight."

Cantrell had noticed that the señora had started calling him Quint, and it seemed to him that she'd said a lot more than her words implied, because he saw Elena blush and drop her gaze to the ground. *Now* what have I missed? he wondered.

It took a few moments to get moccasins from his saddlebags. He always carried them, especially for when he was going to be afoot for any length of time, and tonight a horse would only be in the way, might even get him killed.

He thought of wearing his slicker and decided against it. It made a lot of noise, too much for a man whose life depended on quiet.

He checked his guns, whetted his Bowie knife on his boot sole, wiped his rifle dry, and turned to leave. Elena stood in his way.

She looked up into his eyes. "Quinton Cantrell." Her voice broke. She gripped his forearm. "I don't know why you always seem to feel you are responsible for everyone. You place your life on the line, and in effect yell to the world to come and take it if they are big enough—and I believe you think there's nothing big enough."

Her eyes were swimming in tears; her chin began to quiver. "E-e-even if you just plain don't give a damn," she sobbed, "there are some who do." She turned quickly and, almost running, went to the coach and climbed in.

He stood, a deep frown creasing his forehead as he watched the coach door close behind her.

"Now you know how it is with her, Quinton." The señora's soft words came from behind him. Taken by surprise, he spun toward her.

"Yes'm, reckon I do." He removed his hat and raked his fingers roughly through his thick black hair. "I wish it could be, but I ain't for her, ma'am. I got no book learnin', no nothin', just a ungodly knack for gettin' into trouble. I'm just a cowboy, ma'am, with nothin' much to offer a woman."

She stared at him a moment, then firmly, but just as softly as before, said, "She has probably looked beneath that rough bark, just as I did with her father, and she sees the same thing I did." Then she surprised him. "There's one hell of a man there, and she knows it, Quinton. You'd better realize it too and stake claim to what God meant you to have." With that, she brushed past him and went to the coach.

Cantrell made no sound as he slipped into the brush. Shadowing his way through and around the mountain cedar, he pondered the señora's words.

He was not dumb. Working cattle, or running a ranch, he'd stack up with the best. In the deep woods he'd survive when most would not live through the first day, but the two things he came up with short rations on were book learning—and knowing anything about women.

Until now, the only thing he'd ever really wanted was his own spread. He'd figured on finding himself a woman someday, but he'd looked upon Elena's beauty and pushed the hunger for her into the corner where those things rested he knew were out of reach.

Now Señora Venicia had opened the door a crack, but he didn't figure on doing anything about it until he could talk with Lion. If there was any chance, any chance at all, that Elena would have him for a husband, and now he was certain there was, he wanted to be damned sure he didn't mess it up.

He moved south, paralleling the trail. The wind was out of the southeast; had it not been, the rain would have been snow and the going tougher.

The wind blew in Cantrell's favor too. He would be downwind of the outlaws horses, and with the wind where it was, he should be able to smell the smoke from the road agents' fire before stumbling into their midst.

He paced himself a little faster than a jog. He could run like this all night if he had to. He'd done it many times.

About three hours after leaving camp, when he figured the time to be nigh onto ten o'clock, he caught his first whiff of smoke. It got stronger, then disappeared.

He backtracked a couple hundred yards. There it was again. He slowed to a walk and turned directly into the wind. He was careful now where he placed his feet, feeling through the wet soles of his moccasins for tree branches or twigs that might snap and give him away.

Then he saw fire glow deep in a coulee, but built up along the side, so as to be above the water that might soon flow in ever increasing torrents down the usually dry bottom.

He squatted on the rim, studying the layout below. The outlaws' horses were picketed upstream on the same shelf where they camped. In the fire glow he counted eight horses and knew he'd cut out a chunk of trouble for himself. He peered through half-closed lids to see the camp better.

Finally, the last of the eight riders bedded down.

Reckon they didn't see no need to put a watch on the horses, Cantrell thought. Any horse with the wanderin' fever would have to go through their camp to get out; other end of that coulee's too steep.

He thought of opening up on them with his Winchester but shook his head. He wasn't made that way. He had never drygulched anybody and wasn't going to start now.

He squatted there a good half hour trying to come up with a plan, then nodded. 'Bout as good as anything else, he thought, gotta give it a try anyway. Ain't got much choice.

He scanned the rim's edge, searching along it for a place to go down the wall of the coulee. There were no game trails that he could see, but there were plenty of cedars growing off the sides almost to the bottom, and through the years, wind, rain, and time had exposed much of their root systems. Might be nigh as good as a ladder, Cantrell thought.

He worked his way toward the head of the coulee, upstream of where the camp was located, before he settled down and studied the scrub timber along and down the sides.

The trees were spaced close enough that he judged he could get from one handhold to another without having to turn loose and slide down. He picked the spot where the growth was thickest and slipped over the bank.

Holding onto the tree at the edge, he groped for solid footing on the next one. When he felt he had firm footing, he squatted, took hold of another limb or root, and let his feet drop from under him to scrabble for the next footing.

He repeated this fifteen times. He counted them. Sweat mixed with rain in his clothes until he didn't know which had soaked him the most. But he didn't care; he'd gotten chilled squatting on the bank, and the exercise warmed him.

Crossing the stream, which flowed only a foot deep, caused him satisfaction. He was glad the runoff was light. The wind still blew from the southeast. Luck rode his shoulders.

He inched forward until he could see the horses silhouetted against the firelight. They were about ten feet from him, and none seemed aware he was near.

He took a deep breath. If this didn't work, he was in a hell of a fix, no way out except back up the side of the coulee, unless—unless he could get a handful of mane and ride one of the horses through the middle of them.

Didn't figure on no feather bed when I took on this job, he thought.

His face broke into a grin without his willing it. He couldn't wait to start the music.

He eased up to the first horse and cut the picket rope. Then when the big bay looked around questioningly at him, he placed his hand over the horse's nostrils to keep him from snorting.

Repeating this action with the other seven, he kept the ends of the tether ropes in his hand. The bay, the one he had first released, looked like the best of the bunch, although any one of them could have won first place at a county fair.

Cantrell grabbed the bay's mane and threw himself onto the horse's back. He turned the other ropes loose and at the same time kicked his heels into the sides of the big horse.

Simultaneously, a shrill Jicarillo war cry swelled Cantrell's throat. The seven horses bolted ahead of him.

With his yell, the gunmen rolled out of their blankets, grabbing for guns while trying to get out of the way of the stampeding horses. Some made it, some didn't.

Three gunmen went down with crushed skulls; another fell under sharp hooves, his chest flattened.

Cantrell fired his .44 at point-blank range. Two more went down. Suddenly he was through them. Darkness closed around him as he left the firelight.

He slowed the bay and slipped off its back. The whole thing had taken but a few seconds, yet he knew everything that had happened. He still had work to do. The remaining two had to be put out of action.

He looped the bay's tether around a gnarled, stubby cedar and hunkered down to wait. He felt good. The odds were more in his favor.

Sound carried a long way in the confines of the coulee. He heard the two remaining outlaws thrashing about, trying to get organized; their words were clear, as though only a few feet away.

"Let's get the hell out of here. I ain't sleepin' with no bunch of dead men."

"Ain't we gonna bury 'em? We can't just leave 'em here like this."

"The hell we can't. Wolves, coyotes, or buzzards'll eat 'em. Save us a lot of work."

"What if that ranny's hidin' out yonder in the dark. Let's wait'll daylight so's we can see how to shoot."

"Oh, all right, but I'm movin' my gear away from here. We can build another fire down canyon. Figure that ranny is long gone by now anyway."

"Don't know what makes you figure that. He took on eight of us. What makes you think he won't come after what's left?"

"We keep talkin' like he was some cowpoke, but he shore sounded like a Apache. Did you see him?"

"Caught a flash a him. He wasn't no Injun. Next time I see him, he's gonna get my slug in his gut."

"Oh, all right, we'll move down an' build 'nother fire. Stay there till daylight, but that's all. We gotta find our horses. Ain't gonna do no good to look for 'em in the dark."

"Don't reckon we're gonna find 'em. I b'lieve that's what he hit us for, our horses. He's long gone by now. And we can't hit that coach with the women in it—ain't enough of us left."

"Yeah, reckon you're right, on both counts."

Listening, Cantrell felt his face harden. *You just keep on thinkin' that way, an' we'll bury two more of you tomorrow.* He felt no remorse that he'd killed two of them already and caused four others to die.

They were going to kill him, his men, the ladies—from ambush—so they needed killing. They needed it, and a man did what he had to do.

Cantrell moved along the wall of the coulee until he found a cutbank where the rain couldn't get to him as bad and he'd still be able see everything below.

He sat, his back against a slab of rock. It was not long before a small flame came to life below. He could have tossed a stone and hit it.

He shivered, and thought that if he were a little closer, he might be able to feel the fire's warmth. But then, hell, he'd been cold and wet before. He pressed closer to the slab of rock. The flicker of flame soon turned into a large camp fire.

Cantrell saw them plainly. They'd brought the guns and bedrolls of the other six and thrown them carelessly into a pile off to the side.

Thanks. Saves me the trouble, he thought.

They spread their bedrolls and crawled into them, slickers laid over their blankets.

Cantrell thought of waiting for daylight to attack, but heard them snoring and changed his mind. If he could get off the side of this bluff and into their camp without waking them, he might end this without more killing.

He stood and carefully wormed his way to the stream bank. It still flowed as before. He moved according to the sounds the two sleeping men made; he listened for any change in their breathing. His feet told him what was underfoot. He came within the circle of firelight, never taking his eyes off the two men.

Holding his rifle in his left hand, he slid his .44 from its holster, squatted at the side of the nearest gunman, and carefully laid his rifle on the ground at his side.

He covered the gunman's mouth with his left hand and at the same time pushed the muzzle of his pistol against the outlaw's temple.

"You make one sound, and you'll fry in hell with the rest of your friends." Cantrell looked down into the wide, surprised eyes and pushed a little harder with his pistol.

"Call your friend, low-like, so he don't get excited." The gunny's eyes hardened. Cantrell moved the barrel of his .44 and shoved it, hard, into the gunny's mouth, knocking out a couple of tobacco-stained teeth. "Do it," he ground out between clenched teeth.

He pulled his gun barrel from between the bleeding lips of the outlaw. The man spit out his broken teeth and called, "Hey, Anse, wake up. We got company."

The blankets stirred, and a head poked out. "What the hell's going—" The second gunman chopped his words off and reached for a gun. Cantrell fired. The gunny slumped back. He had a hole for a third eye.

"Want me to improve on your face too?"

"Who are you?" The gunny showed no fear.

"What difference does it make?" Cantrell sat back on his haunches. "Anyway, Quint Cantrell's the name. Take a good look at me so you'll know me next time. Now get up and shuck those clothes."

"Hell, man, it's cold. What you want me to do that for?"

"Do it." Cantrell eared the hammer back.

"All right, all right." The gunny stood and unbuttoned his trousers.

When he had all his clothes off, Cantrell told him to toss them to him.

He picked up each piece and felt for knives and hideouts. Not finding any, he tossed the clothes back. "You can put them on now. In a few days they'll rot off, an' you can get more. You filthy son of a bitch, don't you ever take a bath?"

The gunman dressed, casting Cantrell surly looks. When he was through, Cantrell kicked his guns to the other side of the fire.

"Now lay on your stomach. I don't want to worry about you."

He tied the man securely with rawhide, stood, walked to the pile of gear they'd so graciously gathered for him, and collected all of the firearms.

He slung the pistols and gunbelts over his shoulders, and carried the rifles in his arms. He took them to the bay and placed them carefully on the ground. No point in ruinin' good weapons, he thought, and these are some of the best.

He retraced his steps past the hogtied gunny, went back to their original camp, looked around the shambles, and selected a saddle and bridle that had escaped the stampeding hooves of the horses. He also took the best lariat and headed back to the bay.

After saddling, he tied the rifles in a bundle and secured them behind the saddle. He hung all the holsters and pistols around the saddle horn, mounted, and headed toward his own camp.

He thought he'd make it in time to eat before King had them break camp. He wasn't worried about the gunny. When the rawhide got wet it would stretch and he could escape. As much as he despised the lawless bunch, he'd not leave one of them to starve to death tied hand and foot in a remote ravine.

CHAPTER
13

The new day was dawning gray and chilly when he rode into camp, but the greetings he had from his men put sunshine in his heart.

"Hey, amigo," King said, "you gotta stop takin' these rides 'fore daylight or we ain't gonna hold breakfast for you."

"Reckon I could eat a whole cow—'cept the hooves 'n' horns," Cantrell grunted.

"Make room for a hungry man," one of the men chipped in.

Cantrell looked across the fire at Elena. Her face showed relief, but she looked as though she'd not slept. "Morning, Quint" was her only greeting. Her eyes said more.

The señora walked silently to his side. Their gazes locked. "Thank you, Quint." She glanced toward the bay he had ridden in on. "From the looks of what you brought back I'd say you grew another coat of bark last night."

"A little, ma'am." He nodded, then tiredly reached for his mess gear.

After breakfast the señora leaned out the coach window and tried to convince him to ride inside and get some sleep. It sounded mighty good, but he and King were the best scouts in the party, and in this country they were both needed.

"No, ma'am. Obliged for the offer though." He looked past her, down the trail. "I reckon we're gonna need all the eyes we got to get through without being ambushed." He tipped his hat, mounted, and rode to the front of the coach.

They had no trouble except for the mud the horses slogged through. When they made camp that night, Cantrell figured they were about halfway to Espanola.

"Way I figure it," he said to both Elena and Señora Venicia, "we can stay in Espanola tomorrow night, and then with some hard ridin' we ought to make Santa Fe in time for supper the next day."

"Don't push the boys too hard, Quint. This is harder on you men than it is on us," the señora advised.

"Ma'am, soon's we see the lights of Santa Fe, you won't find a man here that would admit to being tired." He pushed his hat to the back of his head. "Me, now I reckon a good hour in a wooden tub'll wash off any tired I got."

Elena frowned. "Don't you ever complain, Quint?"

He thought a minute. "Well, Miss Elena, reckon if I got somethin' to complain about, then I need to do somethin' about it, an' if I do somethin' about it, I no longer got a reason to complain."

"You see," she stormed, "you're just like I said. You . . . you think you're God. I don't believe there's anything you think you can't do."

He pursed his lips a moment, then nodded. "Yes'm, there's just one thing I figure I can't do."

"Oooh, and what in this world could that be, pray tell?"

"Well, Miss Elena, I just ain't found no way to be around you, for two minutes even, without makin' you mad at me." His voice was serious.

She stood there a minute looking at him solemnly; then her face broke into a smile, followed by that bell-like laugh. Señora Venicia joined her stubborn daughter in laughter. Cantrell joined them.

"Am I really that bad, Quint?" Elena looked at him soberly.

Venicia interrupted, "Yes, my dear, you really are that bad." She took her daughter's arm. "And on that note I think we'd better go to bed. Quint will have us on the trail by daylight." They went to the coach, opened the door, and got in.

Cantrell had King ride drag the next day. The rain had settled the dust, and the day dawned with a flawless blue sky. He rode out ahead, alone. The air smelled clean and pure with a hint of pine in it. A blue jay fussed at him as he rode by, and a squirrel barked from a nearby tree. A big buck, white-tailed deer, stood not a hundred yards from the trail and looked at him. Cantrell never killed game unless he could use it all. They would not be on the trail long enough to make use of this proud animal, so he just looked at the buck, admired his proud stance, and waved as though to say, "Some other day, big fellow. Today I'll not harm you."

Cantrell had been riding perhaps an hour when a rider rounded the bend ahead. Approaching, he held up his hand in greeting. Cantrell returned it and rode on.

A half hour or so passed, and Cantrell came upon a party similar to his own, traveling in the opposite direction. They waved in passing.

"Damn, this country's shore gettin' crowded," he said. "Soon be so's you can look out the window and see your neighbor's house only a mile or two away." He neck-reined his horse around and headed back toward the coach.

He swapped point and drag with King a couple of times during the day, and each time he passed the coach he stopped and told Elena and the señora of the things he'd seen, and assured them that all seemed to be safe.

They rode into Espanola about an hour before sunset. Cantrell had dropped back from point to lead the coach into town. The smells were inviting. The aroma of coffee wafted past his nostrils, and right on the tail of it, spicy smells of tortillas, red pepper, chili powder, and onions invaded his senses to the point that he was starving by the time he went to the hotel and made sure that a good room was available for the ladies. He and the men could sleep in the livery if necessary.

He put Elena and the señora's luggage in their rooms and, before leaving, said, "Need to get on the trail by sunup if we're gonna reach Santa Fe by nightfall. That all right with y'all?"

"That'll be fine, Quint. Do you suppose we'll be able to get breakfast that early?" Señora Venicia asked.

"We'll get it, ma'am." He closed the door softly behind him as he left.

He stopped at the desk and found there were rooms enough for the men. He told the clerk they'd want breakfast by five o'clock the next morning.

The clerk scratched his head. "Don't reckon the cook'll be here that early. How 'bout six?"

"Mister, I didn't ask you if we *could* have breakfast at five. I told you we'd *want* it at five. That's when we're gonna have it." He had not raised his voice. "You don't seem so busy you can turn down business, so you be damned sure the cook is here or you'll cook it yourself." Cantrell disliked being hard-nosed, but was sure as hell going to see the ladies had breakfast before leaving. He went out and told the men they had rooms.

They cared for their horses while he stripped the gear off his and rubbed it down. After seeing the big line-back dun in a stall, its nose buried in a bag of oats, he checked the coach, its wheels and nuts, to be sure they were secure.

Need to grease those wheels 'fore we leave Santa Fe, he thought, and the horses will need to be grain fed two or three days while we're there. He pulled the Winchester from its scabbard, picked up his bedroll, and headed back to the hotel.

Although hungry, Cantrell took a bath first. He scrubbed his dirty clothes, hung them over the bedstead to dry, put on clean clothes, and went looking for the small café he'd seen on the way into town, the one where all the good smells came from.

He was almost through with his meal when Elena and Venicia came in. They walked to his table and he hastily stood.

"May we sit with you, Quint?" the señora asked.

"Please do," he replied, and went around the table to seat them. "Reckon y'all caught the same spicy smells I did when we rode in."

"You didn't think you could keep all this good food to yourself, did you? It is good, isn't it?" Elena asked.

"Yes'm, b'lieve it might be even better'n it smelled." He reached for his hat and tossed it to the empty table next to them. Though many wore hats indoors, his mother had taught him at an early age that it wasn't mannerly.

"Well, tomorrow evening we'll be in Santa Fe," Venicia said, then looked up as the young Mexican girl came to the table. She greeted her in Spanish and asked what she would recommend. When the señorita had made her suggestion, both she and Elena nodded that her recommendation was good. Venicia looked at Cantrell.

"I'd like to stay five, maybe six days," she said. "What will you do in that time?"

"Before anything else, I figure to get the coach back in shape. After all that rain it's gonna need greasin'." He signaled the waitress for more coffee. "After that, reckon I'll see what I can find I might want to buy. Ain't been in a town of much size in some time."

He frowned. "Reckon I oughtta treat the boys to a few drinks. They been mighty close to their jobs the last few months."

"That is a good idea, and Quint," the señora reached out and touched his arm, "you use the money Lion gave you for that. He'd want it that way."

"Aw, reckon I know he'd want me to, ma'am, but figure I'd kinda like to do it myself." He cleared his throat to hide his embarrassment. "You see, ma'am, the BIM is the only place where I ever felt like I b'longed."

He looked up to see Elena staring straight into his eyes, and those beautiful green eyes were sparkling as though tears were trying to start.

"God bless you, Quint." Venicia placed her hand over his. "You do belong there, much more than you'll admit—even to yourself."

"Wonder where the boys are now." He changed the subject. He didn't know how to handle the situation and was beginning to feel all soft inside. "I bet next month's wages they're wettin' their whistle 'stead of eatin'."

Venicia smiled slightly. Cantrell wondered what amused her.

They finished their coffee, with Cantrell being careful to keep the conversation in an area that he knew something about. After they left the café, he escorted them to their rooms and then went to his.

He turned out the lantern and lay in the dark staring at the ceiling. "Damn, double damn," he groaned. "It's gettin' harder all the time to be around that beautiful filly without making a fool of myself." The señora ain't makin' it no easier, he thought. Fact of the matter, she seems to like the idea. He couldn't understand *that*, her bein' such a lady an' all.

He tossed restlessly, thinking, I'll bet Lion would raise hell if he even thought I might be havin' dreams about Elena. Well, what the hell, neither one of us can tell me what to dream. He turned on his side and went to sleep.

While saddling up the next morning, he told the men they would try to make Santa Fe that night. He got no argument, even though it was going to be a long, hard day.

It was just after dark when he led his party into the city plaza of Santa Fe. The windows of the saloons and the hotel were brightly lit, much brighter than oil lanterns would make them. When he walked into the hotel lobby to register for his party, Cantrell saw the reason. Gas lights.

He was surprised, and commented on it to the clerk, who told him proudly that they'd had gas since December 4, 1880. With that kind of light available, he made up his mind he'd buy something to read.

After getting Elena and her mother settled, he assured them he'd check in every day to see if there was anything he could do. He saw that the horses were cared for, settled into his own room, and then went out to look at the town.

He was disappointed. The stores were closed and he could not buy a book, but he did find a copy of Santa Fe's daily newspaper, *The New Mexican*.

The next morning he found a copy of *Ben Hur*, which was written by General Lew Wallace, Territorial Governor of New Mexico. The clerk told Quint they'd had trouble keeping it on the shelves at first, but that had been a couple of years ago. Now they had several copies.

Cantrell carried his book about with him all that day. He prized it as though it were his first gold strike. He wanted to buy Elena, Señora Venicia, and Lion something for Christmas, but he didn't know what.

Hell, he thought, don't even know if a cowboy's s'posed to do it, but I want to, so I'm goin' to.

He had no trouble finding a gift for King. It was a new sheath knife with a slim, beautifully forged blade, a bone handle inlaid with turquoise, and a hand-tooled cowhide sheath.

"Yep, he'll like it 'cause I like it," Cantrell said to the store-keeper. "We both seem to pretty much cotton to the same things."

By late the afternoon of the second day, he had been in every store at least twice and spent quite a bit of time sitting in the café drinking coffee.

He had long made a practice of not sitting around saloons. Drinking whiskey or beer filled him up after two or three glasses so he was at loose ends. Being a loner, he didn't seek out the company of the men.

For lack of something better to do he decided to go by the livery stable and check on the horses, as well as the coach. That didn't take much time. The horses were well cared for. The coach wheels had been greased, and the big, heavy bolts tightened securely.

He walked over and patted the dun on the neck. "Old hoss, I reckon you an' me are sort of useless in a town. Can't figure what all these people find to keep 'em busy. Ain't no cows to push around, can't hear a wolf howl or a mountain lion scream, can't hear the wind sing in the trees, can't smell nothin' here but a whole bunch of people who ain't seen fit to wash up in a month.

"Don't many of them trust nobody. They got to have every-thing in writin' on a piece of paper." He rubbed the dun's ears and reached in his pocket for a lump of sugar. His horse lipped it out of his palm and nuzzled him in thanks. "You're a good old hoss." Cantrell rubbed his mane and walked back toward the hotel. Might as well read awhile, he thought.

He'd read only a few pages when he put the book aside. God, he thought, he'd read an' washed more'n most of these people had in a lifetime. He had to find somethin' to do. He'd not had a drink yet, so he reckoned to have one and eat supper.

He rolled off the bed, buckled his gun on and tied it down, clamped his old, floppy-brimmed hat firmly on his head, and left.

He had a drink in the saloon that adjoined the hotel, then went directly to the dining room. Elena and Venicia were there. He lifted his hand in greeting and turned toward a table in the corner. They motioned him to theirs.

After he was seated, the señora glanced at him. "Are you finding enough to keep you out of trouble?" she inquired, a smile in her voice.

Cantrell felt sheepish in admitting it, but he was just a country boy. "Ma'am, I been in every store here at least twice. I don't do much drinkin' so I 'bout run out of things to do. Been readin' a lot, but I done had my bait of that for a while."

He looked at each of them and grimaced. "You reckon you'd mind too much if I just saddled up an' sort of slept out in the hills tomorrow night? Reckon all these people here in town just don't allow for much breathin' room."

They laughed. He felt the blood rush to his face. The señora placed her hand on his. "Oh, Quint, don't feel embarrassed. We aren't laughing *at* you, but *with* you."

She withdrew her hand. "Just this afternoon Elena and I were saying largely the same thing. We don't think it would be much of a life to be caged into a town or big city. I wish we could go with you." She nodded. "You go find breathing room for a day or so."

Cantrell was surprised. He hadn't expected them to understand, much less agree with him. "Ma'am, I'll be back and check in with you day after tomorrow."

CHAPTER
14

To the northeast was the mountain Cantrell had heard called "Baldy." He headed the dun toward it.

The day was cold and crisp. He breathed deeply when the town fell behind. He wanted to be high on the side of the mountain by nightfall.

The hills folded upon each other, creating meadows in between that narrowed toward the top. He crossed several of these, climbing higher as he did.

A stand of ponderosa pine caused him to stop and try to soak in the scent—as well as the quiet.

"Big hoss," he said, "reckon we'll be makin' camp right soon. Ain't gonna kill nothin' to eat—brought enough with me—even brought you a nose bag full of grain."

The dun twitched its ears. Cantrell laughed. "You like that, huh? I reckon we both like *this*. Promise you I won't get us tied down in no town—ever."

He found where he wanted to camp, unsaddled and picketed the dun out on the meadow, spread his blanket, and placed his slicker where he could get at it. Sudden thunderstorms at this elevation were not uncommon.

Cantrell scraped back pine needles to make room for his fire. He'd seen bear tracks, as well as those of several other animals. Mountain lions were not uncommon down here either, so he placed his rifle in easy reach. He'd not seen man-sign and didn't want to.

After eating, and drinking the last drop of coffee, he cleaned the camp, banked the fire, and rolled up in his blanket. He lay with his head on his saddle and stared up through the pine boughs at the soft, black, star-studded sky, each one standing boldly against the velvety blackness.

Someday, he thought, if more and more people keep comin'
into this world, a man ain't gonna be able to find a place
like this. He hoped he wouldn't be around to see that happen.

He lay there awake through most of the night, smelling,
feeling, hearing. The sweetness of the night air seemed to
have a special taste, and he savored it.

He heard the rustle of small, furry night animals, scurrying
toward the mountain stream not far from where he lay. The
dampness of the night's dew and the fresh odor of the rich earth
engulfed him. The soft cloak of sleep folded about him.

Cantrell was in the saddle when the eastern sky lightened.
Feeling like a man again, he could face a couple more days
in Santa Fe.

He checked in with Señora Venicia as soon as he'd taken
care of his horse. Elena was in her own room.

"Come in Quint," the señora invited. "Glad to see you didn't
just keep riding. The frame of mind you were in the other night,
I assumed that once you got your lungs full of fresh mountain
air you might just head on out."

"Aw, señora, you must know I wouldn't do that," he said,
then realized she wasn't serious. "I was mighty tempted
though."

Her expression sobered. "Seriously, I have a favor to ask
of you."

"Ma'am, I don't reckon you could ask anything of me that
I wouldn't try."

"No. Don't feel that way. This *will* be a favor, and I want
you to do it, but only if you don't mind." She walked over
and sat in one of the two chairs. "Sit down and let me tell
you about it."

Cantrell sat, stiffly, holding his hat in his hands.

"Oh, relax. You look as if you're about ready to bolt like a
scared deer." Venicia laughed.

"Now, to what I wanted to ask you. Lion and I have many
friends in and around Santa Fe. One of them, knowing that
I am in town, is throwing a fiesta Friday in Elena's and my
honor."

She gazed at him with that penetrating look, making him feel she could read his mind. "I want you to escort us there."

He opened his mouth to say something. "No," she said, "hear me out. You will be part of the family if anyone asks, and I want you to act like it—not as you seem to think you must act. You are not, and have not been treated as if you were, one of the hands.

"Lion thinks of you as one of his best friends. I think of you in the same manner. Elena thinks— Well, I had best not say what Elena thinks. At any rate, I want you to go." She frowned. "Do you dance, Quint?"

He nodded. "Yes'm. My ma and pa were from Virginia before they came west. They danced a lot back there. Ma taught me to waltz and polka—reckon I learned most of the Spanish dances down in Mexico."

He rolled his hat brim around in his hands. "You make me feel mighty fine, sayin' y'all are my friends. Reckon that's what these writin' men mean when they say someone's been honored. Yes'm, I feel right honored."

"And we are honored that a man of your caliber would choose us as friends. This will be a day-long affair. We'll be ready about ten o'clock."

He stood. "I'll be here, ma'am. Reckon I better get over to my room and clean up." With that he took his leave.

Thinking he'd better buy another suit, Cantrell checked to be sure he had enough money to do everything he planned. He'd left his good suit back at the ranch. He smiled ruefully, thinking he was getting to be a regular dude, what with owning two suits.

He went to his room, took a bath, and put on fresh clothes. Shopping about the Plaza, he found a ready-made suit and let the salesman measure him so it could be made to fit.

The coat and trousers had to be taken in at the waist, but the clerk told him the town had a tailor who could make it look like it was made for him. He paid for it and left with the promise it would be ready the next afternoon.

He wandered about the Plaza a little longer, then decided to have a drink. There was a saloon around the corner, a large place, with thick adobe walls. Probably been here a hundred years, Cantrell mused. It was a rough place, but hell, he wasn't gonna bother nobody.

There were two empty tables at the back of the room. He selected one and sat, his back to the wall. It was a habit he had. Although he didn't expect trouble, his back was covered if it came. He ordered a glass of whiskey.

His drink in front of him, he realized he hadn't really wanted it, but he figured it was one way to kill time, and if he drank slowly, it would last awhile.

A voice sounded from the front, loud and profane. Cantrell looked up. Two big men stood inside the batwing doors. They were every bit as tall as he, but thicker around the middle. They started toward the back. There was plenty of room in which to walk, but they didn't bother to walk around anyone. They came straight ahead, pushed people out of the way, and stopped at Cantrell's table.

"Get up. Move!" the one on the left growled. "This's our table."

Cantrell felt his insides go quiet. Angry blood started and subsided, and he felt ice replace it. He didn't say anything, but he stared at them quietly, coldly.

"I reckon you're hard of hearin'," the one on the right ground out. "My brother told you to move. Now I'm tellin' you. Get!"

Cantrell knew that if this came to gunplay, or fists, he was at a disadvantage sitting down, so in order to get on his feet without starting anything first, he looked up and smiled. "Hey, don't get all riled. I'm movin'."

He stood, his drink in hand—and, still smiling, tossed it in the face of the first one who had spoken, stepped forward, and backhanded the other across the cheek. They both reached for their guns.

Cantrell was faster. He fired once left, once right, once left, and turned to put another slug in the one on the right.

The heavy slugs knocked them backward. They fired as they staggered back, their bullets gouging creases in the rough stone floor.

The man on the right fell; his eyes, wide in death, stared sightlessly at the ceiling.

The one on the left tried to raise his gun for another shot. He strained. Blood bubbled from his mouth. His neck veins stood out like ropes.

Cantrell stood, thumb holding the hammer back, knowing another shot shouldn't be needed but ready if it was. The man put both hands on the butt of his pistol, tried once more to bring it to bear on Cantrell, then fell facedown at his feet.

Cantrell loaded his .44 and dropped it carefully into its holster. He walked back to his chair, pulled it out, and sat down.

"Bring me another drink," he said to the bartender, "and you better send somebody for the marshal."

"No need to, señor." The bartender nodded toward a tall man standing a few feet from Cantrell's table. "He is here."

Cantrell looked at the man with the star on his chest.

"Do not worry, señor. You must kill them or they will kill you." The marshal walked to the table and placed his hand on the back of the chair across from Cantrell. *"Por favor?"*

Cantrell nodded. *"Sí."*

"I watch when they start the trouble. I think they make the big mistake. Then I see their guns almost out of their holster before you draw. I think then maybe they kill you, but *Madre de Dios* I never see a gun appear so quick as yours.

"You have no trouble with the law, señor. You only defend yourself, and that is, how do you say it? . . . Permissible? *Sí*, that is what I mean."

"Marshal, let me buy you a drink. I shore didn't want this trouble, but they brought it to me."

He signaled for another drink when the marshal indicated that he'd like one. It was then he noticed that a crowd had gathered around the bodies—all talking at once.

His attention returned to the marshal, who took a swallow and leaned forward. "Señor, you 'ave take care of only half your trouble. These two were brothers—and there's two more of them.

"They very bad, been causing me trouble in this town a long time now, but not enough to jail them, or for somebody to kill them, till now. The word will get to the other two, an' they will look for you."

Four brothers! It began to dawn on Cantrell that maybe he had lucked out. If these two were Hardesters, he'd been very lucky to have to face only the two of them.

"You know the names those two go by?" he asked.

"Sí. The one that died so hard, he is Clell Hardester. The first one to die was Owen Hardester. The two that will be lookin' for you are—"

"Bent and Speed Hardester," Cantrell interrupted. "I didn't know who they were, Marshal, but I was gonna have to meet them some time." Then he told the marshal the story.

When he finished, the marshal leaned back and looked at him, shaking his head. "So you're Quinton Cantrell. I hear much of you, señor." He smiled. "I think if they hear the same stories I hear, that maybe they leave you alone. I know when I see you draw you 'ave to be one of those that men talk about."

"Well, Marshal, it's a reputation I don't want, but I got it. I'll be in town till Sunday. If you want me I'll be at the hotel; after that you can find me at the Box I-M, up Durango way."

He stood and held out his hand. The marshal shook it. Cantrell paid for their drinks and left.

Outside, he was surprised to see it was still mid-afternoon. Sure is a lot can happen in a short time, he thought. He glanced at the sky and reckoned he had time to do more shopping. He was glad now that he had asked Lion for a couple of hundred dollars of his money before leaving the ranch. He had had no idea what he might encounter on this trip, and he had wanted to be prepared.

The sun was low in the west, and lights were beginning to paint the windows of homes and stores a soft golden hue.

He put the gunfight of the afternoon behind him. It had to happen sometime, and he'd been lucky to get it done. Now he'd find a good meal and eat before going to his room.

He felt good. He'd found the señora a beautiful tortoiseshell comb and a black lace mantilla, and he'd bought Lion a hand-tooled belt and holster. But he had found nothing for Elena.

He went to a small café he remembered seeing on one of the side streets. He was the only customer, and was glad for it. The lady who waited on him was apparently the owner.

She brought him his order, a half dozen eggs, and a steak that covered his plate, then put a hot pan covered with a clean white towel beside it.

"Them's some of my biscuits. I don't fix 'em like that for everybody, but I figured that a big man like you would appreciate 'em."

She went behind the counter and brought out a steaming mug of coffee for him and one for herself.

"Mind if I keep you company while you eat?" she asked.

Cantrell didn't want company, but he'd not be rude. "No, ma'am, have a seat."

He started to stand, but she waved him back into his chair. She was a heavyset, motherly type of woman, hair snow-white and black eyes sharp as a bird's.

She looked at him with a piercing gaze. "So you're Quint Cantrell. I've heard about you." She sipped her coffee. "You're not like I expected,'cept your looks. I'd have known ya anywhere."

Cantrell frowned, and she continued. "Oh, heavens to Betsy, I ain't one to believe all I hear, especially when it's a bunch of no-accounts talkin'."

She stood, went behind the counter, and brought back a soup bowl, filled with freshly churned country butter, and a pitcher of molasses.

"You better top that steak and eggs off with a few of those biscuits and molasses. I'd shorely hate to think of a big man like you alayin' awake tonight starvin', and it bein' maybe hours till breakfast." She laughed, and Cantrell thought it a nice sound in the quiet little place.

"Well, ma'am, don't reckon I'm likely to starve after this meal." He finished chewing and swallowed, then looked at her questioningly. "How'd you know I'm Cantrell? Nobody around here knows me far as I know."

She laughed again. "Young'un, there ain't many men in the world would fit what I heard you look like. Young, black hair, ice-blue eyes, big as a bear, wide shoulders and lean hips, and to top that off, the handsomest man in the territory. I been hearin' about you for a long time."

He felt his face flush.

"I knowed you soon's you walked in. Ain't nobody I ever seen what could fit that description till I seen you." She laughed again and held her hand across the table. "I'm Kate Mably. If I was thirty years younger reckon I'd hogtie you for meself."

He took her hand and held it. "Kate, I reckon if I was a free man in my heart you wouldn't have to hogtie me."

She looked solemn. "Just my luck. Find meself a man, and his heart belongs to somebody else." They both laughed and Cantrell released her hand.

Kate's eyes locked with his. "Young'un, you done made yourself some friends—and some enemies in this here town."

She stood and brought the coffeepot to the table. She poured them each a cup, sat down, and continued. "Some of the Hardester hands was in here. Some thought you did 'em a favor by killing those two in the saloon this afternoon. Others figured to get even with you. They're the ones who ride for the brand."

She sipped her coffee, never removing her gaze from his. "A lot of the town folks were glad to see it—me included. That bunch wrecks my place about every time they come in here, but once I met you, I would've counted you a friend without you killin' 'em."

She stood, walked to the door, peered out, then came back and sat down. "The two brothers you killed were the rowdy ones. The other two are the ones to watch out for. They're dangerous, worse than a couple of rattlesnakes with their rattles cut off. They'll hit you from ambush or head-on. Don't make no difference to them—but they take the edge where they can get it, so be careful, young'un."

Cantrell's throat tightened with the realization that this big, motherly woman really cared what happened to him.

Some people you instantly like, and he liked Kate. "Kate, this fight today was a long time coming. The only thing it changed was to let them know where I am." He felt his face stiffen. "I'm glad it happened. Ain't lookin' for trouble, but if it happens, then I can look on down the trail to more important things." He shrugged. "Reckon some things happen for the best. Bad as it sounds, I'm glad it happened."

She reached across the table and took his two big hands in her small ones. "Somehow, big'un, I know you can handle it. But be careful."

He stood. "Yes'm, I always am." He dug in his pocket for money to pay his bill and handed it to her. "Say, you reckon you could fill up the boys I rode in here with—an' maybe the two ladies what come with us?"

"Just try me, young'un. I'll fix y'all the goshdangdest supper ya ever wrapped your stomachs around."

"Well then, I can't promise, but if they ain't doin' nothin', we'll be in Thursday evenin'."

"That's tomorrow night."

"Yep, so it is." Cantrell winked and left.

He stayed close to the storefronts as he headed toward the Plaza. His gaze searched every shadow, every roofline. His enemies now knew where to find him.

There were many of them, and only one of him. They had the edge because they knew him and he didn't know them. He was glad he didn't have to worry about anyone but himself during this dark walk back to the hotel.

He twisted to look behind, and simultaneously felt a hot, searing streak across his right shoulder, accompanied by the loud report of a pistol shot.

He hit the ground, rolled, and fired in the direction of the shot. It had come from an alley just a few feet to his right. Then he heard the pounding of retreating footsteps. He held his fire. Whoever it was was gone.

He looked at the slowly growing crowd and holstered his .44.

"You have been hit, señor," a soft voice said. "Is it bad?"

"No. Only a crease," Cantrell replied, and felt his shoulder. "It's bleeding pretty good, but nothing to worry about."

"They shoot at you from the alley," the same voice replied. Cantrell singled out a slight Mexican youth as the one addressing him.

"Yeah, but he's gone. It was only one man. I didn't hit him. I fired to make him run, or return my fire so I'd know where he was—he ran."

Cantrell looked at the still-gathering crowd, and anger welled into his throat. "That's all, folks. Nobody layin' here dead for you to gawk at. Go back to your homes." He walked quickly away from the throng, instantly ashamed that he had vented his anger on them.

If his enemies would try to drygulch him from an alley, he thought, they might try it in his hotel room. Upon leaving his room, he'd placed a small piece of paper between the door and the frame, a couple of inches from the floor. It was still in place, so he felt safer about entering.

Now that the Hardesters knew where he was, Cantrell slipped back into his old habits—the ones that had been a part of him during his hunted years.

He opened the door, went in, closed it, put a chair against it, then stripped his shirt off to take a look at his shoulder.

Just as he'd thought, only a crease.

He poured water from the pitcher on the washstand into a white porcelain bowl and dipped his shirtsleeve into it.

A soft knock on his door stopped his left hand in midair, but it didn't stop his right. Without thinking, he'd palmed his .44. He moved silently to the side of the door.

"Yeah, who is it?"

"Quint, it's me, Elena."

He frowned. It wasn't right for her to be here.

He removed the chair and opened the door, trying to shrug into his shirt at the same time.

"Oh! Quint, what happened?" Elena cried. She closed the door and bolted it.

"Somebody took a shot at me from an alley. Don't know who. Don't matter anyway. They almost missed."

She took his shirt from his arm, which was only partially thrust into the sleeve. "Here now. You're not going to put this shirt back on. It's filthy. You'll get infection. How in the world did it get so dirty?"

"Just wasn't p'ticular where I fell, I reckon."

Elena looked up from inspecting his wound. Her lips tightened. "I don't know what I'm going to do with you. Let you out of my sight for a little while and you have two—yes, not one, but two gunfights. Can't you ever stay out of trouble?

"It's because of the one you had this afternoon that I'm here. I-I wanted to know that you were not hurt." Her eyes blazed. "Now I'm going to ask you again, can't you stay out of trouble for even one day?"

"Reckon not, ma'am. I try. Lord, how I try, but it seems to always be camped right in the middle of my trail."

She started unbuttoning his long johns, and when he opened his mouth to protest, her chin set in that stubborn look he'd come to know so well.

"You're going to peel your tops down so I can see how bad you're hit. Don't argue with me!"

Sighing, he finished unbuttoning the tops far enough to slip his arms out, letting the sleeves dangle around his waist.

Elena looked around and, apparently not seeing what she wanted, looked back at him. "Do you have any whiskey?"

"No, ma'am. I seldom drink, an' even less than that do I keep a bottle with me."

"Stay just like you are. I'll be right back." She left the room.

Cantrell heard her steps go down the stairs to the lobby. Damn, he thought, hope she don't go traipsin' into the saloon for a bottle.

He waited, for what seemed forever, then started to shrug back into his tops. He had one arm into a sleeve and was starting to push into the other one when he heard her returning.

Quickly, he pulled his arms from the sleeves, and when she walked into the room, he stood exactly as she had left him.

"Hmmm, you did what I asked for a change. I had the boy at the desk go find a bottle."

"Yes'm, reckon that's just my nature. I always do what I been told to do."

Elena's snort of derision was totally unladylike. She looked around and, again apparently not seeing what she wanted, lifted her skirt.

Startled, Cantrell turned his head and felt his face flush. Damn her anyway. Don't she know what just being in the room with her does to me? He stared at a spot above the door in an effort to blot out the chance he'd see her ankles.

He heard cloth tearing and looked down. She was ripping a strip from the bottom of her petticoat.

"Aw now, Elena, you shouldn't't've tore up your pretty clothes."

He saw her freeze as she was about to pour whiskey onto the strip of cloth.

She was standing close enough that he smelled the sweet woman scent of her, not perfume, but a scent better than all the scents of the forests he loved so much. Her face tilted to his, lips parted.

"You called me Elena," she whispered, her breath warm on his face.

Without willing it, his arms encircled her and drew her to him. His lips brushed hers lightly, and he felt her thrust her body close to him, her arms closing about his neck while she pulled his head down and crushed her lips against his own.

He held her, his lips tasting the maiden honey of hers. He was like a starving man getting his first taste of food. He couldn't let her go—but some glimmer of sanity filtered into his senses.

Reluctantly he lifted his lips and gently pushed her back so their bodies no longer touched. She stood there, a look of wonderment in her eyes.

"I-I've never been kissed before. It seemed like I was on a cloud, in heaven maybe, only more alive than I've ever been in my life. Even my hair seemed to . . ."

"And I had no right to do it." His voice was rough. "Elena, I've wanted to hold you, to kiss you, since I first saw you, but what I've wanted so bad ain't got 'right' branded on it."

"Don't I have a say as to what you have a right to?" she asked.

He took her shoulders in his big hands. She felt so fragile he thought he might break her, and he turned her loose, as though he'd touched a hot stove.

"Elena, I got things on my backtrail, things you don't know about, things I got to take care of before I can talk to you.

"I got to talk to Lion too. It just wouldn't be right for me to say no more to you till him and me palaver a bit."

She tilted her head toward him again, and he saw that her eyes swam in unshed tears.

"All right, cowboy, we'll ride this bronc your way. You take care of this mysterious business of yours and you talk to Lion, but then that's all the time you have—'cause then I'm comin' after you." Her voice was so soft that he had to strain to hear.

"And one other thing—no more 'ma'am' and no more 'miss,' because if you do I'll tell the boys you kissed me." She was smiling, teasing, through the tears.

"All right. Reckon I'll do it your way. But only because I believe you really would do what you say."

"You can bet a painted pony on that, cowboy."

She looked at his arm. "Oh, you're bleeding again." Still holding the whiskey and the hem of her petticoat, she picked up where she'd left off. It seemed a long time ago, another world to Cantrell, that she had started dressing his wound.

When Elena had finished bandaging his shoulder and gone to her room, he went to bed. He didn't sleep for a very long time that night, and when he did, it was to dream of holding Elena close to him, much closer than she'd been just a few short hours before. And even though he was asleep, the pangs of guilt penetrated his consciousness to cause a restless, broken toss-and-turn night.

CHAPTER
15

Cantrell slept late. The regulator clock on the wall behind the desk indicated six o'clock when he walked through the lobby to the dining room.

He glanced out the front window and saw snow falling. Wind must have changed during the night, he thought. It's that time of year.

Venicia and Elena sat at one of the wall tables and looked up when he entered.

"Come sit with us, Quint," Elena called.

He walked over. "Mornin', Señora, Elena." He nodded, then saw Venicia's eyes widen slightly and just a touch of a smile crinkle the corners of her eyes.

That lady don't miss nothin', he almost grunted aloud as he pulled out a chair and sat down. As soon as he'd said, "Elena," without puttin' the "miss" on the front of it, she'd caught the omission.

When he had ordered, Cantrell commented on the weather, and they talked of that awhile. Then he thought of the promise he'd made Kate.

He looked at the señora. "Ma'am, if y'all ain't plannin' anything special for supper tonight, I'd kinda like to take you and the boys to this little café I was at last night. A lady by the name of Kate Mably owns it, and she shore can cook." He toyed with his cup, then blurted, "I sort of promised her I'd bring y'all an' the boys around."

"Can she cook better'n me, Quint?" Elena pinned him with her gaze.

"Aw, no, ma'am," he drawled, "can't nobody cook like you."

"Quinton Cantrell—I warned you. You want me to tell?"

"Aw, I was just teasin'." He knew his face was red, and he hoped the señora didn't notice.

"Yes, Quint," Venicia said, accepting his invitation, "we'd love to have supper with you and the boys."

The way she hurriedly intervened told him she'd seen him turn red. She might imagine almost anything, and the way Elena had said, "You want me to tell," could have *meant* anything.

What he didn't know was that Elena didn't care what meaning her mother placed on her words, because she intended to tell her the truth as soon as they had finished breakfast and were in their room. They were always honest with each other.

When they reached the señora's door, Elena asked if she might come in, saying she wanted to talk awhile. Cantrell had left to check the horses.

With the door closed and bolted behind them, Elena walked to the center of the room, then faced her mother.

"Mama, Quint kissed me last night," she blurted, "and . . . and, well, I never knew anything could be so wonderful. I, well, I would've never let him stop if he hadn't just pushed me away."

Venicia let out the breath she'd been holding since entering the room; then she folded Elena into her arms.

"Ah, *mi hija*, it does not surprise me." She smiled. "You see, I heard you go to his room last night."

"Mama, after we heard about the gunfight yesterday, I knew I'd not sleep until I knew he was all right."

"You love him very much. I've known this a long time, and for that reason I didn't interfere when you went to him last night."

Elena started to cut in, but her mother held up her hand to stop her. "Oh, yes, I know what love will do to a young woman. The emotions make us lose all sense of propriety, and knowing this, I would have interfered except for two things: I knew Quint would never take advantage of you. Under that rough facade he is very much a gentleman of honor."

She smiled again. "And the other reason? You had to have the opportunity to make him do just what he did. I was beginning to think I was going to have to take a hand in it to, well, to sort of get things started."

Elena laughed and hugged her mother, who was also laughing.

"Mama, he didn't stand a chance, no more chance than a snowball in h—" Choking off the word, she gasped, and looked at her mother apologetically.

"Tsk, tsk." Venicia shook her head. "Your papa has let you attend too many roundups." She cocked her head to the side and smiled. "But then we must say the words that best communicate the thought. You said it very well, *mi hija*."

Elena sat on the side of the bed. "Mama, he had another gunfight last night. At least, someone tried to ambush him from an alley.

"It was when I was cleaning and caring for his wound, a crease across his shoulder, that he kissed me. Then he said he had no right to do it, that he had things on his backtrail that had to be taken care of, and also, he said he'd have to talk to Papa before it would be right."

She stood. "I told him I'd do things his way if he'd stop ma'aming and missing me all the time."

Her mother frowned. "He's right, you know. He'll have to talk with your father, but somehow I don't see that as an obstacle. Your father knows something about Quint, and he holds him above any other man." She rubbed her forehead thoughtfully. "Elena, the things on his backtrail are men, killers, who want him dead. Quint just doesn't want it to be a race between your becoming a widow and consummating your marriage."

"Oh, Mama, I—Isn't there anything we can do to help him?"

Venicia shook her head. "No. Quint is a proud man. He breaks his own broncs. If we offered to help, it would be an insult."

She took hold of Elena's shoulders and shook them gently. "You can take this into your little head, my daughter. You've got yourself one helluva man. Be patient. He'll take care of this in his own way, and when it's over, you'll have a long and happy life ahead of you."

She released Elena, then looked toward the window. "Goodness! We've taken the whole morning, and we have more shopping to do before the fiesta tomorrow."

Cantrell had shopping to do too. He was standing across the Plaza from the hotel, his head pulled down into the collar of his sheepskin, his hands thrust deep in his pockets. He still hadn't found a suitable Christmas gift for Elena.

His gaze swept the Plaza once more. His enemies had tried last night and they'd try again. He didn't know how many there were, nor did he know who they were, but if he could kill the other two Hardesters, he knew he'd not have to worry about any of the Hardester gun-quick cowpokes.

Venicia and Elena came through the doorway of the hotel. They were bundled up against the cold, but he recognized them.

They headed down the street toward one of the larger stores and had almost reached its door when Cantrell saw a rider push away from the wall against which he'd been leaning and step directly in front of them.

He didn't think anything about it until he saw them try to walk around the man and he moved again to block their passage.

Keeping his gaze on them, Cantrell unbuttoned his coat, weaved his way across the street to the square, and angled across toward them.

The rider, a big, rawboned, red-faced man, had his back toward Cantrell, but he could see enough of the man's face to know that he had not had a shave in several days, and that his face was flushed, either from the cold or whiskey.

Red-face said, "C'mon, little lady. We'll leave your mama here and you an' me's gonna go have some fun." Then he grabbed Elena's coat.

Her eyes spit green flames. She slapped the bully's hand away, then raked her nails across his face.

"Damn you!" he spat, and reached for her again. That was when Cantrell arrived.

Grabbing him by the shoulder, he spun the bully around. While he pulled on the man's shoulder, Cantrell's right was coming up from down around his knees. It connected with the point of Red-face's jaw.

He went down, cursing, and reached for his Bowie knife.

Cantrell's knife rested in a scabbard at the back of his belt. It came smoothly into his hand.

Elena and Venicia backed up to the store wall. "Get inside," he ordered, his voice harsh, brooking no argument. Then he gave all his attention to the knife-wielding bully.

Cantrell could have kicked the knife from Red-face's hand, but he didn't. That bastard had touched his woman; Cantrell wanted to hurt him, kill him if he could, and knife fighting was as natural to him as guns.

While Red-face came slowly to his feet, Cantrell shrugged out of his sheepskin and wrapped it around his left forearm.

His adversary planted his feet, and Cantrell stepped in with a slicing motion to his gut. Red-face grunted. The razor-sharp edge had bitten through the coat and drawn blood, but it would take a deeper cut to put this man down.

Cantrell's anger—cold, controlled, calculating—left his mind clear. He planted his feet solidly in the snow. Balance usually made the difference in a knife fight.

Red-face approached slowly, weaving, looking for an opening. Knife fighters, like boxers, played a scientific cat-and-mouse game.

Suddenly, the other man's blade flicked toward Cantrell. He backed up a step, letting it slide past, then sliced again, at the man's wrist. He missed. His swing turned him with his side to the man.

He felt the bite of cold steel along his ribs. Not deep, he thought, and swung his blade again. He slipped on the icy surface and fell.

He rolled to his back, expecting the bully to follow up by diving at him. He was right, but as Red-face started his charge, Elena stuck out her foot and tripped him.

Cantrell rolled to the side and came to his feet. Red-face did the same. Cantrell stepped into him and swung. He saw the other man's blade coming down in a stabbing motion. He threw his left arm up to fend off the knife, and felt it bite into his coat, not reaching his arm.

Before Red-face could draw back for another strike, Cantrell shoved his knife out straight in front of him and felt it start into the man's gut, then he walked into him, pushing his blade to the hilt, and worked it back and forth to each side.

Red-face tried to make another swipe, but his eyes were staring, his mouth open, trying to suck in a breath. A red gusher spewed from between his lips.

He was no longer red-faced. His skin, now a bluish-white, named him—dead.

While the bully fell, Cantrell jerked his knife free, knelt, and carefully cleaned it on the dead man's coat. He slipped his knife into its sheath, then turned to Elena and Venicia, still standing with their backs to the storefront.

"Why the hell didn't you get, when I told you to?" he ground out.

"B-b-because I thought I might help you," Elena answered, her face as white as the scarf around her throat.

The ice inside him melted, and he felt ashamed for having spoken to her as he had. "Oh, *mi amor*, I'm sorry. You did help me. If you hadn't stuck out your foot an' tripped him, he mighta killed me. I just wish you and the señora had not seen this."

"Would it have been better if it were your blood we were looking upon, Señor Quint?" Venicia asked.

Cantrell slanted a look at her. "No, ma'am, reckon it wouldn't."

He looked at the fallen foe. "We shore don't have much of a hog-tied stranglehold on life as we seem to think," he said.

He looked at Elena, then shifted his glance to Venicia. "Y'all go on an' do your shoppin'. I'll get him taken care of; then I got more shoppin' to do too."

"You'll do nothing of the kind," Señora Venicia said, taking his arm. "I'm going to see how much damage he did to your ribs. I know he cut you. I saw you wince. Back to your room, now. Don't argue."

She looked at Elena. "Come, we'll take care of this big man whether he wants it or not."

"Aw, señora, you don't need to do that. Besides, I gotta tell the marshal 'bout all this." He looked around and for the first time saw that a small crowd had gathered. Thank goodness for the bad weather, he thought, or the Plaza would have been full.

Venicia glanced at the crowd, then said to a nicely dressed man of middle age, "Señor, would you see to it that the marshal is notified of this? We will be at the hotel. *Por favor?*"

"*Sí*, señora, I will do this for you."

"*Muchas gracias.*" She took Cantrell's arm and steered him through the crowd to the hotel.

She looked into his face, guilelessly. "I know Elena would like to see you're not hurt bad, and it would not be proper for her to be in your room alone, would it, Quint?" she asked primly.

He felt his face redden. "No, ma'am, that surely wouldn't be proper." He wondered why he felt so guilty. He'd had nothing to do with Elena's visit of the night before.

It took but a minute to walk to the hotel and climb the stairs to his room.

CHAPTER
16

"Strip to your waist," Venicia ordered as soon as the door closed behind them.

"Seems kinda like this is gettin' to be a habit," he muttered under his breath.

"Did you say something?" Venicia looked up at him, her eyes wide and innocent.

"No, ma'am."

She looked first at the angry furrow along his ribs, then, almost admiringly, at the rest of his upper torso. "My, my, so many scars, but this wound is not very bad. The bleeding is almost stopped."

She said to Elena, "Go to your room and bring me some cloth from your ruined—That is, see if you can find some clean material from which we can make bandages."

"Yes, *Mother*." Elena replied.

There they go again, he thought. He'd never heard Elena address her mother as anything but "Mama."

When Elena returned, he sighed, relieved she was back. He didn't have to guess where she'd gotten the bandages. If she'd not gotten back soon, Cantrell thought he might have bolted. The señora had been tracing his scars with her finger, and as she touched each, she guessed at its origin.

Her lips puckered, and frowning, she would say, "Bullet? Knife? Hmmm, this must have been a bear, or cougar perhaps?" Yeah, he was damned glad when Elena returned.

As Elena entered, Venicia said over her shoulder, "Quint has seen many troubles. Just look at all these scars."

He squirmed. "Ma'am, if you don't mind I sure would like

to get my clothes back on. I ain't never felt so uncomfortable in my whole life."

Both women broke into uncontrolled laughter.

"Now what did I say?" he grumbled.

"Do you have any whiskey?" Venicia asked.

"Yes'm, right there on the washstand."

He was glad he had it, or Elena might have been sent for some and it would have been even longer until he could get dressed. On top of everything it was damned cold in this room.

A knock sounded as Venicia tied the last strip around his chest.

Cantrell quickly shrugged into his clothes. "Yeah? Who is it?"

"Marshal," came the soft reply from the other side of the door.

"C'mon in."

When the marshal entered, he looked questioningly at the ladies.

"These are my *two bosses*," Cantrell explained, "the Señora Venicia McCord, and her daughter, *Señorita* Elena McCord. This is Marshal Perez, señorita, señorita."

"We do only what is best for you, Señor Cantrell." Elena's voice was a little too sweet to suit Cantrell.

The marshal smiled at Cantrell's discomfort. "I hear about your fight with the knives, señor. I 'ave come to see how you tell it. This is necessary even though I 'ave already hear it."

"No trouble, Marshal," Cantrell replied, then related what had caused the fight. "Sure sorry, but I couldn't let it ride when he bothered the ladies."

"No, señor, I would not think very highly of you if you had." Perez sighed. "But I sure will be glad to see you leave for a while so I, how you say it, catch up with my paperwork?"

"Well, I'll say it again, Marshal, I'm sorry to cause you trouble."

"*De nada*," the marshal said, then looked at the ladies. "I'm very happy to meet you, ladies." He slanted a glance at Cantrell. "An' I am glad to see you take such good care of this man." He gave them a tight-lipped grin, nodded, tipped his hat, and left.

When he'd closed the door behind the marshal, Cantrell looked at the two women who gave him such pleasure in living, yet so much discomfort.

"Now, ladies, if y'all don't mind, you can go do your shopping, and when you're gone I can put my shirttail in."

Again they looked at each other, laughed, and left.

A puzzled frown crossed Cantrell's face. Seems like when they look at each other, each knows what the other's thinking. He shook his head, unbuttoned his trousers, and tucked his shirttail in. He too had shopping to do.

Cantrell went into every store, along the side streets and bordering the Plaza. It was not until he saw a pair of emerald earrings and a pendant to match that he knew what Elena's gift would be.

"Aw, hell, I'll take 'em," he told the clerk. "Just mean a few head of cows that won't be eatin' on my range. Besides I ain't seen nothin' any closer to goin' with her eyes."

He walked out of the store feeling that Christmas was really going to be a time of joy. He'd never had anyone to give a gift to before, nor had he received gifts.

He most likely wouldn't this time either. He never thought that *he* might receive a gift. He found the pleasure of giving was the greatest gift of all. If Elena liked his gift, his Christmas would be complete.

When he came out of the store, it was late evening, time to get ready for supper at Kate's. He cut across the corner of the square to the hotel. When passing the desk, he asked that a tub of hot water be brought to his room.

While waiting for his bathwater he took out his copy of *Ben Hur*. He'd read only a couple of pages when he frowned down at the book. I read pretty good, he thought. Wonder why I don't talk no better'n I do. He shrugged, and turned the page. Maybe someday, he thought, he could get somebody to teach him how to do it right.

He had stopped by the livery earlier and rented a surrey so Elena and her mother wouldn't have to walk in the snow. He'd told the liveryman to have it in front of the hotel at seven o'clock.

He went to the lobby early. The young man at the desk

offered him a copy of *The New Mexican* to read while he waited. Seating himself and opening the paper, he glanced through the doors and saw the surrey by the hitching rail. Cantrell expected that by the time he got to Kate's with the ladies, the men would be there.

After reading only the headlines, he looked toward the stairs and saw Elena and Venicia descending. Every time he saw them, he marveled at their beauty. Looking at Elena made his throat swell so he could hardly swallow.

Reckon there ain't no two women in the world any prettier, he thought, and there sure ain't none of them's got more backbone. He stood and walked to the foot of the stairs.

"I reckon if everybody in Santa Fe could see me," he said, smiling up at them, "they'd wonder how a plain old cowhand came up with the two most beautiful women in the world, all in the same place."

Venicia said, "You do say nice things, Quint." She turned to Elena. "We like to hear nice things whether they are true or not, do we not, Elena?"

"Mama, ah reckon Quint wouldn't've said it if he didn't mean it." Elena made her voice gruff as she mimicked Cantrell; then she looked at him. "C'mon, big man, ah'm hongry enough to eat a b'ar."

Cantrell looked at her, purposely allowing only his eyes to smile. "Well now, ma'am, I reckon Kate's gonna have a job on her hands,'cause I figured to eat the b'ar myself." He held his arms for them. "Let's see what she's fixed for us."

When they walked into Kate's place, the hands were already there. They sat at a long table Kate had arranged from several smaller ones.

"Everybody here?" Kate asked.

"Yep," Cantrell responded, then introduced the ladies to her. "Reckon you've met the boys already."

"Yeah, we done got acquainted," Kate said and walked to the door to lock it. "Ain't lettin' nobody else in here tonight. If they et what I done fixed for y'all, they'd want me to feed *them* like this, an' I ain't gitten caught in that bear trap."

After seating Elena and Venicia, Cantrell saw there was only one empty chair left. "One thing wrong already, Kate. We need one more chair at this table."

"Thought you said everybody was here?"

He nodded. "Everybody's here. You think we're gonna eat without you?" He shook his head. "We ain't gonna sit an' eat unless you sit with us and eat too. And, Miss Kate, I'm gonna help you put it on the table."

"Naw, now, you ain't gonna help. It ain't fittin' for a man to do women's work."

He placed his hand gently on her shoulder. "Kate, a man what's gotta prove he's a man by the kind of chores he cuts out for himself ain't much of a man."

She tilted her head to look at him. Her eyes glistened. "No, Quint, I don't reckon you got anything to prove, but that lady, whoever she is, that you done give your heart to, is some lucky woman."

He wished Elena, Venicia, and all the hands had not heard this.

"Well c'mon, let's you an' me git the food on the table. That young, pretty lady down yonder already told me she was gonna eat a b'ar, so reckon we better get her fed soon or we're in trouble."

Cantrell wondered, as he put dish after dish on the table, where Kate had gotten it all. She had pheasant, quail, trout, venison, beef, several kinds of vegetables, baked potatoes, rolls, and coffee.

After supper, with a smug look, she went to the oven and brought out two large pans of apple cobbler. "Fixed 'em outta dried apples. Makes a mighty fine dish. Help yourselves."

"Hey, Cantrell," one of the boys yelled from down the table, "you orter marry Kate. Don't know who the gal is you done give your heart but you sure ain't gonna find nobody who can cook like this. After you marry Kate you kin hire us away from Lion, let Kate feed us all the time."

Cantrell felt his face redden. If there'd been a hole in the floor, he'd have crawled into it.

He looked up, straight at Elena, and those green eyes were dancing with merriment. If she says one word, I'm gonna get up an' leave, he thought.

Elena didn't say anything, but Venicia spoke up. "C'mon, men. Leave Quint alone." She smiled down the table at them. "If you don't, he might leave and let us pay for this meal. I'd bet a painted pony none of us brought any money."

Venicia winked at Kate. "Kate, you suppose two weeks of dishwashing each would take care of the meal?"

Kate frowned and pursed her lips as though in deep thought. "Well if I kin stand the sight of that ugly one down yonder who's been hurrahin' Quint, I reckon 'bout three weeks would do it." She smiled. "Besides, I done proposed to Quint an' he turned me down flat. Just to smooth over my hurt feelin's I kinda want him to pay for this meal, so leave him alone."

The evening continued like this—talking, joking. Some of the men had seconds, and some even thirds on the pie. When finally Venicia indicated that they should leave, Cantrell saw that they were all sorry it had to end.

There were not many times in these men's lonely lives that they truly felt like family, but tonight was one of them. Cantrell felt a lump come into his throat. Very much of this and he'd be soft as a feather pillow inside.

After escorting the ladies to their rooms and delivering the surrey to the livery stable, he went to bed, thinking he'd never had a day to top this one.

Venicia had told him she wanted to leave in time to get to the Hernandez ranch by noon. It was only five miles from town, so Cantrell had told the liveryman he wanted the surrey in front of the hotel by ten o'clock. He was lying there thinking of Elena, Venicia, and Kate when a soft knock sounded at his door.

He pulled his .44 from the holster hanging over the bedpost, walked softly to the door, and said, "Cantrell here."

"It's me, señor, Marshal Perez. I must speak with you."

Cantrell unbolted the door and nodded for the marshal to come in. "Trouble, Marshal?"

"Maybe, maybe not, but I think maybe you should know of what I find out."

Cantrell nodded. "If you think so, figure I better listen."

"*Sí*, that is what I think." Perez walked to the bed and back to the center of the room. "You got a lantern in here, señor?"

Cantrell chuckled. "Yeah, reckon I forgot it."

He lighted the lantern, and trimmed the wick. "They got gaslights downstairs. Reckon they ain't had time to put them in the rooms yet."

The whiskey bottle caught his eye. "You want a drink, Marshal?"

"*Gracias*, señor, but no. I must stay on the streets until the saloons close."

Cantrell waved his hand vaguely at the chair. "Have a seat." He pushed his .44 back in its holster and said, "All right, let's have it. What's so big that it takes you off the street on a night like this?"

Perez looked up. "You know, Cantrell, most law officers have people who tell them things they would maybe not know otherwise." He looked at the bottle. "Yes, I will have that drink."

Cantrell nodded from where he was sitting on the bedside. "Cup's right there."

The marshal splashed a small amount in the cup, took a swallow, and put the cup back on the stand. "I find out, señor, that these people who make the try at your life are not Hardester's men. I hear that you have some trouble on the trail not far from Coyote."

"Yep, a little."

The marshal smiled faintly, apparently amused at Cantrell's understatement. Then his face sobered. "That town is very bad place. Many men wanted by the law are there." He shrugged. "But of course you know this."

With narrowed lids, Perez looked across the room at Cantrell. "What you maybe don't know, señor, is that it was men from there who make the try on your life last night.

"That one you killed this morning was also one of them. He was to get you into a fight so he could kill you. He was supposed to be very good with a knife." Perez smiled. "But not good enough, eh, *amigo*? I hear from my people who tell me things that they are going to kill you any way they can get to you."

He tossed down the remainder of his drink. "You must be very careful. Do not trust any man, for you do not know your enemies." He stood, "That is all I have come to tell you, señor."

Cantrell went over and gripped the marshal's shoulder. "*Mi amigo, muchas gracias*. There ain't many men would do this for me."

The marshal's gaze locked with his. "Señor Cantrell, I think maybe there *are* many, so many perhaps you would not believe it." Going out the door, he said, "*Vaya con Dios, amigo.*"

Cantrell bolted the door and sat on the side of the bed. He sat there a long time, staring at nothing, then shook his head slowly, wonderingly. "Don't know nothin' I ever done for nobody to make 'em want to help me, but sure am glad some do. Makes a man know he ain't so god-awful big after all. Can't stand alone agin' the whole world. A man *needs* friends."

He turned the lamp out, pulled the covers up, and went to sleep.

CHAPTER
17

Cantrell awoke, slowly, letting his senses awaken one by one. He had observed this ritual for as long as he could remember.

When fully awake and out of bed, he went to the window. The sun shone brightly. People on the street below hunched into their coats, heads bent as though to ward off a chill wind. Bitterly cold, he thought. Slept till the middle of the day; must be seven o'clock.

He shaved, washed up, and dressed. He felt good. The extra sleep had healed some of his hurts.

With all the cuts and creases he'd gotten lately, he'd have a few more scars, but if he could help it, Venicia would not see them.

He wrapped his new suit, shirt, tie, and boots in a newspaper. Not wanting the snow to mess up his boots, he'd dressed in Levis, thick socks, and a pair of soft, but heavy, moccasins. He'd change clothes when they got to the ranchero.

After breakfast, Cantrell saw the surrey standing at the front door. He had not waited long outside when Elena and Venicia came through the hotel doorway and joined him.

"Mornin', ladies." He helped them into the backseat. "See you done the same thing I figured on doin'." He motioned to the small bags they handed him. "Gonna put on party clothes later."

"We'd freeze in our Sunday-go-to-meeting clothes," Elena retorted.

Cantrell placed the lap robe over their knees. He let them tuck it in, figuring he didn't have any business getting that familiar.

"Ready?" Venicia asked.

"Better tell me how to get there."

"Head north on this street. About a half mile out of town take the right fork; it'll lead right to their gate."

He nodded, slapped the reins against the horses, and guided the surrey into the street.

As they neared the edge of town, a rider spurred his horse from between two buildings, leaving town at a dead run.

Frowning, Cantrell wondered what had spooked the man to such a hurry—unless he'd been watching for them to leave. Cantrell shrugged. He was dodging shadows after what the marshal had told him. He searched for sign of anything suspicious, and careful to hide his movement from Elena and Venicia, he slipped the thong off the hammer of his .44.

He said over his shoulder, "If we have any kind of trouble, you ladies lie on the floorboard and stay there."

"What trouble are you expecting, Quint?" Venicia asked.

"Ain't lookin' for none, Señora, but if it happens, I don't want either of you catching lead meant for me."

Venicia nodded, a small frown creasing her forehead.

The fork in the trail was over a mile behind when Cantrell saw a flash from the side of a small butte ahead.

He wondered if the flash was the sun reflecting off a rifle barrel, or perhaps a piece of quartz; regardless, he looked for a place to leave the trail. Cliffs on his right and about a thirty-foot drop-off to his left wiped out that chance. He thought of trying to turn the surrey and head back toward town, but there was not room for the team and the two-seated vehicle to turn in.

He raised his hand to urge the horses to a faster pace and then changed his mind. If he tried to run the team through them—if there was anyone—a wild shot might hit the ladies.

Closer to the butte he saw movement beside a large boulder at its base.

"Get on the floor, ladies," he said softly. "It's me they want. If they get me, do what they tell you an' maybe you'll find a way out."

They asked no questions; they did as they were told. He slipped the thong from the hammer of his left-hand .44 while palming his right-hand one.

Two men rushed from behind the boulder. Cantrell stood, pulling on the reins with his left hand to halt the horses. He was firing before the men got into the trail.

The one running for the horses dropped. Cantrell swung his pistol to the right and put a slug dead center in the gunman who ran straight toward him.

Slugs whined past from the direction of the boulder. Cantrell had tilted his pistol to fire toward the shots when a blinding pain, accompanied by a brilliant white light, exploded in his head.

He fell from the surrey and tried to bring his arm around to cushion his fall, but he couldn't move it.

His last thought was that he had let the ladies down. He sank into a black void.

Later, Cantrell stirred. His head hurt as if something had stomped it. He never had headaches and puzzled over the hurt before opening his eyes a slit. Everything looked red. Blood, he thought, and tried to sit up. A groan escaped him. Then memory returned—a bit at a time.

Elena, Venicia, gotta see how they are, he thought, and managed to get to his elbows. He couldn't see—couldn't get his eyes open more than a slit.

Resting on one elbow, he felt his face. Blood caked it, glueing his eyes partially shut. He scraped snow into his hand and scrubbed his eyes, removing enough dried blood to clear his vision.

He tried to rise and fell back. Must've lost a lot of blood to be so weak, he thought. Gotta get up—see about Elena and Venicia.

He felt his head and found he'd gotten a deep crease along the side, above his ear.

Cantrell tried again and got to his knees, caught the wheel spokes, and pulled himself to his feet.

A weight at his waist drew his attention. His left-hand gun still nestled in its holster. His gaze traveled to where he'd fallen. His other gun lay there.

He hesitated, afraid to look at the floorboard in the back—but he had to do it.

Holding to the side of the surrey, he moved toward the back, but only reached the front seat before he stopped, sick to his stomach. He had heard that a blow to the head would often cause a man to throw up. Feeling better, he again pulled himself toward the rear. Then he saw it—the empty floorboard.

He stared at the seat and the floorboard, and saw no blood. If the gunmen had taken them, they might be better off dead.

Slowly he worked his way around the surrey. The two gunmen he'd killed lay where they'd fallen. The horses stood in the traces, heads hanging.

Cantrell reasoned that the attackers were fearful the shots had been heard—it was not far to the hacienda. The bandits had not waited to collect guns—or their henchmen.

He checked for small footprints leading toward the ranch and found none—the gunmen had taken the ladies.

Rage swelled Cantrell's throat and beat against his skull. He pounded his fists against the side of the vehicle, then closed his eyes tight.

Don't be a damned fool, Cantrell, he thought. He opened his eyes, his mind clearing. You go blundering after 'em, mad as hell, an' you'll get the ladies killed.

He glanced at the sun and judged it to be about two o'clock. Was about eleven when they hit us, he thought. They had a helluva start.

While thinking, he was unhitching the horses. He got the gear off one and slapped him on the rump, heading him toward town.

He tied the other horse to the seat while he went to get his rifle and other handgun.

Cantrell dragged the two bodies to the side of the trail, shucked off their gunbelts, put the guns in their holsters, and tossed the weapons into the surrey. He was ready to hit the trail—almost.

This was the first time he could remember being glad for snow on the ground. It would make for easy tracking, and he could use it to leave a message for anyone who might come along. There should be fiesta guests traveling this trail.

He walked to the side of the trail and stooped over, then

grabbed his head in both hands. He felt as if his skull were exploding.

He waited for his head to clear, then laboriously wrote in the snow, "McCord ladies taken. Following them—Cantrell."

He unwrapped the reins from the seat, cut them to a length he could handle, mounted, and rode off.

Following was easy. It would have been impossible for the bandits to cover their tracks, so they apparently hadn't tried and were holding a fast, steady pace.

Cantrell studied the tracks closely and judged there to have been four men. He'd killed two, so there were two left, with Elena and Venicia mounted on the dead men's horses.

He rode at a fast trot, intending to ride all night if necessary in order to make up for the time the gunmen had gained. There would not be a moon tonight, but snow gave off its own light, enough to see by.

Still light-headed, the pain in his head made him feel as though the Apache Nation were doing a war dance on it.

Vision blurry, Cantrell stopped at the first stream he came to, watered his horse, and bathed his face and wound in the cold water. He spent a while doing it, but thought it would pay off.

There was sign that those ahead of him had also stopped to water their horses. They'd not spent much time, and Cantrell felt relief that they hadn't. The less time they spent looking at the McCord women, the less chance there was that they would try to force themselves on them. He mounted and rode on feeling better.

They were moving fast, so Cantrell thought he could pursue at a good pace. The outlaws, fearful of pursuit, would ride late and be on the trail early.

Despite hurrying, however, his scrutiny took in everything that might furnish a hiding place for ambush. They would have to stop for the women, for if Cantrell had the McCord women figured right, they'd do anything, perhaps even feign exhaustion, in order to slow their progress. Cantrell smiled grimly. Those two ladies could outride most men.

They probably thought he had been killed during the attack, but they would also figure that the empty surrey, with the horses still hitched, would cause anybody who came along to organize a search for them. He grunted, satisfied that he had things figured right.

The sky was clear, not a cloud anywhere, but it was getting near sundown, and the temperature dropped faster than the sun.

Cantrell tried to recall how the women were dressed, then nodded. They wore plenty of clothes for the weather, but if they stopped for a short siesta sometime tonight, they would need a fire. He hoped the gunnies would build it big enough so he could see fire glow before stumbling on them in the dark.

He continued searching the terrain for signs of ambush, but his chances of seeing them before they saw him were getting slimmer.

Despite the risk, he rode on. He had two chances of catching them before they reached the safety of Coyote: if their horses tired and they didn't have fresh mounts waiting, and if they stopped to rest.

They can ride to hell and back, and they ain't gonna shake me off'n their tail, he thought. Drygulchin', woman-stealin' bastards are gonna look down the barrel of my .44 at the end.

Night settled in, and as Cantrell had thought, he could see their tracks almost as well as during daylight.

Their trail sloped down a creek bank. It was there they had stopped to fix supper. The coals of their small fire still glowed.

Didn't trouble to put the fire out, he thought. Reckon they don't give a damn whether these woods burn or not. He halted the nag, dismounted, and tied it to a juniper. Might as well use what's left of their fire.

He stood over the meager coals warming his hands, wishing he had provisions with him. His stomach was beginning to remind him it was still there. He shrugged. Hell, he'd known more hungry time than full time.

As soon as he thawed the ice from his knuckles, he scooped up several handfuls of snow and doused the fire. He mounted and rode on.

The tracks angled more to the west now, away from the

Sangre de Cristo Range. Just as he had thought, they were heading for Coyote.

He rode on, thinking he might be better off afoot. The old horse had stumbled a few times, and would not stand much hard riding. He could move faster and quieter afoot anyway. Besides, if he did what he figured to do, he would ride one of the gunny's horses back, an' if he didn't—then hell, he wouldn't need a horse for anything.

Thinking that being afoot made a lot of sense, he pulled the nag to a halt, dismounted, removed the bridle, and slapped the animal on the rump. The old horse stumbled off, and Cantrell headed out in a mile-eating jog, glad he'd worn moccasins. With each stride the jar of his foot hitting the ground made his head throb worse. He pushed the pain to the back of his mind.

The snow didn't have a crust. Cantrell was pleased as his feet landed silently on it. The tracks took him around the base of a bluff.

He had not slowed his pace for five hours when out of the corner of his eye he saw a slight reflection against the stone wall of the bluff.

He stopped, searching, his scrutiny not finding what his mind told him he'd seen. Probably a small fire, he thought, maybe caused a twig laying at its side to flare and die out.

If he had seen fire reflection, he was close enough for his handgun. He slung the Winchester to his back and drew his pistol.

The reflection had come from a cluster of rocks. He crouched and inched toward them. There were no trees here behind which he could hide or which he could use to shield his approach. If a bandit sat in those rocks watching his backtrail, Cantrell was as good as dead.

He had to take the chance. He took a step toward the largest rock, froze, and backed off, deciding to go farther up the trail and approach from the west. They most likely wouldn't expect anyone from that direction.

If there wasn't anyone there, he knew he was wasting a lot of time, but if there was somebody there, it had to be Elena and Venicia.

He circled farther to the west and came up hard at the side of the bluff. Cantrell was again glad he'd worn moccasins. He planted a foot, felt with the other for twigs or pebbles, and finding none, planted that foot and moved the other. He went through the routine time after time, one foot after the other.

He moved to circle a large boulder, stopped, and listened to someone talking not far on the other side.

"Jim, we done what we come for. Cantrell's dead, so let's leave these here women an' get the hell out of here," a whiny voice said.

"I done told you, they ain't nobody chasin' us. If they is, we gonna get to Coyote long 'fore they catch up, so quit frettin'," a guttural voice responded. "Besides, think of the fun we gonna have with these fillies when we get home."

"Jim, you ain't thinking straight. This whole territory'll take that town apart if we hurt these women. I don't want no part of harmin' womenfolk noway." There was a long pause. "I done a lot of rotten things, but I ain't never harmed no woman."

"You tryin' to back out on me?" the one called Jim growled.

After another long pause Cantrell heard the response.

"Yeah, Jim, reckon I am. We come a long way together, but I ain't harmin' no woman—not now, not ever."

Cantrell had been moving slowly around the boulder. Elena and Venicia sat on the other side of the fire. They were not tied.

Elena's gaze shifted from looking at the two gunmen, to look straight at him. She gasped, then quickly looked again toward the arguing men.

"Why, you little worm," the one with the guttural voice said, "I ain't lettin' you outta this. You gonna take Mama there to bed. You gonna do it if I have to shove this .44 down your throat."

Cantrell stepped around the rock. They were both in front of him, but one—Cantrell judged it to be Jim—stood facing him. The whiny-voiced one had his back to him.

Jim looked Cantrell in the eye and started to draw. The one with his back to Cantrell obviously thought he was the target. He drew and shot before the other could clear leather. Jim was dead when he hit the ground.

"Don't move," Cantrell said. His warning went unheeded. The gunman spun toward him and caught Cantrell's lead in the throat. He went down, trying to bring his gun up for a shot. Cantrell fired again. A hole appeared where the string from the gunman's sack of Bull Durham hung from his shirt pocket.

CHAPTER
18

Cantrell turned to see if Elena and Venicia were all right, but he didn't have a chance. Elena threw herself into his arms.

"Oh, Quint, are you all right?" And without waiting for his answer, she went on. "We thought you were dead—your face, your poor, dear face, it-it was all bloody."

Her hands searched through his hair, along his jaw. Then she pulled his head down and kissed him full on the mouth.

"I think," Venicia said, "if he can weather that attack, he'll live through the night."

Cantrell felt the blood rush to his face, surprised that Venicia was so matter of fact when seeing her daughter kiss him. He had figured all along that she was in favor of them caring for each other, but Elena kissing him right out in front of her just didn't seem decent.

He wanted to say something but could think of nothing. Anything he said would only make it worse. Then Elena surprised him again.

"If you think this is an attack, Mama, you just wait'll Papa tells this cowboy he can have me; then you'll see a real honest to goodness massacre."

He reached up and pulled Elena's arms from about his neck. He looked at Venicia. "Don't reckon I know what to say, ma'am."

Venicia cocked an eyebrow at him. "Then don't say anything. Just stand still there a moment so I can kiss you too." And she did. Then, despite his embarrassment, she calmly cleaned and bandaged his head.

When she stepped back, he grinned, looked down at his feet, wiped some imaginary thing from the sole of his moccasin, and for lack of anything better to do, pulled his .44, removed the spent shells, and reloaded. He wondered how a man could figure two quality ladies like these.

He glanced around the camp. "Think we better stay here till sunup. Reckon we missed the fandango, so we'll head back to Santa Fe."

"We'll swing by the Hernandez rancho and tell them why we missed the fiesta, but yes, we'll stay the night here," Venicia said, then took him by the shoulders. "Quint, we didn't say it, but we showed it. We're glad you're alive, so very glad, and thank God you got here when you did. I don't believe we had much time left before . . . before . . ."

"Yes'm," Cantrell interrupted, wanting to spare her saying more, "but they ain't gonna be botherin' nobody else."

He looked down at the two gunmen. "I'll drag 'em outta here for the night. Got nothin' to dig a hole with, but come daylight I'll see what I can do. You ladies get some sleep. I'll clean up a little around here."

He threw wood on the fire before dragging the two gunmen out of camp.

Not having a blanket, he curled up as close to the fire as he dared. He thought to use the gunmen's blankets, but discarded the idea quickly. No tellin' what's crawlin' around in 'em, he thought; they're dirty as hell. Nope, ain't that cold, ain't never been that cold. Thank goodness Elena and Venicia brought the lap robe with 'em.

Every time the fire died down, he got up and threw more wood on it. About four o'clock he got up for good. He rummaged through the gunmen's gear and found coffee, beans, bacon, and hardtack.

There was a stream about a hundred yards from camp, so he went down and scoured the cooking utensils he had found. He dipped water into the coffeepot and pan and then went back to the camp to start breakfast.

He was on his second cup of coffee when he heard a sleepy voice from the depths of the lap robe. "You going to drink it all, cowboy, or could I have a cup?" Across the fire Venicia threw the robe back and crawled out.

"Reckon there might be enough left for you to have a cup,"

he said. "If not, I'll sure make more."

He poured coffee into one of the bandit's tin cups. Venicia crossed to where he'd been sitting. He handed her the cup and squatted next to her. She motioned for him to sit.

"Let Elena sleep awhile. It's too early to get on the trail anyway."

"Yes, ma'am. Figured you both as pretty tired. Judged you'd sleep till daylight anyhow."

Silence closed around them, but it was a comfortable quiet. They sipped their coffee, letting it warm them from inside while the fire did its work from without. After a while Cantrell felt Venicia's gaze on him and looked at her. She smiled.

"You like this don't you, Quint." It was a statement more than a question. Then at his puzzled frown, she continued, "What I mean is, you like it out here in the open, hearing the wind rustle leaves, the call of wild things out in the dark, and seeing the night sky high above.

"You like the freedom. The music a stream makes tumbling over rocks seeking its way to the ocean is the only concert you ever need. You're as wild as the geese that fly above, yet as solid and stable as these mountains you roam."

Cantrell frowned, feeling uncomfortable. No one had ever probed into his soul like this, yet he wasn't surprised that Venicia had done so, and he felt good that she had.

"Yes'm. When I'm out here, reckon I feel like the Everywhere Spirit feels. Think maybe if I couldn't get out here once in a while I wouldn't be no good for nobody."

He gathered a few sticks and tossed them on the fire, poured himself and Venicia more coffee, and again sat next to her.

"Ma'am," he continued, "you already know I figger to someday talk to you an' Lion 'bout sayin' you don't care if I court Miss Elena.

"Just so you don't worry none, I want you to know, ain't nothin' I wouldn't do to keep her safe an' happy."

Venicia placed her hand on his arm. "Quint, you didn't have to say that. I already knew it. It's honorable of you to insist on talking with Lion, though. You certainly have my approval."

He slanted her a look. "There's something you need to know, ma'am. I got some things to settle first, before I can talk to you, Lion, or Miss Elena."

Venicia smiled. "Well, Quint, you settle them, because that's the way you do things, but I want you to know now that you wouldn't have to wait. The three of us would take you, trouble or no trouble, and be damned happy to have you in the family."

Sometimes Cantrell was surprised at Venicia's use of damn or hell, but he was not surprised that it didn't lessen her one whit as a lady; for that matter, Elena did the same thing. Cantrell assumed that helping her father during roundup was responsible for Elena's cursing.

They lapsed into another silence. Cantrell emptied his cup and placed his left hand on the ground to push himself up. He froze and held his right hand out, signaling Venicia for quiet. A twig had snapped out in the darkness beyond the rocks.

In one fluid move he stood, signaled Venicia to stay where she was, and silently threaded his way around the boulders.

Staying close to the wall of the bluff, he circled another large boulder. Keeping it between him and the fire, he worked his way into the clear. He wanted to be able to scan the entire periphery of the campsite and at the same time keep himself hidden.

His eyes searched the cleared area between the rocks and the trees so as to not miss anything. He saw no one. Then he did it again. This time, patience rewarded him.

A man, flat on his stomach, emerged from the tree line. He had his rifle laying in the crook of his elbows as he snaked his way toward the campsite.

Knowing the whereabouts of this one, Cantrell continued his search and was soon satisfied that the man had come alone. He waited, not wanting to chance missing a shot.

The man claimed Cantrell's admiration. Except for the sound of the broken twig, he moved as silently as any Indian Cantrell had ever seen. He slithered to the base of one of the rocks, stood, and worked his way around it toward the fire.

Cantrell, only a shadow, moved toward the same rock. Upon reaching it, he moved in the same direction the other man had taken.

Out of the darkness the man's shape materialized in front of him. Cantrell pushed the muzzle of his .44 into the man's back.

"Hold it right there. You even blink, you die." Cantrell pushed his gun harder. "Come warm yourself by our fire; it'll be the last one you ever see."

He prodded his prisoner into the firelight and glanced about the camp. Venicia and Elena were gone. The prisoner looked around, then faced Cantrell.

"Señor, if you have harmed those ladies, this territory is not big enough for you to hide in." His eyes, like black agates, bored into Cantrell's. He stood poised as though calculating his chances even though the big bore of Cantrell's handgun covered him dead center.

"Turn around," Cantrell ordered, then removed the rider's knife from its sheath. "Now drop the gun an' step forward."

When the man had done as told, Cantrell flicked a searching glance around the perimeter of the firelight. Venicia and Elena stepped from behind a large rock, both carrying guns. They must have taken the ones belonging to the dead gunmen.

"C'mon up to the fire." He cocked a crooked grin at them, then said to the prisoner, "Who are you? What were you slipping up on our fire for?"

The rider drew himself up straight as a bowstring, his head held proudly. "I, señor, ride for the Hernandez rancho. They will all be here to give you the big party soon. I think maybe you call it the necktie party. *Sí?*"

Cantrell asked Venicia, "Do you recognize this man?"

Before she could answer, the rider cut in, "Señora, Señorita, I am Juan Sanchez. Has this man harmed you?"

Venicia laughed. Cantrell noticed that she and Elena laughed with the same musical lilt.

"No, Juan," she answered, "this is Quinton Cantrell, our most trusted friend. He saved us from the *bandidos*."

Deciding the man was who, and what, he said he was, Cantrell holstered his .44 and stepped forward, hand extended.

Juan's face lit up in a broad smile as he shook Cantrell's hand. "Señor, what I tell you is true. Many riders from our rancho will be here very soon. Is good you are not the enemy."

Cantrell walked to where he had put his cup down and poured coffee for Juan. Handing it to him, he said, "Here, c'mon to the fire and get warm."

Cantrell threw more wood on the fire so its light could be seen from the trail, then walked over and sat by Elena.

Juan told them that a party from town had come upon the empty surrey and read the message written in the snow. They made haste to report it to the Señor Hernandez, who had immediately organized a search party. Hernandez sent Juan ahead of them to follow the tracks left by the bandits.

Juan said he had known that another lone rider followed the bandits and, apparently, was hurt, because he found bloody cloths at the side of the trail.

Not long after finding the cloths, he crossed the trail of the horse Cantrell had turned loose. He told them he thought perhaps the wounded rider had fallen off to the side of the trail but had not stopped to look for him.

"Now you found us you reckon mebbe you ought to find your boys and bring them here?"

"No, señor," Juan said and glanced at the sky, "it will soon be daylight. They will be here within the hour."

Cantrell nodded and cocked an eyebrow at Elena. "What'd you figger to do with those guns if Juan turned out to be one of the outlaws?"

"Well, big man," she mimicked, "ah reckon I'd've blowed his damn haid off."

Cantrell had just taken a swallow of coffee. He choked and spewed it over the fire, and for the next few seconds, with tears in his eyes from withheld laughter and misdirected coffee, he alternately laughed and coughed.

When he could control his laughter, he shook his head. "You sure got more'n just a little of your mother in you."

Before Elena could answer, Venicia spoke up. "Very little of me, Señor Quint. I think that's the Lion side of her you are seeing."

Abruptly, Cantrell cocked his head. "Whole passel of horses comin'. Juan, just so's we don't get all shot up, you better ease out of here an' tell 'em you found the ladies, and that they're safe."

Juan smiled, his teeth snow-white in the half light. "*Sí*, I think you are right, Señor Quint. I go now." He stood and silently melted into the maze of rocks that surrounded them.

Quint looked at Venicia. "You know, I feared that vaquero would try me while my .44 looked right down his gullet." He shook his head in wonderment.

"Quint, you amaze me," Venicia said. "You sound surprised, yet I know you would do the same thing. Foolhardy gallantry is the brand most men out here carry as their shield—"

"Yes," Elena broke in, "and it terrifies your womenfolk to death, but makes us so very proud that you are our men."

Before Cantrell could respond, horses were pulled to a halt outside the rock enclosure. He stood, as did Venicia and Elena.

The first rider to enter their camp, followed closely by Juan, was a tall, handsome man, probably in his mid-fifties. Cantrell saw him sweep the area with a flicking glance, then with long strides head toward Venicia.

"Ah, Venicia, old friend, it has been much too long." He spoke in pure Castilian Spanish, but Cantrell understood. He was fluent in Spanish.

He and Cole Mason had worked south of the border a couple of years. Cole already spoke Spanish, but Cantrell learned it while there. His only problem had been in getting the border Mexican language out of his vocabulary and putting in good Spanish grammar. Cole had told him that he used much better grammar in Spanish than in English.

Don Hernandez embraced Venicia. After their greeting, Venicia motioned Elena and Cantrell to her side.

"Federico, you remember Elena." Venicia spoke in English. Cantrell knew she did it as a courtesy to him.

"Elena! But you are as beautiful as your mother. I would not think it possible."

"You're still the same old flatterer, aren't you, Uncle Federico, but I thank you." She hugged his neck and held a hand out to Cantrell. "Mama and I would like you to meet our dearest friend, Señor Quinton Cantrell."

Cantrell saw Hernandez's eyebrows lift slightly, and knew he had heard of him.

"Señor, I am happy that *my* friends have a friend such as you. I have heard much of you and like what I have heard."

Cantrell felt his face turn red; then, in Spanish fully as fluent as the Don's, he replied.

"Thank you, señor. I am honored that you think well of me, and I too am pleased, that the señora and señorita have a friend such as you."

He gripped Señor Hernandez's hand and looked at Venicia. Laughter slipped out despite his attempt to stifle it. Her expression of surprise at his use of fluent Spanish caused him joy. Suddenly realizing he'd been rude, he turned back to the señor.

"Pardon me, señor, but I had to laugh at the expression on the señora's face."

"You . . . you big fraud," Venicia sputtered. "Why did you never tell us that you spoke very, *very* good Spanish?"

Cantrell tried, but couldn't wipe the grin from his face. "Señora," he lapsed into English, "I just don't reckon you ever asked me." He still grinned. "I had a friend once who told me I talked better in Spanish than English." He looked at the don.

"We started fixin' breakfast. If y'all brought any provisions with you, we better get 'em so everybody kin eat."

Federico nodded and told Juan to get the food and bring it to the fire.

After breakfast, Juan took a couple of men with him and buried the dead gunmen. That done, they headed for the ranch.

Federico told Cantrell he'd had the surrey taken to the ranch and that their clothes were still there, just as they had left them.

Venicia, Elena, Federico, and Cantrell rode at the head of the column of heavily armed horsemen.

The sun hung just above the eastern horizon when the ranch came into view. They were more than a mile from it, but Cantrell could see that the buildings were all of Spanish architecture, and very old.

"My ancestors built the hacienda and outbuildings in the early sixteen-hundreds," Federico told Cantrell proudly, apparently having read his thoughts. They spoke Spanish.

"It is very beautiful, señor," Cantrell responded. "It seems almost a part of this land, so old, yet so new."

Venicia reined her horse closer to his in order to be heard above the "clop" of the horses' hooves. "It is even more beautiful than the exterior promises, Quint. Elena and I have loved this rancho of Federico's as though it were ours. For that matter, I believe Elena thinks that it *is* partly hers. She laid claim to 'her room' when just a toddler, and whenever we've visited, it has been there for her."

CHAPTER
19

Hernandez decided to hold the fiesta, albeit a day late. Most of the guests had delayed leaving until they knew the McCords were all right.

When Cantrell came from his room, freshly shaved and bathed, there must have been a hundred guests gathered in the garden area despite the cold.

He was glad he'd bought a new suit. The ladies were resplendent in their party dress, and many of the men had donned snow-white shirts, bolero jackets, flared trousers heavily embroidered with silver, and the traditional flat-crowned, flat-brimmed black hat.

Cantrell felt he was back in the middle of Old Mexico, a land he loved. The people here, as in Mexico, were so gracious it would have been hard for him not to give it a special place in his heart.

The guests began drifting into the great room of the hacienda. Even though the night wind had stilled, the setting sun took with it the warmth that had permitted being outside.

Elena stood with a group, apparently old friends of the family. She spotted him.

"Come, Quint, I want you to meet our very dear friends, the Alberons." She identified each of them by first name. She then asked their pardon and led him around the room, introducing him to group after group.

He was surprised that he felt so at ease with these people; it didn't occur to him that his fluency in their language had broken the invisible, informal barrier that seemed to hover over any multilingual gathering.

As he and Elena circulated among the guests, he marveled at the amount of food the servants piled on the long tables. Had the tables not been so massive, in the style of most Mexican furniture, he was certain they would have collapsed. Some of the guests were already eating.

When the music started, Elena looked at him. "Quint, I never thought to ask, do you dance?"

"Some," he answered, not telling her that Venicia had asked the same question before they left town. "Want to try?"

At her nod he took her hand, led her to the space cleared for the purpose, and held her in his arms. The piece was a romantic old Mexican ballad.

After a few steps she tilted her head to look at him, her eyes wide; then she closed them and floated with him across the floor.

The next piece, a lively Mexican tune, started as soon as the ballad finished. Many of the older couples drifted off the dance floor. Elena followed until Cantrell took her elbow. At her surprised look, he grinned.

"Aw c'mon, a old cowhand ain't afraid to try nothin'. You got to understand, though, that I ain't never seen this done afore." He lied.

She picked up the rhythm and they danced. When the piece finished, he and Elena were the only couple on the floor. There was a burst of applause. He grinned and nodded to those surrounding them. Then he looked at Elena.

Her face, a frozen mask with a pasted-on smile that didn't reach her eyes, chilled him. Her chin had that proud, arrogant tilt he knew so well.

What the hell have I done now? he wondered.

"Thanks for making a fool of me," her words, like ice, backed up the lances of emerald fire hurled by her eyes.

"Well now, ma'am . . ." He choked back anger that swelled his throat. "Yore Mama asked me if I could dance, an' I allowed as how I was passable." He steered her to the side of the floor. "Didn't know I was s'posed to put it in the daily paper." He released her elbow, and bowed. "Thank you for the dances, ma'am."

"Oh, Quint, I'm sorry. I had no reason to get a burr under

my saddle. Y-you just continue to surprise me, and most times I'm just not ready for it."

She placed her hand on his forearm. "You're angry with me, and rightly so, but please don't be. I really am proud of you. You're clearly the best dancer here."

"You gotta understand, ma'am, there's a lot of me you don't know. Don't reckon I want you mad at me every time you find out somethin' else." He never stayed angry but an instant, and certainly could not do so with Elena. "Ma'am, now you're about to slide off the other side of your saddle. You don't ever have to ask me not to be mad at you. I ain't."

He glanced around the room. "We better find Señora Venicia. Reckon I'd like to see if she can dance as purty as her daughter."

"All right, cowboy, but if she can, you'd better not tell *me*." She tucked her arm intimately through his. "If we can find Señora Hernandez, you should dance with her also."

They danced until breakfast, during which they watched the sun start its warming trek across the heavens. After eating, the guests packed sleepy-eyed children into buckboards, surreys, and buggies for their long journey home.

Many had come from as far as fifty miles, and would have come even farther if necessary. The hard, ofttimes boring life on an isolated ranch demanded that you take and enjoy the good times when you could.

Cantrell had hitched a team to the surrey; he'd borrowed the horses from Hernandez. When the last of the guests had departed, he and the ladies said their good-byes, offered their thanks for the gracious, hospitable evening, and headed back to Santa Fe.

Cantrell gave the surrounding country more attention than he did the horses. Of their own accord the team stayed in the deeply rutted trail while Cantrell searched for any sign they were not alone.

Both Venicia and Elena rode on the front seat with him. He had stowed the luggage and gifts from the Hernandez family in the rear. Cantrell reckoned he'd never had a nicer ride. For them to be sitting there on the same seat with him was about as much as he could ask, especially since Elena had to sit close to him to make room for Venicia. An unintended chuckle escaped him.

"What's funny, Quint?" Elena asked.

"Aw, nothin'. Reckon I was just thinkin' how good everything is."

"And that caused you to chuckle?" She gave him an unladylike dig with her elbow. "I don't believe one word of it."

"Aw, well, I was just thinkin' that it shore is nice sittin' here on the same seat with you, sorta like I b'longed here."

"Why you big . . . ," Elena started, but Venicia interrupted.

"If Elena isn't going to say it, I will. You do belong here." Then a puzzled frown creased her forehead. "Quint, you know that 'bark' I once mentioned to you, well I didn't see a sign of it at the fiesta. What happened?"

He shrugged. He didn't know the reason any more than she did.

"What in the world are the two of you talking about?" Elena looked from one to the other of them. "And what is this about 'bark'? Honestly, I have to wonder if you and Mama haven't done a lot of talking that I'm not aware of. If she wasn't my own mother, I think I'd be jealous."

Cantrell looked across his shoulder at her, gave her a smug grin, and slapped the reins against the horses' rumps. "Elena, yore mama don't use up a lot of words, but she shore can say a lot with the few she does use." He chuckled again. "No, ma'am, we ain't done a *lot* of talkin', but I reckon she set me straight with what she did say."

Venicia, apparently wanting to change the subject, commented, "Santa Fe's just over yonder the other side of that hill. We should be back in time for a late nooning."

They rode in silence the rest of the way, but Cantrell felt Elena studying him, and when he would occasionally glance at her, he found the same puzzled frown between her brows.

He held his hand for the ladies to grasp as they climbed from the surrey, then walked them to the door, and, while holding it open, asked, "Want I should have everything ready to travel in the mornin'?"

"Yes." Venicia nodded. "Let's try to get an early start." She looked tired. "I'm ready to go home, Quint. I'm missing that big man of mine."

"I'll have the coach here 'bout six, ready to load. Y'all can have breakfast while I'm gettin' that done. We'll ride soon's you're through."

After returning the surrey to the livery, Cantrell looked for King. He glanced in four or five saloons with no luck and decided to swing by Kate's place for something to eat.

When he opened the door, he saw King and about half the crew. He grunted with satisfaction; most of the job of rounding them up was done.

"Soon's you're finished eatin', find the rest of the men," he told King. "Tell them to be sober and ready to ride about six in the mornin'."

King snorted. "Don't reckon they's 'nuff money left 'tween 'em to buy a drink. Kate's been feedin' us for two days. Told her to keep a tally on what we owe 'er and you'd pay whatever it come to."

Cantrell looked at Kate. "Howdy, Kate, gimme a bowl of that stew I smell, an 'figger up what we owe yuh—No, better wait till after supper. I'll eat late an' take care of what it comes to then."

He glanced at King. "Tell the boys to eat in here tonight if they want, but try to make it by seven so's we don't leave owin' Kate nothin'."

She brought him a bowl of steaming stew and sat across from him.

"If that ain't enough there's a lot more where it come from. You want your coffee now?"

"I'll wait till after I put this away. This bowl just might be enough. It's about the same size as the one they brought up to my room for me to bathe in."

"Ah, quit joshin' me, Quint. I seen you surround more grub than that in the middle of the mornin'—just to tide you over till noon."

Their conversation continued in the same vein until Cantrell saw the humor leave Kate's face. "Reckon you'll be headin' out soon, huh?"

"Yeah, reckon so, Kate, been loafing long enough. Time to start earnin' my pay."

"Shore hate to see ya go, cowboy." She sort of sniffled, and Cantrell saw a suspicious hint of moisture in her eyes.

"Aw, Kate, I'll bet you a painted pony we'll be back for shoppin' next Christmas."

"I hope so, cowboy. You all sort of seem like family to me. All of you been awful nice."

"You're an easy lady to be nice to, Kate. You're special."

He slicked out the bottom of his bowl with his last bite of biscuit, grunted in satisfaction, and decided to forgo the coffee, mostly because he figured a pinto bean would play hell finding room in his stomach.

He stood. "See you later," he said, "little after seven for supper." Then, not thinking what he was doing, or why, he walked around the table and hugged Kate to him, a lump in his throat so big he dared not say anything. Embarrassed at his show of emotion, he spun on his heel and walked toward the door.

"God bless you, Quint," he heard Kate murmur as he headed out.

It was still no later than mid-afternoon. Cantrell walked to the livery and checked the coach wheels. They had been greased and the wheel bolts tightened. He should have known everything was ready to go; hell, he'd checked several times and the coach hadn't been anywhere since their arrival.

He looked at the horses. They were well rested and sleek. From there, he walked to the Plaza and went in several stores, not knowing why he was restless.

When he came out of the last store, he snorted, thinking that this was the first Christmas he'd ever been around anybody he gave a damn about and he would do things his way. He turned sharply and headed for the hotel, only two doors away. He went directly to Elena's room and knocked.

"Yes?"

"It's me, Elena. Jest wondered if I could ask you to do somethin' for me—or with me?"

The door opened. "Whatever you ask, Quint. Yes."

"Would you take a little while an' go with me to buy a

present for someone what's awful special to me. Got no idea what would be fittin'."

"I'd be glad to, Quint. Wait a minute and I'll get my coat."

In front of the hotel, Elena cast a quizzical look at him. "Who is this mysterious person we're buying a gift for?"

"Well, it's sort of for a special lady, least she's special to me. Don't reckon they's gonna be nobody around to help make Christmas much for her. I figure a little old present from me might make the sun shine some on her day." He stared at Elena, defensive and embarrassed.

"Oh, Quint, it's a beautiful thought." Her eyes glistened suspiciously. "You haven't said who this special lady is. It's Kate, isn't it?"

A lone tear rolled down her cheek and he wanted to kiss it away.

He wondered that a lady who could hold a .44 in her hand, and calmly state that she intended to blow an outlaw's damned head off, would get so soft over other things.

"Yes'm. Don't reckon I know but two other special ladies".

They looked in several stores and didn't find anything they could agree on.

Elena decided to buy a gift for Kate also, from her and Venicia. This didn't prove to be as much of a problem as finding one for Cantrell to give.

Elena bought a nightgown and warm robe, pretty but serviceable. Cantrell grunted that he didn't think it would be "fittin' " for him to give Kate anything like that. When they had had it wrapped in pretty paper and gone back outside, he was about ready to give up.

"I shore didn't figure it would be as hard as findin' a white buffalo when we set out to buy a li'l ole present."

Elena laughed. "Oh c'mon, be truthful, you just don't like to shop."

"Reckon I wouldn't mind so much if I knew what I was doin'. But bein' truthful, if it's anything more'n a pair a Levis or a new gun, I'm just plain lost."

They were walking down the street, looking in store windows for ideas, when Cantrell stopped abruptly, causing Elena to bump into him. "Now, why didn't I think of that before?

She ain't got one, an' she needs to have one."

"What in this world are you talking about?" Elena stood with hands on hips.

"Why, I reckon I'm gonna buy her one of those scatterguns. Won't nobody hurraw her cafe if she lays *it* across the counter, loaded with buckshot." He laughed. "I can just see 'em now, comin' outta her front door like a covey a quail what'd been run in a hole."

"Oh, Quint, you're not going to give her a gun?"

"Why, I sure am, little girl, an' I bet a painted pony she'll like it."

Elena stared at him a moment, a faint smile showing in her eyes. "And you know what, cowboy, I'll lay odds you'd win that bet. Yes, as unconventional as it is, I know she'll like it."

She took his arm. "Let's go find Kate a gun."

They went in two gun stores before Cantrell found what he wanted. It was a sawed-off American Arms 12-gauge. He also bought a couple of boxes of shells—buckshot.

He had it wrapped and wrote Kate a note. "Kate," it said, "don't let nobody rawhide you none, no more. Wish I could be here to tame 'em down but I can't, so Merry Christmas. All the BIM crew will think of you a lot. Me too. Quint."

That night Elena, Venicia, the crew, and Cantrell went to Kate's for dinner. After eating and settling the bill, Elena and Cantrell gave Kate her gifts, extracting a promise that she wouldn't open them until Christmas morning.

"Well dadblast it," Kate said, wiping her eyes. "Reckon don't none of ya mind makin' a old woman cry right in front of everybody."

She hugged each of the crew, hugged and kissed Elena and Venicia, and then kissed Cantrell full on the mouth.

"I-I reckon I love all of ya like ya were ma own flesh and blood. Now shoo, y'all get outta here an' let me cry in private." She wiped at her eyes, and as they were leaving, she said, "I better see y'all next time you get to Santa Fe or I'm gonna come way up yonder where you're at."

They had been on the trail about an hour when the first sliver of sun edged over the mountains.

Venicia edged her horse close to Cantrell's. "That was a real nice thing you and Elena did last night."

He pushed his hat back and wiped his forehead out of habit; it was too cold to sweat. "I'm findin' out I like doin' things for nice people. Never had no chance before. Matter of fact, don't reckon I ever knew nobody I give a d—" He stopped, feeling his face turn red. "Sorry, ma'am, what I meant to say was, I never had no friends before. Now I got a whole bunch of 'em."

"You can bet on that, cowboy.' If she had kept looking at him like she was, Cantrell thought he might kiss her.

They rode in silence. Venicia and Elena had chosen to have their horses saddled to begin the journey home. They would change off and ride in the coach only when they got cold, or when Cantrell thought they might be approaching an area suited for ambush.

When they reached Tierra Amarilla, he looked for the old man he had promised a job and found him squatted in front of the saloon.

"Still want that job, old-timer?"

"Yep."

"Ready to ride?"

"Yep."

"Got a horse?"

"Nope."

"Sure don't want you wearin' your teeth out with all that talkin', but what handle you go by?"

"Nat Straker." He squinted at Cantrell. " 'Fore you take me on, they's somethin' you oughtta know."

"Yeah? Well, s'pose you tell me."

Straker squirted a stream of tobacco juice far enough that it cleared the boardwalk. "Ain't much good for ridin' broncs, or stayin' in the saddle all day. Reckon I been throwed once too often, but I don't mind juicin' cows." He nodded. "Yeah, I know most riders don't like doin' that kind of work, but I don't mind. An' I'm pretty good at fixin' things up around a place. They's usually a pretty good bait of things needs fixin' round a ranch. S'pose they's any of that kind of work at yore place?"

Cantrell saw that Straker was braced to hear the words "Sorry, we can't use you," but his open, honest face was almost childlike in reflecting the hope for words of acceptance.

Cantrell held out his hand. Straker grabbed it, and Cantrell pulled him from his squatting position. "Better get your things together if you gonna leave here with us."

Straker danced from one foot to the other. "By golly, big'un, got 'em right here in this here gunnysack, had 'em with me ever since you went south."

"Reckon you kin sit a horse from here to Chama?"

"You bet I kin."

Chama was just a short distance from Tierra Amarilla, so Cantrell didn't look for problems of any sort.

A couple of miles out of town, he had King ride ahead to make sure a flatcar for the coach was on the siding, along with a boxcar for the horses. He'd gotten a train schedule when they came through the week before. Barring trouble, the train would be in the next day.

He wondered how he was going to explain Straker to Venicia. When he saw Chama ahead, he decided he'd better tell her, flat out, that he'd hired him.

King rode to meet them before they got to town. He said the cars were available, and the train was expected to be on time— "on time," meaning that it would be in sometime the same day it was scheduled for.

It was not until supper that evening that Cantrell had a chance to talk to Venicia. He looked up from his plate. "Ma'am, reckon I got somethin' to tell you."

"Well, my goodness, Quint, it can't be as serious as your expression would lead me to believe, so tell me."

"Well you see, ma'am, I reckon you done seen we got a extra rider with us?"

The corners of her mouth strained at a smile. "Yes, I had noticed." Then she did smile. "What did you do, Quint, buy him a ticket to Durango?"

"Reckon I done worse'n that, ma'am. I give 'em a job."

Venicia didn't say anything, so he hastened to add, "It ain't like it's gonna cost y'all nothin'. I told 'em he could do the milkin' an' fixin' up around the place. I'll see he has plenty to do an' don't get in nobody's way."

Venicia fixed him with that straight-on look. "Quint, that's a proud old man. He wouldn't take a handout down yonder in Tierra Amarilla, and I don't believe he'd take a job like you've described. He'd have to be getting some pay as a way of telling him he was worth something to us."

She sipped her coffee, carefully placed her cup back on the table, and cocked a quizzical eyebrow at him. "Now, cowboy, what did you offer him?"

He squirmed again. Venicia always seemed to be able to read his mind, seemed to know what he was going to do before he did it. Well, he reckoned, he might as well tell her.

"Ma'am, figured I'd give him half of my pay an' he'd get that feelin' you was talkin' about." He swallowed. "An' besides it wouldn't cost nobody much, 'cept what he et, an' I'll pay for that too."

Venicia laughed. Damn, double damn, he thought, that there is a pretty laugh, but what the hell's she laughing at? Then, as if reading his thoughts, she said, "So the big, bad man has a heart as large as he is." She placed her hand over his, and their gazes locked, her eyes soft as a doe's.

"You shouldn't be ashamed for being just a little soft once in a while. I'm so proud of you." Her eyes filled with tears. "We have a heart too, Quint. Do you think Lion would let you pay that old man's wages?" She shook her head. "Not on your tintype he wouldn't."

"Aw, well, I just don't want Straker beholden to nobody, an' I don't want to put Lion's money in the pot when he ain't even seen his poker hand—I'll pay Straker."

"No." Elena spoke up, and she had that stubborn tilt to her head. "Mama has said how it's going to be, and I'm adding my say to hers."

"I'll talk to Lion about it. I—"

"*We'll* talk to Lion about it," Venicia said. "Now let's get a night's sleep so we can enjoy our train ride tomorrow."

CHAPTER
20

To say they enjoyed their train ride would be stretching the truth. Even those who'd had only the one ride, from the ranch to Chama, griped about the smoke and cinders on this return trip.

When the railroad put its track through to Durango, Lion had had a spur laid about four miles from ranch headquarters in partial payment for the right-of-way. Cantrell had the cars shunted onto it; then the engine, with a great billow of black smoke, puffed its way to the main rails.

"Riders comin'," King said.

Cantrell squinted into the distance, then said to Venicia, "It's Lion, ma'am. Want I should saddle a horse for you?"

He talked to the wind. Venicia was running toward the approaching riders as though a few more seconds would be more than she could stand.

"Better have one of the horses saddled, King. She ain't ridin' no coach back."

When King turned away, Cantrell continued, his voice scarcely above a whisper, "Shore wish I had a woman care that much for me."

"You do, Quint."

He spun. Elena stood at his elbow. "I-I didn't know you was standing there, Elena."

"I'm sure you didn't, because you never see fit to say nice things to me. Quint, let your backtrail rest. You've got the whole BIM between you and it. We'll never let anything happen to you."

His felt his face harden. "You know I won't do that, Elena.

Would you settle for ridin' back to the ranch with me?"

"Well now, cowboy," she mimicked, "ah reckon if that's the best I can get, I'll take it."

It didn't take long to cover the four miles to the ranch, so when Cantrell had things from the trip taken care of, he reported to Mann. His report omitted all of the gunplay. Finished, he said he would go back to work after reporting to Lion—but he didn't get to see Lion until late the next morning. Lion and Venicia had secluded themselves in their room and told Elena they didn't want anything short of an Indian uprising to disturb them.

The next morning Cantrell removed his hat and entered at Venicia's invitation. "He's back in his office, Quint, and, uh, I've told him all that happened on the trip."

"Thank you, ma'am." He stepped toward the office.

"Quint, I want you to fully understand what I've said. Lion and I have no secrets from each other. I've told him *all* the things that happened on the trip."

"Reckon the fat's in the fire then. Suppose he was madder'n a skunk-sprayed coyote."

"Well maybe the best thing to do is face him with it."

Cantrell, feeling queasy inside, knocked softly on Lion's door.

"C'mon in, boy!" Lion roared.

"Got a few things to tell ya, Lion," Cantrell said straight out, "an' reckon I better account for all of your money I spent on the trip. The señora said she done told you about most everything that happened while we was gone."

"Yeah, boy—she did."

Cantrell noticed Lion hadn't taken out his bottle of good whiskey and took that to be a sign he wasn't pleased with what Venicia had told him.

Well, what the hell, Cantrell thought, when you got trouble sittin' in your path, just walk right up to it and see what happens.

"Lion, they's somethin' I want to talk to you about . . ."

"Wait a minute. Let me say right off, Cantrell, I'm mighty beholden to you for takin' good care of my ladies. Figger if anybody else had been ramrodding that trip I'd have lost 'em for sure."

Cantrell felt a flush of guilt; his guts roiled. Maybe Venicia hadn't told Lion after all. Whether she had or not, he knew he had to. He couldn't look at this man knowing something lay between them. "Lion, I got somethin' to say, an' maybe you better listen before you say any more."

Lion raised his eyebrows. "All right, boy, say it."

"First off, I got a few things that's got to be done. After I get rid of my troubles, I'm askin' you to say I kin come courtin' Miss Elena. Ain't got much for her but me, but I promise you they ain't nothin' in the world she could ever want but I'd try to get it for her."

Lion stared at Cantrell, eyelids narrowed. "Venicia told me you was gonna ask me that. Don't know as how I could say yes to you. Seems like, from what I seen around here before you left, she was spittin' mad at you most of the time."

"Well, yes, sir, reckon she was, but somethin' happened, don't rightly know what it was, but she ain't been mad at me nearly so much lately."

Lion leaned forward and slowly pulled his right-hand desk drawer open.

Well, damn to hell, Cantrell thought, he's gonna go for a gun and shoot me. Ain't no way I'll pull a gun on him; he'll just have to kill me.

Lion opened the drawer wider, reached in—and pulled out two glasses. His bottle of good whiskey followed. "Reckon if you're gonna come courtin' my little girl, you an' me oughtta have a drink."

"You sayin' yes, Lion?"

"Hell yes, I'm sayin' yes. What the hell you think I'm doin'?"

Cantrell exhaled slowly. He hadn't realized that he'd been holding his breath. "Damn, Lion, I thought you was gonna shoot me when you opened that drawer."

He heard it start, way down deep in Lion's gut, and then it erupted—the damndest belly laugh he'd ever heard. Then Cantrell laughed too.

Lion poured two water glasses to the rim with his good

whiskey. Cantrell had never drunk that much whiskey at one sitting before. He wasn't sure he could do it, but he was going to give it one hell of a try.

He raised his glass and touched Lion's. "*Salud*, Lion."

"*Salud, amigo,*" Lion responded. "And, Cantrell," he said and hesitated, "I don't reckon they's anybody I'd rather call friend—or son—more than you."

He leaned back in his big, ornately carved chair, eyes boring into Cantrell's. He took a swallow of whiskey, cleared his throat, and leaned forward again. "Tell you a little secret, boy. It wasn't long after you come here that me an' Venicia was sittin' in the kitchen drinkin' coffee, nobody else around.

"You'd come to the back door to tell me somethin', and gone, when Venicia looked at me and said, 'He's the one, Lion, *mi amor*, so don't get a burr under your saddle about it. Elena doesn't know it herself yet, but he's the one.'"

He shifted in his chair and squinted at Cantrell. "Know what I said, boy?" He waited a minute, obviously not expecting an answer. "Well I said, 'Hell, *querida*, I knowed he was the one the day he showed up an' Elena spit at him like one of them big mountain cats with cubs. If you'll remember, you done me the same way when I come to work for yore papa.

"She just smiled at me, sort of like she had some woman secret. She told me later she knowed I was her man the very day she first laid eyes on me. I'll bet some day Elena will tell you the same thing."

Cantrell stood, paced the floor, and returned to his chair. "Lion, I reckon I'd like you to keep this under your belt till I take care of the Hardesters—an' Curly Farlow. Don't want nothin' gettin' in the way of Elena's happiness."

"No need to do that, son. You got the whole BIM to back you."

"You know better than that. This is my bronc to ride. Ain't gonna bring no trouble down on the BIM. After the señora's New Year fiesta, gonna go to Durango an' send a wire to them as wants my hide. When it's over, I'll be back."

Lion sipped his whiskey and looked at Cantrell over the rim of the glass. "Knowed it was gonna be this way. We'll be here when you get it done."

Cantrell tossed off the remainder of his drink, reached across the desk, shook Lion's hand, and left.

Christmas dawned gray and snowy. The crew had come in off the range the night before. To Cantrell's surprise, Mann told him that every Christmas morning the whole crew went up to the hacienda for a couple of drinks and to exchange gifts. There would be no other guests. Then for the nooning the señora and Elena served a meal they alone prepared. The gifts were, for the most part, carvings the crew had whittled around the fire of an evening, or leather goods they had cut and tooled.

Each of them had a gift for his range partner and something for the señora and Elena.

Knowing the gifts he had for the ladies and Lion were more than the others would give, or could afford, Cantrell decided to ask Lion to let him come to the house that evening after the others had gone back to the bunkhouse.

Cantrell finished shaving, and having bathed in water that he'd had to break the ice on, he followed the lead of the hands, who were putting on clean Levis and denim shirts, along with their best neckerchiefs.

They'd rolled out of their bunks about four-thirty in order to be ready in time to go as a group. Cantrell had to smile as he watched. Sometimes as many as four men tried to shave at the same time, using one bowl of water.

A lot of good-natured cursing and pushing and shoving took place, and he felt especially good when they cursed and pushed him.

If they had not considered him one of them, they would have left him space, as men seemed to do everywhere, he thought. "You men ready?" Mann yelled. It was about eight o'clock. They went to the cookshack, ate breakfast, and then went to the hacienda. Before Mann could knock on the door, the señora swung it wide.

"Entrar, amigos. Mi casa es su casa. Felices Navidades."

Cantrell's chest tightened, and he found he couldn't swallow very well as he watched the señora give each man a hug as he entered.

Not so strange, Cantrell thought, she and Lion probably

raised most of the young'uns from colts, and many of the others had helped raise both Venicia and Elena.

When it came his turn for a hug, he reached up and wiped his eyes. "Reckon I got somethin' in my eyes," he explained.

"Yes, Quint, I seem to have the same trouble at times like this."

He wondered if Venicia would ever cut him any slack. All he could do was grin foolishly and mutter, "Yes'm."

Lion called them to the bar as they entered and handed each a drink. When they all had their drinks, which Quint noted none had touched, Lion took Venicia and Elena each a drink and held his aloft. "Merry Christmas to all," he shouted. The response from the men was so loud that it almost raised the roof.

"It's like this every year, Quint," Elena said from close to his side.

"Don't reckon I ever seen anything like this before. The way you all treat the men, sort of like they are family, an' me right along with the rest of them."

"Quint, every man here *is* family to us." Then she shot him an impish grin. "And you even more than the rest." She cocked her head to the side, her face lifted toward his, teasing. "Want me to show them?"

"You-you wouldn't—would you?"

That tinkling laugh bubbled past her lips. "No, Quint. I wouldn't embarrass you like that. Besides, you still have to talk to Papa."

Cantrell knew then that Lion had honored his request to keep silent.

Lion, Venicia, and Elena circulated among the men with a few words for each, and every man there felt special as a consequence.

Before they gathered around the fireplace to exchange gifts, Cantrell managed to corner Lion for a moment.

"Lion, if y'all have time later on this evening, I'd sort of like to come for a few minutes 'cause, well, I got Elena a little gift, an' I want to give it to her when all the men ain't lookin' on."

"Can Venicia an' I look on?"

"Yeah, Lion, I, uh, I'd like for y'all to do that."

Lion had asked only as a joke, but Cantrell was glad he had, because he didn't think he could handle being alone with Elena.

Most of the men had wrapped their gifts in brown paper bags, or the remnants of old newspapers. The firelight accented their sun- and wind-browned faces, each a little wide-eyed, almost childlike, in anticipation of the reaction his gift would bring.

Cantrell, fearful that Straker would be given no gift, had wrapped a pair of suspenders he'd bought for himself while in Santa Fe.

Lion indicated that it was the magic time, and each searched out his partner, or special friend, and almost shyly handed him his gift.

Cantrell cornered King and handed him his present; King in turn gave him one.

Then Cantrell looked for Straker, who'd eased his way to the back of the circle of men, apparently feeling that he was not part of this.

"Hey, Straker, I brung you a little somethin'." He thrust it at him. "Here 'tis."

"Aw, Cantrell, you shouldn't't've."

"Why not, old-timer? You're my friend." Quint's gift from Straker was the look on his face. If a man can be beautiful, right now that old man is beautiful, he thought. Then he heard King burst out laughing at his shoulder.

"What's funny?"

"Hell, partner, open your gift an' you'll see." King held his gift from Cantrell behind his back.

Puzzled, Cantrell tore at the old newspaper, first making certain that he'd already read it. When he had stripped his gift of wrapping, he held in his hand a sheath knife exactly like the one he'd given King.

Stunned, he gazed at it, feeling a slow smile crinkle the corners of his mouth; then he burst into laughter and grabbed King's shoulders. When they had controlled their laughter down to a chuckle, King shook his head in disbelief.

"I sure knowed we thought about things the same way, but

out of all the things those stores in Santa Fe had, damned if I woulda b'lieved we'd hit on the same thing."

"When I saw them knives alayin' there in that store, partner, I got to thinkin' I'd like to have a knife like 'em, so I figured you would too," Cantrell said. "Now danged if we ain't both got one."

"I was thinking the same way, amigo. We sure can know what we give is liked, can't we?"

After dinner they drifted back to the bunkhouse, all still basking in the glow of a perfect day, not thinking about the day that would follow, one of backbreaking work that each would curse yet wouldn't swap for any other.

It was nearing sundown, if there had been any sun this Christmas day, when Lion stepped out on the *galería* and bellowed for Cantrell to come up to the house. Said he needed to see him.

Cantrell was laying on his bunk whetting his new knife on his boot sole. He rolled over, shoved it in its sheath, and went out, going by way of the stable, where he'd cached the gifts he'd bought.

Before Cantrell could knock, Lion pushed the door open and quickly closed it after him.

"Come on in. Set by the fire."

Venicia and Elena were there. Cantrell nodded his greeting and sat, and then abruptly stood and handed them their gifts. "Hope y'all like 'em. Ain't much used to gettin' things for ladies."

Lion brought him a drink, went behind the bar again, and brought out three packages. "Our Christmas to you, son."

"Aw, didn't figure y'all would get me nothin'. I just wanted to say how much I'm beholden to you for makin' me part of the BIM."

He handed Lion his gift and glanced at the three of them; he felt like a kid. This was the first time he'd received a gift since he'd left home. "Can I open mine now?"

They laughed, and Lion replied, "Yeah, s'pose we all can do just that."

Cantrell had a pair of gloves from Venicia and a new dress shirt from Elena. There was a small but rather heavy package that he'd saved till last. He carefully unwrapped it.

While he was worrying it to the point of distraction, trying to keep from tearing the wrapping, Lion sat with a smug smile.

"That there one's from all three of us. Elena said she saw you stop and look in the store window at 'em 'bout every time you passed. Said you was sort of like a kid with his nose pressed agin window glass, lickin' his lips for some of that penny candy they always have stacked inside."

When he had removed the paper and carefully folded it, he saw that whatever it was, it was encased in a hinged hardwood box. He snapped the latch and opened the top.

"Ooooh, son of a gun," he breathed, "ain't they beautiful." He removed one of the matched set of Colt .45s from the case. They were engraved, ivory-handled, double-action six-guns, perhaps the finest gun Sam Colt had ever produced. The handles had Cantrell's name and the year's date, Christmas 1882, engraved on them.

He shook his head in disbelief. "Y'all knowed I wanted these so bad I would've gone hungry a year for 'em."

Elena nodded. "Yes, and Papa had given us explicit directions that we were to get you something you'd like. So we all had a hand in it."

Cantrell didn't really know what to say, and not being too much of a talking man anyway, he just smiled and said, "Thank you."

"Now I reckon we better see what our gifts are, but seein' you open yours was just about all the Christmas I could want," Lion said.

Cantrell tried to watch them all as they tore into his gifts.

"Hot damn!" Lion exploded when he opened his. "You must've knowed I was disappointed at not being able to make the trip with y'all. I wanted to get down there where them Mexican bootmakers was so's I could get me a new belt and holster." He looked over at Cantrell. "Shore thank you, boy."

It was then that Cantrell heard Elena gasp.

"Oh, Quint, they're beautiful. I saw them and wanted them, but Mama said 'no.' Then suddenly, one day when I went by the store to look at them again even though I knew I couldn't have them, they were gone."

She looked at her mother. "Mama said if I had been meant to have them, they would still be there."

She stood and walked over to Cantrell's chair. He stood, thinking it was the proper thing to do, and then she surprised him. She threw her arms around his neck and kissed him—right square on the mouth.

He stood, rigid, his arms at his side, so embarrassed that he would have run if her arms hadn't prevented it.

"Hot dammit, boy! You gotta do better'n that," Lion roared. Then the three of them laughed. If he could have just by wishing it, he would have turned to smoke and drifted away. Elena stood back from him. "I'm sorry, Quint. I have embarrassed you, but . . . but, well, ah reckon ah jest wanted to do it, cowboy."

Cantrell didn't know how to react. He was glad they knew about him and Elena, and glad they all accepted it, but, hell, this just wasn't the way he had planned it. He looked around at the three of them.

"Reckon everybody knows what everybody knows," he said and felt stupid with the words. "But I still got somethin' to do 'fore I come acourtin'."

"Oh stop that, Quint. Put your arms around me and hold me close for just a minute. I need that to hold me until you get your job done."

"To hell with the whole world,'cept you an' me, Elena." He pulled her into his arms. This time Lion had no comment.

Venicia came up and put her arms around both of them. "Thank you, Quint, for the beautiful comb and mantilla. I'll wear them to our fiesta." Then she kissed him on the cheek.

"Whoa there, boy, you can have my daughter, but leave my wife alone."

Cantrell looked at Lion, only to see him smiling.

CHAPTER
21

Winter laid its icy grip on the land. The warm and wonderful respite of Christmas Day had proven to be only that. Snow continued to fall, and on the morning after, Mann rolled them out of their bunks to fit the wagons with sled runners.

The cattle needed hay, and ice on water holes broken so they could drink. Another danger was suffocation from ice formed in their nostrils, or they could simply drift before the blowing snow until they came to a fence line, where they would stand and freeze to death.

Cantrell and King's job was to find cows in danger of suffocation. The job then was to hold the cow's head and run a finger around the inside of its nostrils to clear them of rime-ice. The job could not be done wearing gloves.

Back in the bunkhouse, well after dark, Cantrell, like the others, soaked his hands in brine and rubbed animal fat into them. Every crease in his knuckles and hands was cracked and bleeding. This had happened many times in the past, and would again, countless times.

Despite the weather, every man on the place anticipated a good time at the fiesta. They had to double up on their work in order for all to attend. They worked from before daylight until well after dark each frigid day.

Ranchers, and townsmen from Durango and small towns close by, began arriving two nights before the fiesta. Although the hacienda was large, the beds only went so far. As a result many of the guests slept on pallets, as did their children. They expected this and considered it a small price to pay for attending the gala affair. The afternoon of the party Lion sent for Cantrell.

In his office the look on Lion's face indicated trouble. "Pull up a chair an' set, boy. Got some news for you."

Cantrell swung a chair around and straddled it. "All right, Lion, reckon I kin tell from your face it ain't *good* news. Lay it out here so we both kin look at it."

"The Hardesters are in Durango an' somebody's done told 'em where you are."

Cantrell went quiet inside, with just a spot of white-hot anger that it had to be this way.

"Been a long time coming. It was gonna happen sometime, Lion. Reckon that bein' the case, it's a good thing it's now."

"I'm sorry, boy. Wish it didn't have to be, but the BIM's behind you."

Cantrell was shaking his head before Lion finished. "This is my fight, Lion. I put my saddle on this bronc a long time ago." He shot Lion his most stubborn look. "If one man from the BIM got hurt in this fracas, I'd figure it was me hurt him."

Lion leaned across his desk. "Now, you listen here, boy. The Hardesters have teamed up with Curly Farlow and his men, along with Moose Lawson. I ain't standin' still for you goin' against five men—we're goin' with you. Don't argue."

"Damn, Lion, Elena's hardheaded, but she ain't nothin' compared to you. Anyway, I'm stayin' here until after the fiesta. Ain't gonna spoil Elena's fun."

"Good. We'll ride in with you. Start early, day after tomorrow. Now let's have a drink." He reached in his top desk drawer.

Cantrell stood. "Thanks for the offer, Lion, but I'll pass this time." He hesitated. "Don't know who told you this, but I'd take it kindly if you don't say anything about it to nobody. No point in spoiling the party."

"I'll do what I can, boy, but I'm afeared maybe some already know."

"*Que sera, sera.* Thanks for telling me." Cantrell shook Lion's hand and left.

He danced most of the dances with Elena and Venicia. He enjoyed each of them, but made his excuses and left about eleven.

He slipped into the bunkhouse and got his guns, the new ones the McCords had given him for Christmas. He'd been practicing with them and believed he got off his second and third shots faster than with his old single-action Colts.

He picked up his Winchester, then put it aside. No need for a long-range weapon. King had an old American Arms 12-gauge shotgun, double barreled, sawed off. If he had to face five guns, he couldn't choose a better weapon.

He went to King's bunk, picked up the shotgun, and stuffed a pocketful of buckshot-loaded shells in his pockets.

After penciling King a note telling him he'd borrowed his gun, Cantrell went to the stable, saddled the dun, and rode out. He had never felt so alone in his life. He wanted the BIM with him, but he wouldn't let himself have it that way.

A cold, hard anger built in him. It wasn't right that he had this to do when he'd only now found Elena. He thought about the friends he'd made, particularly Venicia and Lion. If he didn't come out of this, he had at least found that it was a good world, with a lot of good people in it.

When Cantrell left the dance, it had hurt Elena. She knew he had anticipated this dance with pleasure. Maybe he didn't feel well, or maybe the party hadn't been up to his expectations, or . . . or . . .

Something was wrong. She cornered Venicia. "Mama, did Quint seem to be having a good time?"

"Yes," Venicia nodded. "When he danced with me I didn't notice anything wrong. For that matter, he seemed more outgoing than I've ever seen him." She glanced around the room and found Lion. "Let's ask your father. Perhaps he'll know."

They cornered Lion, and when they both asked at the same time what was wrong with Cantrell, he just stared at them a moment. His glance dropped from their eyes and he looked at the floor. "Might's well tell you. He probably put on a good-time face long's he could and then went to bed. The ones who want him dead are in Durango. Gonna take the boys and ride in with him in the morning." He put his hand on Elena's shoulder. "Honey, we ain't gonna let nothin' happen to him. Don't worry."

Elena looked at her father and mother a moment, willing her

face to freeze, not wanting to cry here before the guests. She turned and went to the kitchen. Venicia stepped toward her as she walked away, and Lion took her arm. "Let her go, *mi amor*. She needs to be alone. She's gonna cry it out by herself."

"Oh, Ian, she needs me now."

"In a little while. Leave her alone for now."

Venicia nodded and reluctantly followed him onto the dance floor.

Elena didn't stop in the kitchen. She went up the back stairs to her room and changed into riding clothes. If she knew anything at all about Quinton Cantrell, and she thought she did, he wouldn't wait for the BIM crew to side him in this fight.

Dressed, and with a gun strapped to her waist, she went down the back stairs and headed for the bunkhouse, thinking it would be empty. Most of the men were still at the dance.

Despite the snow and cold winds, Cantrell drew rein in front of the livery stable about ten the next morning. The doors swung open as he was about to dismount. Rawhide Doby stood there, holding one of the doors open against the wind.

"Ride on in. Heard ya come up. Sort of figured ya'd be here this mornin'."

Cantrell rode in. "Howdy, old-timer, Happy New Year." He took care of his horse and said to Doby, "Feed him good, Doby. I'll be riding out this afternoon sometime."

The old man cocked his head. "Reckon you know they's five of them done teamed up to nail your hide to the wall."

Cantrell nodded. "I heard."

"C'mon in. I got hot coffee. You need to warm a mite."

In his living quarters, Doby poured coffee while looking Cantrell straight in the eye. "I'm goin' with ya."

"No. You ain't." Cantrell looked at the old man and saw no hint of indecision, or doubt, in the wrinkled old face. He softened his voice and took Doby's's bony old shoulders in his grasp. "Thanks, old-timer. I know you're my friend, but this is my fight. I got to do it alone."

"Well gosh dang it, Cantrell, you need somebody to keep 'em off'n yore back."

Cantrell shook his head.

"Well ya need to know where they're at, an' I kin tell ya."

"All right, tell me."

Doby's eyes widened. "Been awatchin' 'em. They been doin' the same thing every day for the last three days, so way I figger it they gonna keep on doin' it the same way.

"Curly Farlow's sittin' inside of that upstairs winder, across from the Golden Eagle. He's got a Winchester. Moose Lawson, he's been standin' 'tween them two buildin's this side of the general store. He's got a shotgun. An' the two Hardesters been stayin' in the Golden Eagle. They just sit there adrinkin' at a table in the middle of the place.

"Most town folks been stayin' away from there, knowin' they's gonna be 'nuff trouble there to paper hell a mile." He shook his head. "No siree-bobtail, they don't want none of that trouble on their backs." He frowned, and scratched his head.

"Well now, figgered I knowed where all of them was, but that's only four. I just plain don't know where that skinny rattlesnake's been hangin' out—the one what's been trailin' around after Farlow. Reckon he's the only one left of them. I heard you done eliminated the rest."

Cantrell broke the breech of the shotgun, looked down the barrel, shoved two shells into it, and snapped it shut. Next he took his .45s out, checked each one, spun the cylinders to ensure they were fully loaded, and slipped them gently into their holsters. He drew them a couple of times for the feel of it.

"Woo-wee," Doby breathed, "I figgered five of them was gonna be too many, but I never seen a gun come out so fast." He put his cup to his lips for the last swallow, then looked secretively at Cantrell.

"They's a door at the back of the Golden Eagle. I was you, that's the one I'd go in. Leave here at the back of the stable an' go down the alley. Them ones on the street ain't gonna see ya that way till after you take care of the Hardesters. You can take care of them what's left one at a time."

It was only a short walk to the back of the saloon. Cantrell didn't think about the possibility of the door being locked until he reached for the knob. If it was, he'd have to go in the front.

The knob turned smoothly under his hand. He pulled it, the hinges squeaked once, and the door swung soundlessly toward him. He stepped in and eased the door closed. A long hall stretched before him, with game rooms lining one side. He came to the end of it and recognized the door to his left as the one through which Faye had taken him after his fight with Lawson.

When he stepped around the end of the wall, he would be in the main room of the saloon, with the bar to his left. He took a deep breath, eased his guns in their holsters, and, holding the shotgun in a pistol grip with his left hand, stepped into the saloon.

The room, as Doby had described it, lay before him. The two Hardesters sat at a table in the middle, facing the front door. Each had a drink in his hand. A bottle, almost empty, sat on the table between them. Faye stood behind the bar staring at them. Cantrell saw no one else in the room. He'd not been seen.

His back to the wall, Cantrell slid toward the wall to his right so he could see the whole room.

"You lookin' for me?" Voice quiet, heart pounding, Cantrell waited.

Faye gasped, her breath sounding loud in the still room. The Hardesters turned as one, each throwing himself to the side, hands streaking for their guns. Cantrell's right hand dipped to his side and came up spewing flame and lead.

Bent Hardester rolled and got his gun clear. He was fast—very fast. Cantrell had already put lead into each of them, but not enough. He thumbed off another shot at Bent and saw another black hole appear in his shirtfront. He swung the .45 toward Speed and squeezed off another shot; Speed's throat spouted a stream of blood. Then Faye screamed. She sounded far away.

"Quint—the balcony!"

Cantrell swung the 12-gauge toward the balcony, at the same time a skinny gunman under it brought his .44 in line with the room. A stream of fire erupted from the muzzle of the gunman's pistol. Cantrell didn't feel the shock of a bullet and thought Skinny had missed.

The gunny swung his pistol a little to the left. Cantrell squeezed both triggers of the 12-gauge. Skinny fired again. Cantrell's left hand went numb. The slug turned him half around.

Skinny straightened. Cantrell's buckshot loads cut him almost in half, knocking him back a step. With a surprised expression, he buckled and fell across the banister to the floor below.

Cantrell swung his pistol back toward Bent. He'd already put two slugs in the man, either of which should have killed him, but they might not have been enough. They weren't.

Bent struggled to bring his .44 up. He held it with both hands. The only thing keeping him alive was pure, naked hatred.

The venom in his eyes struck Cantrell like a physical blow. They fired at the same time. Cantrell's left leg went numb. It buckled. The force of the blow turned his side toward Bent as he fell.

He rolled and brought his gun up for another shot. Bent lay stretched out on the floor, his eyes staring at the ceiling. Cantrell held his fire.

The batwing doors in front burst open. He swung the muzzle toward them, his finger squeezing the trigger. At the last second he pulled his shot toward the ceiling.

Elena, King, stick McClure, and Rawhide Doby crowded into the room. Cantrell tried to stand. It was then he realized where he was hit—his left leg had taken lead. He thought he must be hit somewhere else too. He couldn't hold onto the shotgun and looked at his arm—finally his eyes locked on the shotgun. The breech and stock were shattered. The blow of the bullet against the breech had numbed his hand and arm. That must have been what turned him when Skinny fired his last shot.

Elena reached him and helped him stand. "Where are you hit, Quint?" Her face was flushed. Her eyes spat green fire. "Oh, damn you anyway. Why did you have to do this without help?"

Cantrell's gaze searched the room. "Where's Faye? She

called a warning to me when she saw that slime yonder under the balcony about to fire."

"I-I don't care where your woman is," Elena stormed.

He pulled away from her, hobbled over to look behind the bar, and saw Faye on the floor. Blood, a lot of it, was on her side. He limped over, squatted, and held her head in his arms. She was alive.

"Get a doctor."

"Know where he might be this time of day," Doby answered. "I'll fetch him."

Quint looked at Faye. Elena kneeled at her other side. "Where are your clean towels?" she asked, her anger at Cantrell forgotten for the moment.

"Under the bar," Faye answered, then looked at Cantrell. "I knew you didn't see him, and when I warned you, he fired at me first, hit me somewhere, then fired at you."

Elena was back with a stack of towels. She began tearing the material away from Faye's side.

"I'm sorry, Quint. I'm to blame for all of this," Faye continued, her voice only a whisper, "When . . ."

"Don't talk now, Faye," he cut in.

"No. I have to tell you. You were the only man I ever really wanted, and . . . and when I offered you all I had to give and you turned me down it made me furious." She stopped and breathed deeply, her breath ragged with pain.

"Aw c'mon, Faye, you're hurtin'. You don't have to tell me all this. Lay back an' let's wait for the doctor."

"It has to be said and I might not have the courage to tell you later." She gasped, then continued. "When you wouldn't have me, even after I lowered myself to acting like a hussy trying to get you, it . . . it made me mad. I'm the one who wrote and told Bent Hardester where you were."

She took a long, shuddering breath. "I knew where he was, because I was once married to him. My full name, a name I never use because I detest him, is Faye Barrett Hardester." She fell silent.

Her eyes begged him not to hate her.

"Faye, don't rawhide yourself like this. Reckon I understand how you feel, but I had already seen Miss Elena, and there just wasn't nobody else for me. Besides, you just made this happen sooner. It had to happen sometime."

Elena placed another towel against Faye's side; then she looked at Cantrell, her eyes swimming. "I-I'm sorry for all the things I thought about you, Quint. I think I loved you the first time I ever saw you and it made me mad to think I was sharing you with Faye—with anybody. I wasn't even sharing you, because I had no part of you at the time. I-I guess it just made me mad to think somebody else had laid claim to you."

"Elena, you won't ever have to worry about Quint," Faye said. "You better grab him and hold tight. There's not another like him anywhere."

Elena, still looking at Quint, tears running down her cheeks, said softly, "You can bet a painted pony on that, Faye." It was then that Doby returned with the doctor.

"Reckon the doctor can take over here," Cantrell said. "Still got this job to finish."

"Whoa there, Cantrell." King caught his shoulder. "It's done—finished—through."

"What the hell you mean? Farlow and Lawson are still out yonder somewhere."

King shook his head. "Cantrell, listen to me. Your woman done killed Lawson; an' me 'an Doby 'an McClure took care of Farlow. Don't rightly know which one of our bullets killed 'im, but he was sure as hell deader'n a butchered steer when we got to him."

Cantrell stared at the floor a moment, then raised his eyes to look at them all. "It's over then—really over. No more runnin', no more lookin' over my shoulder."

The doctor kept Elena to help with Faye. Cantrell told him that when he got through with Faye, he'd be at the hotel; he had a hole in his leg.

By then, people from all over town, who had heard of the shooting, were beginning to fill the saloon. Cantrell pushed his way to the street, only to see a larger crowd there. He finally had to accept King's help in walking. He had just draped his arm across King's shoulder when he saw Marshal Nolen.

"Marshal, gotta get somewhere and sit down. C'mon down to the hotel an' I'll tell you what happened. If you got any charges again me I'll just have to talk about it there. I'm hurtin'."

"Knowed it was gonna happen, son. Wanted to stop it but warn't nothin' I could do. They hadn't done nothin' I could arrest 'em for."

"Arrestin' 'em wouldn't've helped. They'd a been out in a few days anyway. *Then* it woulda happened. Now it's over."

Cantrell limped a few steps, stopped, and said to King, "How the hell did you, McClure, and Elena get here so fast, and what did you mean when you said Elena killed Lawson?"

"Keep walkin', partner. When we get you settled in the hotel and the doctor has patched you up, I'll tell you about it."

The marshal walked on the other side of Cantrell. "Sure glad to see they just ventilated you a mite. Figured you'd have holes all over you." Nolen shook his head and forced an exaggerated sigh. "Reckon you're gonna be around to cause me more trouble."

Cantrell knew the marshal was joshing. He shook his head. "No more trouble, Marshal. I'll wear my guns, but I don't figure any more are lookin' for my hide. I know I ain't lookin' for trouble—never was."

They came to the front of the hotel and turned in.

A couple of hours passed. The tall man Cantrell remembered from the newspaper came and went. Elena arrived and reported that the doctor had said Faye would be all right in a couple of weeks, barring infection.

She persisted in fussing over Cantrell like a mother hen. He was glad when the doctor told her to leave while he looked at Cantrell's leg. When everything settled down, King suggested they go to the café for coffee and something to eat. None of them had eaten since the night before.

They had no sooner reached the lobby when, led by Lion and Venicia, the entire BIM crew streamed through the door.

"By damn!" Lion roared. "What the hell you mean runnin' off like that? Told you last night we was comin' with you."

"An' I told you it was my fight," Cantrell cut off Lion's tirade.

Lion sputtered.

"Settle down, Ian," Venicia told him. The way she said it wasn't a request. She turned that penetrating gaze from Ian to Elena. "And why did you run off without saying a word to anyone?"

"I did, Mama. I told Art I thought Quint had gone to Durango to face five men alone."

"Where did you find Art, young lady?"

"In his bunk."

Lion choked. "In-in his goddamned bunk . . ."

"Ian," Venicia didn't raise her voice, "hush! You know blamed well I would have done the same thing if it had been you. Now hush and let's hear what happened."

"S'pose we let King tell it," Cantrell said. "I want to know how Elena happened to tangle with Lawson, an' how you three took on Farlow."

Cantrell looked at Lion and would have bet even money that he'd have a stroke. Too, Cantrell knew he'd thrown an old she coon on King's back. He'd probably never been called on to say ten words at one sitting in his life.

King stood, as though saying, "If I gotta do it, I'll take it standing."

"Well," he started. "I felt somebody shakin' my shoulder. I sort of squinted up to see who the hell . . . 'Scuse me, ladies . . . Anyway there was Miss Elena. I crawled under my covers far as I could go. Ain't never been no ladies in the bunkhouse before, so I didn't know what to do, but she took care of that.

" 'Get outtin that there bunk,' she says, 'Quint's done gone in town alone.' I allowed as how he was a plumb growed-up man, an' he'd been in town alone before. Then she throwed it on me, like throwin' a Texas rig onto a sore-backed hoss.

" 'He's done gone in to meet the Hardesters—an' Curly Farlow—an' Moose Lawson,' she says. Well now, I come up outta that there damned bunk—'scuse me, ladies—blanket an' all, like she'd done blowed me out with a tub full of black powder."

He squinted around the room, apparently to see if everybody was listening. He seemed to be satisfied that they were, and now that he'd started, he also appeared to like talking. He glanced around again and saw that even the open-mouthed desk clerk hung on his every word.

"Reckon I dressed so fast Miss Elena didn't even see me get outta that there bunk. I slung my gunbelt on, and while buckling it, I looked for my shotgun. Then I seen the note Cantrell left. Well it's the first time in my life, but I just plain took somethin' of somebody else's. I took a shotgun. Don't know whose."

"Better get another one, King," Cantrell interrupted. "That skinny gunman yonder in the saloon done ruined yours."

"Shhh." Venicia shushed him before anyone else could cut in.

"Well," King continued, " 'fore we could get outta there, I seen McClure was dressin'. He must've heard us, 'cause he was ready to go by the time I was. Didn't stop to tell nobody. Figured to take a day off'n work. Besides, we sort of figured Cantrell would take care of most of them and leave us the soppins. That there is 'zactly what happened.

"In town, Doby herded us into the livery stable an' perceded to tell us what was goin' on—an' where everybody was doin' it. 'Bout then, Miss Elena disappeared.

"We hurried out on the street. Didn't see her nowhere so we started walkin' toward the Golden Eagle, keepin' a eye on that there upstairs winder Doby done told us about. Then all of a sudden I heard a shotgun belch, twice, behind me. I was still in one piece so I allowed as how they wasn't nobody shootin' at me. Then I seen it.

"Lawson was alayin' there, cut slam in two, an' there was Miss Elena, standin' there holdin' that there shotgun, both bar'ls still asmokin'." He looked at Elena admiringly. "She just looked at me like she was gonna say how pretty a day we was havin'. Then she said, 'Lawson was drawin' a bead on your back. He didn't get off his shot.'

"About that time, Doby squalled an' fired. Me an' McClure hit the dirt arollin' an' come up firin' at that there winder where Farlow was standin' leverin' shots outta that there Winchester of his so fast you'd a thought it was a pistol. The three of us all got lead in him."

King cleared his throat. "Sort of in the back of my head, while all that was goin' on out in the street, I heard all hell—'scuse me, ladies—breakin' loose in the saloon. It was then that Miss Elena an' we'uns run in the door.

"It was all over. Cantrell done depop'lated the town some. Reckon that's 'bout all I got to say." He shuffled his feet nervously and looked at Lion, whose face slowly softened, then broke into a grin.

"What a damned crew," Lion roared. If there had been anyone left at the ranch, Cantrell was sure they could have heard him. Lion continued. "If anyone fights a BIM rider, they got to figger on takin' on the whole crew." He cocked an eyebrow at Elena. "Includin' my daughter."

Her chin came up in that proud tilt. "Well, I reckon, Papa," she drawled, mimicking Cantrell, "anybody figgers on fightin' my man, they got to whip me too."

Every mother's son standing there burst into uncontrolled glee. When the laughter finally subsided, Venicia looked at Cantrell straight on.

"Does this take care of *all* of your business, Mr. Cantrell?"

"Almost all, ma'am. I figger I got some serious courtin' to catch up on though."

Before Venicia could answer, Elena walked to the middle of the floor. "Cowboy, they ain't gonna be no courtin'," she again mimicked. "If you figger on acourtin' *me*, you done took the wrong fork in the trail."

Venicia's mouth hung agape, Lion frowned, and the crew shuffled their feet in embarrassment.

"Now," Elena continued, "if you woulda said you was gonna come amarryin', I reckon you woulda topped that bronc off right slick." She turned to Venicia.

"Mama," then to Lion, "Papa, I reckon it's gonna be a lot of work fixin' for a weddin', so just so's we don't waste a lot of time while we're here in Durango, y'all can get started."

She looked at Cantrell. "And you, cowboy, can start the shortest courtship in history—starting right this minute, so put your arms around me."

If you enjoyed this book, subscribe now and get...

TWO FREE

A $7.00 VALUE—

If you would like to read more of the very best, most exciting, adventurous, action-packed Westerns being published today, you'll want to subscribe to True Value's Western Home Subscription Service.

Each month the editors of True Value will select the 6 very best Westerns from America's leading publishers for special readers like you. You'll be able to preview these new titles as soon as they are published, *FREE* for ten days with no obligation!

TWO FREE BOOKS

When you subscribe, we'll send you your first month's shipment of the newest and best 6 Westerns for you to preview. With your first shipment, two of these books will be yours as our introductory gift to you absolutely *FREE* (a $7.00 value), regardless of what you decide to do. If

you like them, as much as we think you will, keep all six books but pay for just 4 at the low subscriber rate of just $2.75 each. If you decide to return them, keep 2 of the titles as our gift. No obligation.

Special Subscriber Savings

When you become a True Value subscriber you'll save money several ways. First, all regular monthly selections will be billed at the low subscriber price of just $2.75 each. That's at least a savings of $4.50 each month below the publishers price. Second, there is never any shipping, handling or other hidden charges—*Free home delivery*. What's more there is no minimum number of books you must buy, you may return any selection for full credit and you can cancel your subscription at any time. A TRUE VALUE!